DUTY STRONG

SUBPLOT™

www.mascotbooks.com

Duty Strong

For more information, please contact:
Subplot, an imprint of Amplify Publishing Group
620 Herndon Parkway, Suite 320
Herndon, VA 20170
info@mascotbooks.com

Library of Congress Control Number: 2022921267

CPSIA Code: PRV1222A
ISBN-13: 978-1-63755-606-1

Printed in the United States

To my wife, Lecia; son, Zane; brother, David; Kohl; Mauryn; and many wonderful friends for their love and support.

DUTY
STRONG

STEVE SHOCKLEY

SUBPLOT

CHAPTER 1

"It's over, Zinny," said Major General Hugh Haywood.

The decorated general, all business in his dress uniform, delivered the bad news uninflected. He didn't have to explain his decision to a subordinate. He followed up with an authoritative stare to let me know he was serious. There was no leeway. I was on the list.

After the Vietnam War ended, rumors spread around the Pentagon of staff cuts. Career soldiers were edgy, as if a trapdoor awaited us all. The stunner of my release left me speechless—a cold wind finding out I wasn't indispensable. Raging expletives filled my thoughts, demanding answers. But noncoms, even sergeant majors, limited their emotional reactions to superiors, especially a general.

"Zin, this isn't sixty-nine, with all those draftees. Everything's changed. Now we're RIFing good soldiers in seventy-five."

RIF: Reduction in Force—meaning, "You're fired!"

I fixated on his slow, deep voice, which lingered in my head like the last song I heard on the radio. The encircling photos on his wall—him with two presidents, key senators, and Pete Dawkins—was a noted reminder not to be at ease in his office.

General Haywood tapped me for his staff during my third tour in

Vietnam. He depended on the unit we organized to carry out covert missions. He demanded unquestioned loyalty and absolute success. My grunt work was a counterbalance to his deft politicking. He attached me on his fast-track trajectory to major general—me, a command sergeant major.

"Twenty years in. A good soldier's career. Be proud of your service."

His praise without explaining why I was RIF'd made it impossible to hold back my emotions. I balled up my fists, tightened my jaw, locked my eyes on his resolute demeanor.

"You're pissed. I get it. Your divorce and breakup with Sally—it's a lot."

His attempt at empathy found no home in my stonewalled expression. I suppressed my anger out of respect for the stars on his collar.

"I gave Sally the day off. She won't be happy with me. Oh well, that's it. Let me know if I can ever help you out."

I translated his meaningless offer as if he wanted to say, "Never call me for any reason."

He handed me the paperwork every life soldier dreaded to receive. I stood there, remaining silent. The general labored to stand and then extended his hand. I backed away, saluted, did a smart about-face, and left his office. He seemed surprised by my rude gesture—a man accustomed to obedience and esteem. I fast-stepped around our floor at the Pentagon to burn up a portion of my anger. Colleagues noticed my unfriendly manner. It felt awkward ignoring their concerns. Back in my windowless office, I hurled a stack of top-secret dossiers against the wall. It seemed right at the time to be out of control.

A major was ahead in line at the first-floor finance office to receive his RIF pay. No matter how much money I received, it would never be enough to compensate for an abrupt end to a career. I rose in rank from private to sergeant major, which was a long service ladder to climb. I did my duty to the best of my ability. These days I couldn't outpace young legs but could still energize young soldiers with my "wow" stories.

"Sergeant Major George Zachary Zubell," said the finance cashier with my RIF papers in her hand.

"It's just Zinny now."

"Huh?"

"Never mind."

She unstrapped a stack of new hundred-dollar bills to pass under the glass window shield. "Five hundred . . . one thousand . . ."

I left the Pentagon with a wad of cash but in no mood to talk to anyone. I was uncomfortable telling colleagues of my RIF, which would unnerve them, thinking they might be next. And I couldn't handle anyone saying, "I'm sorry." At my retirement, I expected a send-off in a banquet room for storytelling, drinks, and a steak dinner. I never imagined a hasty brush-off.

I drove to my one-bedroom apartment in Arlington to change into civilian clothes to mix in with any vocal antiwar crowd. Returning veterans were disrespected for serving in an unpopular war. And I didn't trust myself to react rationally after being RIF'd. I drove to an upscale bar where NCOs hardly frequented. Drinking alone wasn't my norm. Today was an exception. I made no eye contact, no conversation with anyone at the long bar—brooding occupied my time between beers while I reminisced about my career; my ex-wife, Jeannie; and my ex-girlfriend Sally.

Loud talking isolated me. It drove home the thought that a life around strangers, coupled with the loneliness of no responsibility, wasn't acceptable. With no calling or family obligations, I decided to take a risk that was out of character for a grounded soldier. I needed to be around someone with a similar background and experience, someone who might join me in searching for new possibilities. I knew where he was.

I slept off the heavy drinking the night before. I fried the only food in my refrigerator—eggs and bacon—then collected my clothes and personal files in four duffel bags. For the first time since leaving home for boot camp, with my parents' blessing, I headed out with a not-thought-through-in-detail plan in mind. No one, if honest about the uncertainties, could prepare for a sudden end to a way of life.

I dropped off the keys at the apartment management office with a note to keep the security deposit, then notified the rental company to pick up my furniture. I departed the DC area without telling anyone where I was headed. Rude as it was, I didn't want the opportunity to rant to friends about why I was angry with the service I loved.

Six hours later I pulled into the VA hospital in Salisbury, North Carolina, to see my friend Major Jack Klinkscales. I had fleeting doubts about a hasty decision to take him along for new possibilities. I wanted someone who knew the challenges of living without the army.

Major Jack was a life soldier. We first met at Ranger School in Fort Benning. The rigorous training made us competitive, not friends. I stayed on the noncom career track; he applied for Officer Candidate School. We were reunited when General Haywood recruited him to lead our special ops team on our third tour in 'Nam. He heard of a gung-ho major—older than other officers at his rank after graduating from Officer Candidate School—with kinetic energy and the "it" leadership skills.

To this day, I don't know much about the major's past. He wasn't close to his alcoholic parents. Concerning them, he said, "Never look back. Always forward." He never married, never committed to a long-term relationship. His life was everything the army offered.

Despite our personality differences, we bonded serving on General Haywood's special ops team. As if plugged into a high-voltage circuit, each mission deep behind enemy lines energized him. When hell came calling, we wanted him at our side. It was my job to keep him grounded on a mission. I failed him on our last mission in 'Nam. I had to live with the guilt of allowing his zeal to accomplish the mission overtake good sense.

Sitting in my 1972 Chevrolet Cheyenne, it was impossible to keep that fateful mission out of my thoughts. I recounted the events of that afternoon. We had an op order to assess the deployment of M48 tanks on a search-and-destroy mission along a known Vietcong trail. When the mission bogged down, he climbed on the turret of the lead tank to be the eyes of the unit. He shouted commands while I remained in the hatch of the lead tank to relay his directions to the crew. Hours into the mission, Major Jack spotted a Vietcong trip mine—similar to our claymores—set up in a low limb of a black star tree. "Get down!" he shouted. I crouched, slamming the hatch shut. Major Jack only had time to drop flat to the armor plate in a frantic attempt to slide behind the turret. Seconds later the tank tracks tripped the wires to the mine. Shrapnel sprayed the tank; shards ripped apart the major's steel-plated boots and impacted his lower legs.

I hurried to aid him, calling for a medic to apply tourniquets to stop the bleeding. Deep gashes cut up his feet. Shrapnel exposed both tibias. The medic shot him with morphine to ease his anguished screams. I radioed for a medevac to fly him to a mobile surgical hospital.

Major Jack was in and out of VA hospitals after multiple surgeries. I stayed in touch when I returned to the States after my third tour of duty. I visited him as often as I could during his extended stays at the VA. He pushed himself to walk as normal as possible, a testament to his will. But he grew sullen and difficult to be around as he faced the reality of a pain-filled life. He described his stay at the VA as a slow death. For the past few months, our conversations consisted of his one-word grunts, like a teenage boy to his parents after a date. In our last conversation, he said he wanted to end it all. Major Jack refused my calls the past four weeks—my reason to take him with me.

After waiting over an hour in my truck, I went inside to ask for the major. Seeing him in a wheelchair saddened me. In 'Nam, his slim, athletic body was a contrast to my lumberjack build. He was slumped over, pale, with fading blue eyes. It was gut-wrenching to see him stand and walk like opening a foldable yardstick. The surgeries removed the shrapnel and scar tissue, altering his personality along with it. His immobility devastated him, his spirit broken.

He grinned when he noticed me with more hair than usual and a slight bulge over my belt. I heard him mumble, "Hippie." No longer hardened soldiers, we stood together shaking hands, then hugged. He looked away when I stared at the long scars on his legs. He cleared his throat, fighting for a measure of dignity. "Well?"

My response was without regret: "Let's go."

An hour and a half later, Major Jack signed the release forms and checked out with a slight grin. His possessions were two duffel bags of clothes and crutches. I carried both to my truck. He walked unassisted and stumbled twice, once falling to the concrete, but he refused my help. It wasn't a long walk to my truck—less than a football field—but it seemed longer at Major Jack's pace. He halted twice to catch his breath.

I bought a six-pack of beer at a nearby convenience store to start up a conversation. After we gulped a beer apiece in the parking lot, I told him about the general's decision.

"Asshole. Always gets what he wants," he said.

"Generals do."

"Where're we heading, Zinny?"

"Charlotte."

"Why there?"

"Got nothing else in mind."

"That's a reason?"

"You got a better idea?"

"No. What's your plan?"

"Don't know yet."

"You got money when you were RIF'd?"

"Yeah."

"So you got no job, no plans, no woman to spend money on. Sounds pretty good."

On the drive to Charlotte, I saw an occasional smile as Major Jack stared at the terrain along the highway as if the light and color of the outside world were fresh to him. Living with another man in civilian life challenged my comfort level, but I'd make it work.

We checked into a motel on the four-lane Independence Boulevard. We had nothing to do and nowhere to go. We knew nothing about this city. We told each other every army story we had shared many times in the past. There was nothing else to talk about. We eased beyond boredom to comatose. Our meals—breakfast at the Knife and Fork, lunch at McDonald's, snacks at Krispy Kreme, and dinner at the South 21 Drive-In—were all in the vicinity of our motel. At night we drank beer in our room. It only took four days of the same routine to derange my disciplined bearing. I yelled at the major for no reason. I paced back and forth in our room, with push-ups the only worthwhile activity. I wasn't ready for retirement.

Another day passed. The major got frustrated with my circular path around the small room. "What's your problem, man? You're driving me crazy."

"I gotta do something I'm not comfortable with."

"Then don't do it."

"Got to. I just can't sit around."

"What's so important you have to do?"

"Look for work."

"Why? You got money."

I had a career in mind after my army service was over. I completed criminal justice courses at Fayetteville Tech Community College years back while stationed at Fort Bragg. A job as an investigator for a law firm might be of interest. No way to be certain that career choice was the right path to follow. I had to find out.

"I'm gonna look for work as an investigator."

"You qualified to do that?"

"When you say it like that, no. But I'm willing—"

"Good luck with that."

———

The best way to find my footing was to get out of the motel and locate a one-day print shop for one hundred black-and-white business cards with only my name and army rank. With no experience, I had to impress a potential employer with my service record. Was that enough? I would find out.

The following day I left the motel for a job search. I wore my best civilian clothes: a red plaid jacket, cream-colored slacks, white short-sleeved shirt, and an army airborne necktie. I parked my truck in an uptown lot and walked to the center of Charlotte. I waited on the sidewalk watching the civilian world stroll by—men in dark suits, white shirts, and ties, and women in heels—and realized I stood out like a grease pencil among fountain pens. Being an outsider to their world was like the first day of boot camp, only without a drill sergeant in my face.

I gazed up at the tall buildings, concerned about rejections. I had no experience asking strangers to pay me for work. I mustered the courage to go straight to a tall building and open the door to the first law firm I found, armed with a stack of business cards. That was the jumping-off point. To the receptionist and each one thereafter on the first day, I asked, "Does your firm have an open position for an investigator?"

"No," or, "What?" or, "I have no idea," or simply confused stares were the responses I got on my first day of the search. The last firm I visited asked for my résumé. I had the worst possible reply: "I don't have one."

I tramped on the hot sidewalks to various-size law firms, a bit slower with each passing day, searching for an opportunity for investigative work. I greeted each receptionist with a smile I shared only with friends. Everyone

I spoke with was cordial to a fault. Charlotte, at first impression, was a big, small city, whose citizens were gracious and smiled more than I was used to. *There is money to be made here*, I thought, but so far no opportunities for a man with no résumé and only a desire to work. It was too early to assume I had made a dead-end career choice.

On the last afternoon of the workweek, I remembered a top-floor law firm that I avoided at the end of a discouraging day. I put on my brassy civilian coat and tie to return to the humiliation of rejection. "You're reaching for something that isn't there," the major said.

I opened the door in a barren corridor on the top floor of the Baugh Building. I cleared my throat to get the attention of the sixtyish, bespectacled receptionist. Engrossed in a house and garden magazine, her nameplate askew from any visitor, Mary Lou Johnson looked up with a Friday-afternoon attitude.

"Yes? May I help you?"

"Ma'am, I'm here to meet with your headman."

"Who? Do you have an appointment?" Mary Lou spoke with the cool drawl of a woman on the front line.

"Uh?" was my response, since I forgot the namesakes of the law firm. I backpedaled to the firm's door, peeked around the corner to study the names on the wall—Sedley, Cannon, Dalton, and Miller—then returned to her desk. "Please ask Mr. Sedley for a few minutes of his time."

"Mr. Sedley senior or junior?"

"Just a few minutes with Mr. Sedley Senior."

"Mr. Sedley doesn't see anyone without an appointment."

Blocked again. I could no longer mask my anxiousness. The crippling frustration was hard to hide. "I guess you're in the business of crushing dreams."

I was out of line snapping at a subordinate doing her job. I put my business card on her desk anyway. She glanced at it, then dialed an extension to whisper her displeasure about having to deal with a perceived jerk.

Her irritation reminded me of my ex-wife, Jeannie. She became weary of a marriage of little compromise; the passion and friendship ebbed to an irreconcilable state. She served me divorce papers on the day I returned from my last tour in Vietnam. The storied romance of a man going to war three times was lost on a modern woman.

Jeannie was too pretty and demanding for a roughneck like me. She wanted someone I wasn't and told me so during a heated argument. Instead of going through a pricy divorce, I gave her everything—our sofa, chairs, bed, furnishings, knickknacks I never wanted, and half our savings. I had no use for anything to remind me of our failed marriage.

Six months after our divorce, Jeannie married a naval officer and got pregnant with her first child.

I walked out to the hall to see if there was another law firm on the floor. My slow walk revealed only closed unmarked doors. After a lengthy stop in the public bathroom, I returned to the law firm's lobby to find a young man in a dark gray suit and starched white shirt at Mary Lou's desk tearing up a business card. She gasped when I cleaned my throat. The young attorney realized who I was, then dropped his grin, complicating his upper hand. Mary Lou lowered her head in hope that their indiscretion wouldn't lead to a reprimand.

"Excuse me, sir. That card costs money."

A lapse in his judgment moved him to consider an approach to allay his rudeness. His face lit up with a sound plan in mind. He reached into his pants pocket for his coins.

"This should cover it, sir."

He handed me a dime, then smiled as if he had regained an advantage. He shook my hand to seal his recovery. Fate offered the perfect circumstance to play out a ploy my dad maintained he pulled on a rude customer. Selling expensive *Encyclopaedia Britannica* copies door-to-door, Dad said, required an arsenal of clever comebacks. I reached into my jacket pocket, counted out four business cards, and handed them to the young attorney.

"They're five for a dime."

I laughed, but Mary Lou and the young attorney stared expressionless. Ploys like that were why Dad stopped selling encyclopedias and parked his huge body on the hoods of Fords to sell cars. He worked at the same dealership until he collapsed and died of a heart attack five years ago on a sweltering July afternoon.

The man appeared embarrassed about what to do next and exited the lobby with my business cards. They would be in pieces before he got to his office. I sat down on the sofa in the lobby for no good reason. Mary Lou ignored me like she would the unemployed gathered on vacant lots. I set my mind on sitting in their lobby a while longer.

Ten minutes later, Mary Lou answered a call. "Yes, sir, he's still here . . . No, sir . . . Yes, sir."

I watched a sixtyish balding man approach the lobby with a bulldog scowl and the confidence of a man able to handle any situation that presented itself. His slow walk exuded controlled intentions.

"So, Mr. Zubell, I'm Claude Sedley Senior. How can we help you?"

He approached the sofa with his hand extended. He sized me up as he greeted me. I stood up and shook his hand. He was at least six inches shorter and had a strong grip.

"Good afternoon, sir. Nice to meet you."

"What can we do for you, sir?"

Mr. Sedley didn't engage in small talk. I had no clue if his presence was an opportunity or a rebuff. I stated my pitch for work. "Looking for work as an investigator."

"We don't hire investigators on staff."

His controlled gaze dropped to a cold stare, the kind a person got right before the boot. The doubt I had struggled to keep in check for days leaped off my face. I was career army. I never asked anyone for anything. Nightmares did come true.

Mr. Sedley read the uncertainties on my face. Yet, as outmanned as I was, he released his stare, dropped his head, stayed with a troubled thought for what seemed like ten seconds. When he looked up, our eyes met, and he said, "Mr. Zubell, Mary Lou will keep your name on file in case we ever need your services."

A delayed rejection? There was interest in his demeanor; something about his thought process spoke of his desire to know more about me. But he needed to save face with Mary Lou and the young man.

"Let me work for you one day, sir. Prove how hard I can dig for answers. No charge. Nothing to lose, okay?"

Mr. Sedley had a contemplative frown. Thoughts churned. I read his expression: *Could he trust a stranger with sensitive firm matters?* He looked as if he would buy me a beer if no one he knew saw us together.

With his head tilted, he said, "Who sent you here?"

"No one, sir. I'm just looking for work."

"I have a conference call. If you don't mind waiting, I'll give you a few minutes."

Mary Lou, still standing out of respect for Mr. Sedley, sucked in enough oxygen to keep three fat men walking up stairs. He smiled at her. She acknowledged his grin, sat back down, and refused to look up. He exited the lobby.

Did I go fishing in the right spot? I felt a surge of excitement for the first time all week. Mary Lou pretended to be busy organizing an uncluttered desk and was relieved when Mr. Sedley called me to his office after waiting only ten minutes.

A middle-aged smiling secretary in a blue floral print dress with a piled-high updo escorted me down the hall past the stares of attorneys and staffers. My intuition told me the joust with the young staffer had made the rounds in the firm.

Sedley's office was large, powerful: an enormous presidential oak desk, three leather chairs facing him, oak cabinets on the near wall, a row of diplomas and wildlife paintings around the room, and a leather sofa and two high-back chairs in the far corner of the room. The outside walls had floor-to-ceiling glass and panoramic views of the city. He likely had the ear of many corporate executives in view from his top-floor office. Mr. Sedley stood up when we entered. His secretary closed the door behind her. He invited me to sit as he returned to his leather chair behind his desk.

"Why did you come to our firm today? Why do you think we need an investigator?"

"Just looking for work, sir. I'm interested in a position with your firm."

"Tell me about yourself."

"I'm an army command sergeant major. Last stationed at the Pentagon."

"Impressive."

"Twenty years in, sir."

"Vietnam, I'm sure."

"Three tours."

"Oh wow! In combat?"

"All the way, sir."

"We owe you a lot. So, retired?"

"RIF. Reduction in force. Cutbacks in senior staff who reached retirement age after the war."

"What a shame."

Mr. Sedley gazed out his window longer than I expected. I was uncomfortable. No need to say something that would impede the opportunity. He was frowning. Was this a delayed rejection?

"What're you looking for, Mr. Zubell?"

"Work."

"Why do you think you can help us?"

"I don't, sir. I'm not even sure being an investigator is the right career choice." That was a stupid mistake spoken at the worst possible time.

"And no one sent you here, right?"

"I've been in town a week and a half. I don't know anyone who would send me anywhere."

"I see."

"I'm knocking on doors all week. I thought it would be like dating. Ask enough girls out, one is bound to say yes."

He sank deep in thought, sighed, without a grin at my glib reply. He seemed to be struggling with a difficult decision. How I was involved was beyond my knowledge.

"Sergeant Zubell, do you have references I can check out?"

I came prepared. I reached into my wallet to hand him a business card with General Haywood's office number embossed on it. "General Haywood's office at the Pentagon, sir. They'll assure you that I am who I say I am."

Mr. Sedley buzzed his secretary, Edna, into his office and ordered her to call the phone number to check me out. About time my search for work moved in the right direction. First Sergeant Sally Aberdeen would praise my work without prompting. Good turn of events, although she might be upset if she had to pick up, sort, and file the folders I hurled across my former office.

After an awkward silence, he said, "I always supported the Vietnam War."

I had an immediate reaction to his attempt to be supportive of my service with a tone of a parent giving comfort to their child after a huge disappointment. "I was a life soldier, sir. No need to—" I stopped, mid-sentence, and looked away. No reason to be defensive. "Mr. Sedley, is there something I can do to prove my worth?"

"I'm willing to take a chance on you, if your service reference checks out. It's a risk. But I may be willing to take it."

A risk? What did he want me to do? I chose not to ask questions. Instead,

I squinted to read the impressive diplomas on his wall while he studied me as if I was a war memorial statue. Mr. Sedley asked a question I would ask in an interview.

"Did you do investigation work in the army?"

"I conducted intel for General Haywood and got answers. I'm good at being persistent."

"As investigators go, Mr. Zubell, you don't dress the part. More like a used-car salesman." Unknowingly, he insulted my late dad. But I kept quiet.

His stiff jaw loosened up a bit. A casual jab at my attire was his way of building up a comfort level before he told me why I was here. There was an uncomfortable pause in our conversion, followed by comparisons of the modern army to his experiences years ago, then another pause as we waited for Edna's report from my reference.

He broke the silence with a pertinent question: "Were you this persistent with other law firms?"

"Sir, to be honest, you're the first person to show any interest." Another uncalled-for mistake. I was on a roll.

"You've never been hired by anyone else to do investigative work, right?"

"No. Come Monday morning, I'd like to start doing that here."

"I'm not sure. You're telling me the truth, right?"

"I have no reason to lie, sir." His leap of faith would be careful, suspicious, one small step at a time. "So you have a job, Mr. Sedley?"

"If your reference checks out." He hesitated, leaned forward. "Let me be clear: I've built a successful law practice. You won't jeopardize our reputation. Understood?" With an ominous tone, he said, "Being a military man, you'll appreciate where I'm coming from. Don't disappoint me. You do what I ask, and no more, and we'll see where we go from there."

"Understood."

His phone rang. Mr. Sedley listened without comment as Edna related the information she received from my reference. He hung up without any appreciation for her effort. He swiveled around to unlock a cabinet behind his desk, located a nine-by-twelve manila envelope, and dropped it on his desk.

"You'll only be working for me. Don't talk with anyone else about what you're doing. Not to anyone in my law firm. Understood?"

"Yes, sir. Got it. One condition, sir: I won't do anything illegal."

"Don't insult me, Mr. Zubell."

"Okay, we understand one other."

"I want you to go to Stuartville, down east. There's a guy there named Damon Slade. Give him this envelope. No one but him. No one else sees the contents. Agreed?"

"Yes. What background information do I need to know about Mr. Slade?"

"Nothing. Just give him the envelope. His hands only. And then leave."

"Does he have to sign something?"

"No."

"What if he wants to know why a stranger is giving him an envelope?"

"Say nothing."

"What if he refuses to accept it?"

"He'll take it."

"Okay. And just leave, right?"

"Do you want the job or not?"

"Yes, sir. You know, I could hang around and watch him from a distance."

"No."

"No? Okay."

"Don't make this out to be something more than it is. And don't discuss Damon Slade or me with anyone. No one." He shook his head like he changed his mind. "You sure you wanna do this? It's not really investigative work."

"Yes, sir. I'm your man."

"Good. You'll get twenty-five dollars per day, plus twenty-five dollars for travel expenses. You'll only need one day."

"When do you want the envelope delivered?"

"Tomorrow. He's there now."

"Okay." I reached for the envelope, but Mr. Sedley moved it out of my reach. "Anything else, sir?"

"Deliver it without incident."

"You made that perfectly clear, sir."

"You'll have to sign a form."

Mr. Sedley flipped on his intercom to tell Edna to bring him an NDA. It took him too long to explain the acronym: nondisclosure agreement. For the next few minutes, I read over "don't" statements warning me not to speak or disclose to anyone about the firm's business or its clients. I initialed each paragraph in the document.

"Anything else I need to know, Mr. Sedley?"

"No."

After handing him the signed form, I said, "Why do I get the feeling Mr. Slade isn't gonna like what I'm delivering to him?"

"No arguments, no discussions. Just give him the envelope and leave."

"Will there be more work?"

"Call my secretary, Edna, next week."

Mr. Sedley rose, buttoned his suit jacket, came around his desk, and walked to his door to shake my hand with a concerned stare. He gave me a day's work without burdening me with need-to-know information. Civilian work was more like the army than I realized. He could've given the envelope to Edna for a postal delivery, but for some unknown reason he wanted a stranger to deliver something important to Damon Slade. Could the messenger be as important as the message?

Then I remembered Major Jack. I left him in my truck in the parking deck before job searching, not expecting to spend an hour at Mr. Sedley's law firm. Major Jack told me that he had to get out of the motel room but insisted on staying in the truck after I parked in an uptown lot. I hurried out of Mr. Sedley's office building and jogged across the street to the elevator to the top floor of the parking deck. Major Jack was still sitting where I left him in the passenger's seat of my truck with the windows down. It was humid and hot in the direct sunlight. His olive drab T-shirt had turned dark from the soaking sweat.

"Sorry, man. Good news. I got a job."

"You'd never leave beer in heat like this."

"Real clever."

"What kinda job?"

"Hired to make a special delivery out of town."

"What's a special delivery?"

"This." I held up the manila envelope.

"A letter? That's what you're doing now? A postman. Put a stamp on it and let's get a drink."

"There's more to it. A big-time attorney wants me to deliver this to a guy out of town. He wants to trust me."

"Shirt-and-tie crowd ain't your calling, man. We're grunts, Zin. Tall buildings and fast talkers got you all jacked up about a shit job, and you don't even realize it."

"I'm up for a beer. Tomorrow, road trip."

CHAPTER 2

At 0500, I was awake. It was more than nerves. I was thinking too much, going over questions I had, making assumptions with no knowledge of the situation. Mr. Sedley struggled hiring someone he didn't know for a one-day job. Understandable. As a green investigator, an in-office task was more appropriate to assess my abilities. The puzzling question was why send me on my first job with his firm out of town to deliver a document. The importance of the document was clear. So why not send a staffer he trusted?

He could trust me to perform the simple assignment as directed. Nothing more. *Don't overthink the job*, I thought. I could be relevant in the world of suits and high heels. I was well versed in adapting with a clear head. Earn his confidence.

I woke Major Jack at 0600 for breakfast at the Knife and Fork. He reluctantly agreed to ride along to Stuartville, even though he grumbled about his legs cramping on a long drive. Each night he would stiffen up to where he moved like a turtle the following morning.

An hour later I was on the job, ready for the four-hour drive to Stuartville. I was curious what was in the manila envelope, sealed with three strips of wide tape. Major Jack asked about the contents. Serve process papers, he reasoned.

"I'm not in his confidence yet."

"Why pay a guy he doesn't know to deliver something important in person? Makes no sense. Ya know what? He paid you off just to get rid of you. Now he's done with you."

He had a point. I hadn't considered that assessment.

We traveled along state highways through the eastern backcountry of the state, past rich, breathing tobacco, corn, and cotton fields, inset in thick forests. A sunny day trip in early fall. The major stared at the miles of farmland as if he had an interest in crops. Not talking was his way of demonstrating his displeasure over the forced road trip. On a long, straight stretch, I swerved my truck off the banked asphalt to get Major Jack to say something. He was that stubborn to maintain his mood.

Turning onto NC Highway 87, we passed signs for Fort Bragg. I made a passing reference about detouring for a brief stopover at Bragg to revisit the good ole days.

Major Jack said, "No fucking way."

—

The "Welcome to Stuartville" marker was adjacent to the speed-limit sign warning twenty-five miles per hour was in force. Stuartville had a row of clapboard homes on each side of the highway leading into town. After a hard brake for a double set of railroad tracks, we were in town. A plank-board diner advertising the "Best BBQ in Eastern NC" and a two-pump Gulf gas station crowded with parked cars and pickups were neighbors after the railroad tracks. A group of men lined up in an uneven semicircle outside the door to the station for vacuous stares at passing cars.

I slowed to twenty miles per hour, studying both sides of the street for a parking spot to begin my search for Damon Slade. The name *Slade* fit a small town like Stuartville. The one-stoplight town had a general store, a small grocery, boarded-up buildings, and a combo bank-police-city hall. I stopped at the traffic signal. I then eyed two elderly men sitting on a bench outside the general store staring at us like we were a float in a Christmas parade. I leaned out the window. "Excuse me, fellas. Is there a phone booth around here?"

"Don't need one," said the guy in overalls, smoking a pipe.

"Store behind you open?"

"Old George is always around," said the smoker's friend.

"I'm trying to find someone."

"Who you lookin' for, mister?"

"I got business with Damon Slade. You know him?"

The signal turned green. With no traffic behind me, I stayed at the intersection to wait for an answer. Major Jack leaned forward, cursing under his breath.

"You're the only man in town lookin' for him," said the smoker's friend. Both guys got a chuckle out of an inside joke.

The smoker shook his head and smirked as if I had asked the dumbest question imaginable. "Go straight ahead to the motel."

"Straight ahead to what motel?"

"You'll find him. He's all the excitement this weekend, and that ain't saying much," said the smoker's friend.

"It'll be pretty obvious, mister."

One question asked of a stranger, and I found Slade. We drove through Stuartville, passing four huge warehouses outside the city limits. They were the moneymaker sustaining the town. Ahead I saw the Stuartville Inn, a small L-shaped motel, with cars and pickup trucks double-parked. I weaved through the lot to an adjacent parking space at the roadside restaurant next door. After parking, I watched groups of women exiting the motel rooms with large shopping bags.

A scrawny guy in a faded blue shirt and loose tie was the manager in the motel office; his attention was glued to a small black-and-white television under the sign-in counter.

"Yes, sir?" He got off his stool when I entered.

"You booked up?"

"Yes, sir, booked solid through the weekend. Sorry about that," he said, slow enough to leave no doubt he was in no hurry to get the words out of his mouth.

"What's going on?"

"Mr. Slade's in town." He spoke of him as if he were the most celebrated man to ever visit here.

"What room is he in?"

"He's rented 'em all."

"All of them? He needs every room?"

"Yes, he do. He kind of goes from room to room." He grinned like he found a wad of money when speaking of Slade. The townspeople of Stuartville had a Hollywood spotlight on him. I walked out of the motel office listening to the clerk apologize over and over for no vacancy.

Major Jack, still not talking, stayed in the truck while I walked to the center of the motel parking lot to watch for anything giving me a clue as to what was happening. I saw two groups of women exit the end room with shopping bags. They all smiled, talking to each other at the same time. I walked to room twelve with the special delivery in hand to knock on the door. A grinning middle-aged woman with her hair pulled back in a tight bun opened the door. I stayed in the doorway witnessing five women rummage through racks of dresses situated all over the small room. The woman who opened the door returned to her chair at a foldout card table with a small metal lockbox for cash transactions. When a woman came out of the bathroom displaying her new dress, she got compliments from the other kindhearted women.

I strolled to room number ten and found the same thing: a similar-aged woman sitting at a card table watching other women paw over dresses. In the next room I visited, number seven, I found a man who I assumed was Damon Slade—broad-faced, with pronounced cheekbones, a stout build, and an unfriendly gaze. His brown eyes looked me up and down. We sized up at six feet tall, around 225 pounds. After a staring contest, he forced a salesman's smile, reached out to shake my hand, and flexed his grip to overpower me. I resisted with equal firmness. We had instant chemistry, disliking each other from first impression. I was curious why he was unfriendly.

"What's your problem, mister? You don't think a man should do work like this. Something like that?" he said.

"Yeah, but that's my issue, not yours."

"A friend set me up in the business. He said there is good money to be had." He continued to size me up. "You're not from around here, are ya?"

"Why'd you say that?"

"No man from these parts would be caught dead at my sale. Plus, you got things on your mind. What's your business here, mister?"

"You." Doubtful he would display this level of poor salesmanship to his female customers. His body language told me that he wanted me out of his element.

"It don't matter what your problem is, mister. Gotta show you something."

He motioned me to follow him to the back corner of the room. There he reached behind the door for a leather briefcase with a yellow manila envelope the same size as mine. I held on to my delivery a while longer.

Whispering, he said, "This is what lots of cash brings. An ugly man can only dream about having a woman as fine as this. You gotta know that." He laughed to ratchet up our mutual dislike.

Slade's way to coax me to open the envelope was to press it hard against my chest. I opened the unsealed flap to find an eight-by-ten photo of a tan young blond woman with dark eyebrows and lustful green eyes, lying on her stomach on an animal-skin rug in black garters and nothing else. Slade grinned and slapped my back as a sign of male one-upmanship. The women shopping in the room seemed oblivious to us.

"I'm my own boss, and I got her in my bed every night. Buy something for your woman—that is, if you have one."

I had no idea what a pretty girl saw in him. Coincidental timing sometimes brought on an awkward moment. The woman in the photo opened the door and walked in all smiles, appreciating the busy room. She strutted up to us in a tight red dress and black pumps. She caught me staring at her.

"Hi, Silver," Slade said. "How's my baby? This man was just admiring you."

"Hi there," she said with youthful innocence.

She glanced down at the photo in my hand, dropped her playful grin, and let out a mild shriek when she saw her nudity exposed to a stranger. She grabbed the photo out of my hands to tear it in half.

"How could you, Damon? I'm not some slut you get to show off." She aroused the attention of the buyers in the room. "How many other guys have you showed this to?"

Slade grabbed her arms and lifted her up close to his face, lighting his quick fuse. "Go back to work. Now."

Customers were shocked when hostility invaded the relaxed shopping environment. The women in the room gaped at each other for an explanation and watched Silver as she stomped out of the room and slammed the door. Slade recovered from the unseemly incident with a vibrant smile to keep sales moving along. He addressed his customers in a salesman's "everything's under control" manner.

"I apologize, ladies. The stress of working on the road for weeks at a time gets to young people who aren't used to hard work. Tell you what. Everyone gets an additional 10 percent off any purchase in this room. See me right now for the best deal."

Delivery time. I extended my left hand to press Mr. Sedley's document against Slade's chest. I held it there until he jerked the envelope away.

"What's this?"

"Special delivery from Claude Sedley."

"Claude Sedley?" He knew the name. He was shocked; anger and anxiety blended in the same expression. He flipped the envelope over in hopes there was something distinguishable posted on the back side.

"What's this? Who are you?"

"Messenger."

Stunned beyond comment, Slade checked both sides of the envelope again for a clue to its contents. Though curious about the document, I left the room without incident.

Outside, in the early afternoon heat, the women of Stuartville kept coming to the motel in packs. The steady flow of shoppers was a validation of Slade's enterprise. In Stuartville, like many small towns, the thread of day-to-day life offered little change; a sale of fashionable attire would be the talk of the town all week.

I coaxed Major Jack out of my truck, where he sat sweating with his eyes closed. He could stay stubbornly uncomfortable for hours. I talked him into coffee and apple pie at the restaurant next door. We sat down in a booth with a clear view of the comings and goings at the motel. I wanted to watch for Slade's next move.

"What's this guy about?" Major Jack said after we ordered.

"Selling dresses."

"What's in your hand? Return mail?"

I still had the manila envelope Slade handed me. "Nothing."

"You find out what's so damn important about a personal delivery?"

"No."

"Don't make sense, Zin. Why the personal delivery to a guy selling dresses in nowheresville? Some job, Zin."

"I was paid to do it, Major."

"What did the guy say to you?"

"He didn't like me much."

"Why?"

"Maybe he thinks I'm some badass sent to push him around. But I don't think he's the kind of guy who can be pushed around."

I went over my encounter with Slade in detail to amuse him. He smiled when I told him about the nude photo. I turned my head in time to see Slade hurrying across the parking lot. He rushed inside room number two, strong-arming Silver on his way back outside. She resisted, but his strength kept her moving beside him. He went into the first room next to the motel office and unlocked the door while struggling to hold on to Silver, who wiggled and resisted as a child would to avoid a spanking. He kicked open the door and searched in all directions for anyone who might be witnessing the scene. Not noticing me, he positioned Silver in the doorway, slapped her, and shoved her hard into the room. He again checked all around for witnesses, but this time saw me in the restaurant—an eyewitness to his brute behavior. Slade scowled, rushed toward us, never losing eye contact, with Mr. Sedley's envelope folded up in his pants pocket.

Inside the restaurant, he yelled at us long before he reached our table. "This supposed to scare me or something? Sending a goon to intimidate me. Ain't gonna happen." His shouting alarmed three families in the restaurant.

"What's wrong, Damon?" the heavyset cashier asked when he walked past her. He stopped momentarily, looked back at her, but said nothing. He continued to our table.

He might overplay his hand and give me a clue into the dispute with Mr. Sedley. *Stay calm. Don't ruin any future employment*, I thought.

"Stay out of this, Jack," I warned him.

Without hesitation, Slade grabbed my shirt with his left hand to jerk me to my feet. "I won't be intimidated—"

"Get off me." I forced his hand off my shirt.

Slade thought through what he was doing and where he was after looking at the stunned faces of the families in the restaurant. He was too well known in Stuartville to have an incident ruin his business. He then addressed us with a quieter tone. "I don't know why Claude Sedley has it in for me. Tell him that I don't respect a guy who sends a goon to threaten me."

The major said, "Don't you just love being called a goon?"

"Listen, smart-ass, I'm a former marine. I don't take shit from anyone."

"Remind me, Zin, why we should be afraid of a marine selling skirts," Major Jack said.

Slade leaned down to stare at him. "That's big talk. Anytime you wanna back that up."

"Let's go." Major Jack locked his eyes on him. His irritable temperament would accept a challenge and initiate a fistfight. I feared bringing him on the job would be a risk. As Major Jack started to push up to get at him, I reached across the table with a stiff-arm to hold him back. Over Slade's shoulder, I saw the three families stand up and head for the door to escape the expected fight.

"You wanna make noise, fine. We'll tell the local cops what we saw you do to your girl." I violated Mr. Sedley's caveat not to confront him.

He crumpled the envelope I delivered and held it to my face. "This means nothing. If he wants to intimidate me, tell him to get a pair and come face me."

Major Jack let out a mocking laugh. "Zin, it's a hoot messing with a jarhead."

"I'll remember you boys."

Seeing the cashier and the families huddled at the door ready to exit if violence broke out, Slade grinned like a salesman to a customer and walked toward them with his arms reaching out in their direction, sensing word-of-mouth stories would spread if not explained. Making a scene in a family restaurant during his sales weekend was bad business.

"I'm sorry y'all had to see this. Sometimes you gotta stand up to city tough guys who wanna push around us simple folks. Everything is okay now." He greeted the families with calming handshakes.

"I called Fred, Damon," the cashier spoke up.

An advancing siren shifted everyone's attention to the arrival of the local police. A cruiser slid into the parking lot, where a police officer in a khaki uniform came running in to halt the reported disturbance, leaving his siren blasting and his squad car running. Shoppers at the motel came out of every room like exposed ants.

Slade stepped toward the approaching town constable. "Fred, I'm sorry about all this. No need for concern. It's just business associates I've had bad dealings with before. Ain't no big deal."

The frowning officer shook his hand, then addressed us in a loud tone with his jaw set, his stomach sucked in, and his right hand on his revolver. "What's your name, fella?"

"Sergeant Major Zubell, sir."

"And your buddy there?"

"Major Jack Klinkscales."

"What's your business here?"

"We had a special delivery from an attorney for Mr. Slade. He's the one doing all the pushing. Ask around, Officer."

The constable turned to him. "Damon, you say it ain't no big deal, then it ain't no big deal. I'll take your word for it." Turning to the woman at the cash register, he said, "Mabel, you see it the same way as they say?"

"Yeah, I guess so. I thought there was trouble brewing, but I guess not. Sorry to bother you, Fred."

"Okay, okay, if there's no big deal, then there's no big deal." He looked back at us. "You boys got any further business in town?"

"No, sir."

"Leaving won't be no problem, will it?"

"Suppose not. We'll eat our pie and leave."

"Fred," Slade said, extending his hand, "tell your wife to come see me personally. I'll give her 25 percent off every dress she buys. You too, Mabel, and any of you other fine folks here. Come enjoy the savings. Sorry for the disturbance."

He covered his tracks with deep discounts in hopes the locals would ignore the incident and continue to support him. The families warily returned to their tables. Slade again stepped up in a salesman's effort to greet everyone at each table. As he left with Officer Fred, patting him on the shoulder, he craned around to say to us, "I'll see you guys again. Count on it."

Major Jack smiled after they departed. "My apologies, Zin. Road trips are fun."

Slade shook hands with Fred, then walked to the motel to continue with his weekend sales. Twice he stared in our direction. Officer Fred stayed in his cruiser waiting for us to leave.

Ten minutes later, I gave two dollars to the uneasy cashier. We strolled to my truck for the long ride back to Charlotte. Fred tailed us to the town limits and followed us for ten more miles before returning to Stuartville.

The legal maneuverings between a small-time marketer and a prominent attorney were difficult to comprehend. In time, I would find out why. In the short term, I was the go-between for Mr. Sedley, who had to know how Damon Slade would react to the delivery. I was willing to stand in the middle of the fight to stay employed without any facts about their dispute.

I was familiar with the venom in Slade's eyes. I had seen that look on men with rage issues. They showed a controlled manner until challenged.

CHAPTER 3

I left two messages with Mr. Sedley's secretary, Edna, for a return call. No callback. On the third call, I told Edna to relay the message that I was successful in delivering the document as requested. She sounded confused but would give him the message. The major's doubts about ongoing work with Mr. Sedley rang true.

I had worrisome thoughts about finding work without a history of serviceable civilian skills. I decided to give Charlotte one more chance. Any success finding work depended on how fast I became comfortable job searching. The sour thoughts of seeking clients from a motel room wasn't the path to a sustainable career.

The major and I grew frustrated living in the cramped white walls of a motel. We had skewered each other about our personal habits and character flaws to the point of almost coming to blows, then agreed a residence was the logical decision to avoid more verbal spats. The following morning we headed into the heart of Charlotte for a rental property. Even with a map in hand, I got confused driving around the city, where street names changed without notice, with too many named Queens Road. The setting we found were spacious homes under canopied streets of towering oaks and shaved yards kept free of nature's weed siege. Most had late-model cars and no trucks in the driveways. We were out of place on this side of the city. I could never imagine earning enough money to buy a home in never-afford land. And my wallet knew it.

We crossed Independence Boulevard near the motel where we were staying in search of a working man's neighborhood. Within an hour, we located a for-rent sign on an untended yard of a wood-framed two-bedroom house on a side street off Central Avenue. Homes in this neighborhood were small and bunched together, had dated cars in the driveways. I felt comfortable on a street with unkempt homes.

I called the landlord's number on a yard sign for a walk-through of the house we were interested in renting. Comparison shopping was never appealing to single soldiers who moved often and had no desire for roots in any community. Rent for the fourteen-hundred-square-foot house was cheap: no fresh paint, small holes, scuff marks on the walls and floor. Furnished with used, unmatched furniture, the house was right for uncaring single men. Two hours later I signed a six-month lease with a month's security deposit. We moved in that evening.

———

The next morning I phoned Mr. Sedley's office again from a pay phone to set up a time to review my encounter with Damon Slade. Mr. Sedley wouldn't take my call. Edna asked me to detail a message to him.

"I'm not permitted to discuss my assignment with anyone," I said.

"Oh," she said. My bluntness surprised her.

"Can I set up a time to speak with him?"

"What is your number?"

"Well, my phone will be set up in a few days."

"Call us back then."

"Okay. But let me ask you this: Did Mr. Sedley give you instructions to pay me?"

"I don't know anything about that, sir."

"Did he tell you about my trip to see a client?"

"I don't know anything about that either, sir."

I wanted to ask her the color of Mr. Sedley's tie, but I doubted she would tell me. Her irritated responses convinced me that she was in the dark about my assignment for her boss. Strict confidentiality was the way a law firm operated. Got it.

I thanked Edna and hung up. I decided to pay Mr. Sedley an unannounced visit.

———

Mary Lou allowed me into the firm on my word I had an appointment with Mr. Sedley. Edna wasn't happy to see me. "A brief meeting with him," I told her. I waited by her desk while she continued typing.

Mr. Sedley emerged from behind closed doors with two men showing confident grins, the look of executives who always got their way. He wasn't happy to see me. He turned away to escort the gentlemen to the lobby.

Upon his return, Mr. Sedley demanded an explanation. "Mr. Zubell, why are you here?"

"Can I have a minute, sir?"

"You looking to be paid?" He looked at Edna. "Advance him fifty dollars out of petty cash."

"It's not about pay. Can I speak with you in your office?"

He hesitated, wanting to say no, but relented. "Briefly." Mr. Sedley walked ahead and closed the door behind me.

His office was again showroom neat and without paperwork. The man was a power broker who moved deals forward with persuasive conversations. His associates cleaned up the details.

"I don't want you just showing up here, Mr. Zubell."

"Yes, sir. But I do have a phone in my motel for a callback."

"I don't have to."

"Point taken. The document was a complete surprise to Slade. In fact, he said it meant nothing. I thought things might get testy."

"What did you do?" He leaned forward in his chair and rubbed his forehead, worried about my response.

"Nothing happened. I'm likeable some days; he's not."

"Okay. Anything else?"

"No, sir." Might he want to know about Slade hitting his girlfriend? He might not. I decided to hold back on more information. "I'd like more work, sir. How can I prove I'm trustworthy?"

"You've done enough."

"No, I haven't. Otherwise, you'd have called me back."

He stared like too many issues crossed his mind at once. He lowered his head and stroked his face with both hands. I expected another no, then being told to leave. But he surprised me. "Okay."

I waited for what seemed like a minute for more instructions.

"Go to the Pothole. Go a couple of times. Just observe what goes on there. Just observe. Twenty-five dollars per day." He turned to the credenza behind him and opened a folder to review. I was patient for further information. Receiving none, I left without shaking his hand.

A bizarre assignment to sit at a bar and watch.

———

The Pothole was a carbon copy of the sleazy bars outside army bases. The small, paint-chipped building suffered for years with apathetic owners. It was an orphan amid a row of industrial buildings and vacant lots. Developers risked no investment on the rundown western edge of the city.

Walking inside the dimly lit bar with Major Jack, I expected to see topless women or an array of pool tables. I saw neither. Instead, there was a long, semicircular bar in the center of the room with high-backed wooden booths wrapped along the three walls surrounding the bar. The establishment aged with obvious neglect everywhere. The pine floor had ground-in peanut shells and popcorn scattered about. The wallboard—discolored by layers of cigarette smoke and stains of an unknown substance—was unsanitary for touching. The Pothole was long overdue for demolition.

At four in the afternoon, the Pothole had no waitress, just a big man behind the bar. I suspected patrons of the Pothole stayed for a while to connect with folks of similar ilk. A man with a three-day beard and a stained white shirt bearing a company logo called out to the guy behind the bar. "Hey, Lugs, the toilet is backed up."

"Then go piss someplace else."

Lugs's response to the customer told me that he had no respect for the day drinkers in the bar. Built like a boulder, he resembled a pro wrestler who ate an entire meat loaf for dinner. He never looked up as we took a seat in a booth near the front door. I needed to start up a conversation with the man called Lugs. I had to find out about Mr. Sedley's baffling interest in a place he wouldn't frequent.

"Two beers, Lugs," I shouted.

He poured two draft beers, lumbered to our table, and flopped down the mugs with little regard for niceties. "One buck. I ain't no waitress. Fifty cents extra for making me walk over here."

"How'd you come to be called Lugs?" I reached into my wallet to hand him one dollar.

"Don't matter. Fifty cents for nuts or popcorn. And a dollar more to be a regular 'round here."

"This place don't even qualify as a dive," the major mumbled to me.

"Haven't seen you in here before. Why you actin' like we're familar?"

Major Jack said, "We don't wanna know you."

Lugs frowned and returned to his stool behind the bar. When I glanced around, he was staring in an unfriendly way.

"Tone it down, Jack. I'm working."

"Hassling a jarhead out of town and then getting paid to drink beer is a damn good job. Congrats, Zin."

We had no conversation of interest. He was bored. I was bored. Lugs ignored us as he argued with drinkers about a recent football game. After an hour of boredom, the major said, "Let's get outta here, Zin."

"You got nothing else to do, Jack."

About thirty minutes later, after another round, a bony, long-haired guy in his late twenties wearing a grimy mechanic's uniform entered the bar. "Ed-die," patrons nearest him hollered out. I couldn't tell if they were laughing with him or at him. But Eddie reveled in their shout-outs, smiling when he heard his name. Eddie walked to the far end of the bar to sit with smiling faces. He yelled at Lugs to bring him a beer. Lugs ignored the request for service, opting instead to continue his conversation with other drinkers. Lugs gave in to Eddie's demand after he shouted for service twice more.

"If you get outta control again, moron, I'm gonna kick your ass."

Gulping the beer, Eddie said between swallows, "I-I-I got a right to be here."

"No. No, you don't."

"Slade said it's—it's okay. 'Member: you—you work for him."

"It ain't his call, dipshit. And you ain't welcome here." Lugs waved a warning finger in his face. Foreshadowing his threat, Lugs swung a jab with his right fist past Eddie's nose.

"All right, already, all right." Eddie downed the rest of his beer in one gulp.

After Lugs turned his back on him, Eddie flipped him off, mumbled something under his breath, then sputtered, "Ass—hole."

Without facing Eddie, Lugs said, "Grease monkey."

"At least—at least—least I wasn't some con's bitch."

The conversation near Eddie stopped. Lugs came around the bar counter. Without speaking a word, he grabbed the back of Eddie's belt with one hand, clutched the back of his shirt collar with the other, then manhandled him to the front door. The patrons standing near the door stepped out of his path. Lugs used Eddie's head and arms to open the bar door. Outside, in the parking lot, I heard a thud like a heavy sack hitting a wall, then a loud moan. When Lugs returned with a bully's smirk on his acne-scarred face, the bar crowd ignored what had just happened with no expressed concern for Eddie. They returned to drinking and casual conversation.

I gestured to Major Jack it was time to leave. I hurried ahead of him to the parking lot, where I saw Eddie rubbing his jaw and lying on his side beside my truck. He heard my approach without turning to see who I was, grabbed a handful of gravel, then cocked his arm to use the rocks in his defense.

"Whoa, man," I said. "We got no beef with you."

Eddie looked scared. He was bleeding from the mouth. I stepped toward him. I halted when he threatened to throw the gravel our way. "Drop the rocks, man. You want the police?"

Eddie shook his head. He moved his jaw around in a semicircle, rubbing it.

I said, "What's the deal with Lugs?"

He staggered away and headed across the parking lot. He fumbled with his keys before unlocking the door to a mint-condition green 1964 Mustang convertible. Eddie never looked around. He got in his Mustang, squealing his tires, spraying gravel as he drove away.

Eddie mentioned Damon Slade. There was a connection—the Pothole, Slade, and Claude Sedley—of a strange group of disparate characters. More reason to hang out here.

———

The following afternoon the major and I again took a seat at the Pothole in the booth near the front door. I saw the usual crowd: guys drinking and avoiding meaningful work. Lugs, sitting on his barstool, eyed us like we were unwelcome nobodies. I raised my hand with two fingers extended for beers. Lugs moseyed over to our booth.

"You guys left with that moron, Eddie Kelter. What's your story?"

"What's it to you?" Major Jack pushed back.

Leaning down toward the major, Lugs said, "You got a real mouth for a gimp. That's not good for your well-being."

Major Jack said, "Superb customer service. You guys expanding soon?"

I spoke up. "We're just hanging out, Lugs. No trouble here."

"Listen, I say who stays and goes around here. Got it?"

I gave Major Jack a disapproving frown to avoid any further confrontation. He read my expression and kept quiet. Lugs leaned toward us, wanting the major to say something to aggravate him. Hearing no comeback, Lugs returned to his barstool behind the counter.

After another round of beers, little conversation, and no interaction with Lugs, Eddie Kelter walked in, halting at the door before committing to enter. The right side of his face was swollen and bruised. He had a black eye and favored his left side with a stiff leg. He skimmed the crowd for a friendly face, looking for an invitation to join someone for drinks.

Lugs stood up and shouted, "Get, moron."

Seeing us, Eddie came over to our booth. Fearful, he looked back at Lugs, who didn't approach but stared like a stalking lion.

"Surprised to see you back here. It's Eddie, right?" I said.

Eddie nodded, glancing again at Lugs.

"What's going on?" I was curious about his connection to Slade.

Angling his hips away from Lugs's view, Eddie reached in his pants to pull out a lug wrench. He held it tight against his left leg, only exposing it to us, and sat down beside me, placing the tool between us. He reached into his greasy mechanic's shirt pocket to drop two dollars on the booth table.

"Beers, yeah, on me. No more—no more shit from—from that asshole."

"You got balls coming back here," Major Jack said. "And I gotta respect you coming back armed."

"Eddie, that's not smart taking on Lugs. Why come back here? There're plenty of bars around."

"Gotta come here. Gotta." He bit his fingernails and turned back to check on Lugs. Biting the back of his hand, he thought over his decision to return here.

I peered again at Lugs, who was now standing up to pour beers for a customer.

"You guys—you guys—seen my mom, Mosie Kelter?"

"We don't know her."

"Yeah, yeah, but—but she used to come here."

"We haven't seen a woman in here yet," I said.

"Your mom hangs out in a place like this?" the major asked, an obvious query.

"Listen—listen—asshole—my mom ain't that kind. If—if—if you think that, then fuck ya."

"Eddie, it just seems like a place no woman would want to hang out in," I said.

"Well, yeah, well, she came here—with Pastor Billy Sedley."

Sedley, huh? The conversation was getting interesting—my curiosity percolating. "You're telling us a pastor and your mom came here? What's the story?"

"The—the pastor—yeah—" He turned to check on Lugs's whereabouts, then continued. "Came here to save souls. Good—good luck with that bullshit. He—he—he was some talker. Got Slade and Lugs and me to—to—to go to his church."

Stunned, I leaned against the booth back. "Wait a minute. Wait a minute. You're telling me that you, Slade, and Lugs sit in the same pews?"

"Yeah. Ain't—ain't what ya call—what ya call the religious crowd."

"What kind of church is it?" I asked.

"A shitty one, I say. But—but Slade really—really took to it. And Mom too. Billy Sedley got Mom so interested—uh, he gave her a job there."

"Something doesn't make sense. You and Lugs go to the same church, but he roughhouses you outta here. That don't make sense," I said.

"I'm—I'm waitin' for Mom here. He don't like it."

"What do you mean waiting for your mom?"

"Last—last—uh, she was last seen here. And—and—when she comes back, I gotta know. Slade said—Slade said she'd check in here with me—with me. I gotta be here."

"Why here?"

"'Cause I'm here a lot. A lot."

"Why does Lugs not want ya here?"

"'Cause he's—he's an asshole. Yeah, that's right—Slade said Silver will call when Mom returns. And she will—she will. I know it. Yeah, I do."

"How long has it been since you heard from her?"

"A couple of months."

"Months? Have you thought about calling the police?"

"They—they don't know shit. Everyone says—says it's all right, even the pastor. But—but—but I say different. The way Lugs—the way he acts—he knows something. I feel it. Yeah, I feel it."

"So that's why Lugs keeps beating on you. You keep accusing him of knowing something about her disappearance."

"I agree with you, Eddie. Lugs looks like the type," the major said.

An untimely comment. I wasn't pleased.

"Your buddy's right. Lugs—Lugs does shit to hurt people."

40

"You can't be blaming a guy without proof, Eddie."

"Yeah, I can, and I—I do." He downed the rest of my beer.

"Pastor Sedley hired your mom, right? He knows where she went. Talk to him."

"Can't."

"Why not?"

"Don't ya know? He's dead."

"Pastor Sedley?"

"Yeah. A big deal."

"Was he sick?"

"Died—died in his garage."

I couldn't hide my shock. "Suicide? You're telling me that he killed himself."

"Yeah—yeah—I said it—I did. But folks won't hear it."

There was a common thread. The Pothole had ties to the Sedley tribe. I envisioned Mr. Sedley's brother being the senior pastor of a huge, rich, staid, first-something church without the likes of Lugs and Slade and Eddie. Pastor Billy Sedley trolling a bar for Jesus was a different calling than a traditional Christian minister's path. With Slade and Lugs in his congregation, he must foster willfully sinful souls.

I had to know more. I raised my hand with three fingers up for service. Beer might keep Eddie talking. Not unusual for someone to ramble on to a stranger with a beer in hand. Eddie looked around at Lugs, who was behind the bar keeping a close watch on us. He raised a clinched fist as a warning to Eddie.

"Eddie," I said, "you mentioned someone named Silver. Who's that?"

"My sis. She—she goes with Slade."

"I met her," I blurted out.

Eddie had an immediate disturbed reaction to me knowing his sister. He had good reason to be suspicious of my ill-timed disclosure. He became edgy and shook both legs rapidly. His body language told me that he was shutting down the information tap. He shook his head from side to side, then slid across the wooden seat, clutching his lug wrench, and stood up.

"Why you—why you prying?"

"We're just talking, Eddie. That's all."

Major Jack jumped in the conversation. "I'm with Eddie on this one, Zin. Is this what that lawyer is paying you to do?"

"Lawyer? You assholes. Just—just like the rest of 'em. All assholes. Yeah, you're pryin'. I ain't done nothing."

"It's not like that, Eddie."

"Well, fuck ya. Yeah, just fuck ya. I've cleared parole, so you—you got nothing on me. So fuck ya."

Lugs strolled to our table with two beers, not three, and plopped them down, sloshing the foamy heads across the booth table. He scoffed at Eddie, waiting, wanting him to say something he deemed justification to take him on again. But to Eddie's credit, he looked away. Eddie gulped a beer in three swallows.

"You guys friendly with the nobody, huh? I'm keeping my eyes on y'all." Lugs then noticed the lug wrench. "You plan on using that on me? Huh, retard?"

In response, Eddie stood up, swung the wrench, rested it at port arms, and began slapping it against his open left palm, sending a clear message to Lugs. Eddie grinned with confidence, believing his wrench evened the odds. Eddie walked backward, eyeing Lugs the entire time, then did an about-face near the bar door. Lugs rushed him when he opened the bar door and kicked him hard enough to send him sprawling outside.

Lugs turned to a patron sitting at the bar counter. "Sammy, get my shotgun. Below the beer tap. Hurry up, boy. The moron might be stupid enough to come back in."

Sammy, an obese, sloppy man, leaned over the bar counter to reach for the twelve-gauge shotgun out of sight of customers. He hustled to hand it to Lugs.

"You sure can move for a fat ass, Sammy."

The insult pleased the toady.

"Let's go, Jack. Eddie might be mad enough to come back in."

Major Jack wouldn't allow a smoldering situation to die out. Angling toward Lugs, Major Jack said, "Hey, asshole, try kicking my ass."

Lugs stepped back and raised the shotgun over his head in derisive surrender. "Well, the gimp's got a pair. Shame I don't pick on the lame."

Major Jack stared with the gaze of a man unable to control himself. "Let's go, fatso. Right now."

"Like I said, I don't get off stomping on gimps. Retards are a different matter." Lugs dropped the shotgun to his side and headed back behind the bar. "I'm going back to my stool, girls. I don't wanna see either of you in here anymore—ever. Get me?"

Everyone in the bar turned to gape at the commotion. Arguments weren't unusual in a bar, but a shotgun put alarmed stares on the patrons' faces. Major Jack and Lugs continued to lock eyes on each other; neither masked their intentions. I saw Jack's legs struggling to respond to his pumped commands. His labored movement gave me ample time to block his path to Lugs.

"Let the gimp go. Let's see what he's got." Lugs chuckled, watching Major Jack struggle to push me aside.

"Goddamn it, Zin, let me go."

The major leaned against me, lost his balance, and slid sideways. I hauled him like a large sack of fertilizer to the bar door. I twisted around when I heard Lugs laughing, waving us off with a ridiculing hand gesture and a bully chuckle.

"A gimp dancing with his boyfriend. Cute. Real cute."

Too many patrons shared a laugh with him.

Major Jack erupted with a stream of run-on obscenities as I guided him out the door. Outside he pushed away from my grasp and tried to reenter the bar. I blocked his path no matter how much he struggled to get past me. He raged with louder obscenities. *Lesson learned: don't bring Major Jack on an assignment involving beer consumption.*

Over Major Jack's shoulder, I saw Eddie backing up in his Mustang. He braked when I gestured drinking an imaginary beer. I hoped the lure of free beer would trump suspicion.

"Fuck ya. Stay away—stay away. I ain't done nothing."

Eddie flipped me off and drove away, spewing gravel. My constant investigative questioning made him distrust me. I had to learn how to be more tactful when asking people for information. I was a stranger investigating Eddie with a barrage of personal questions—too many too fast.

And then there was the Major Jack problem. "Jack, I'm getting paid to do this. You're interfering."

"You're pretending to be what, Zin?"

"I get what I'm doing."

"Shooting the shit with people and asking a bunch of personal questions just to be nosy. It ain't your business."

"You were an asshole in there. And this isn't the army. You don't pick a fight with a civilian. You could go to jail for that."

"You're just screwing around and fucking with people's lives."

"Give me some credit."

"You ain't clever enough to pretend to be some legal-type guy."

Major Jack could push me to overreact. And I did. I shoved him harder than I meant to, then grabbed his arm before he collapsed to the ground. He gave me an understanding nod. Major Jack realized it was time to back down. He got the response he wanted.

"Really stupid to pick a fight with a guy simply because you don't like him. You can get seriously hurt," I said.

"I'm already seriously hurt."

On our way home, the major offered his opinion of Eddie. He summed up his predicament in one sentence: "He'll step in shit tomorrow the same way he did today."

He was right. Eddie would return to the Pothole. A black eye and a swollen lip wouldn't deter him from trying to get to the truth about his mom's disappearance. He was stubborn and concerned enough to pay that price.

CHAPTER 4

Earning Mr. Sedley's trust wouldn't come easy when I was a backdoor man. I had a hunch Mary Lou, Edna, and the young lawyer would spread the gossip about a person unknown to them meeting with the headman. Mr. Sedley had his reasons to keep his agenda confidential and enough control over his firm to maintain the no-need-to-know basis.

In the army, a sergeant's job was to build skills and teamwork—the framework of an effective unit. It took time and training to the point of exhaustion. An investigator's job didn't require similar physical demands, but it did call for attention to details, persistence, and reading people. I could be successful with those skill sets, if given the time and opportunity.

The following day I left my new telephone number with Edna. Four hours later, I got a call from her to come to Mr. Sedley's office at the end of the business day. No reason for the meeting.

I expected the same cold reception when I arrived at Mr. Sedley's firm. But this time Mary Lou was pleasant. I walked through the body of the firm with my plaid blazer and wrinkled cream-colored pants, drawing little attention from the secretaries and lawyers. Edna invited me to sit in her office, then announced my arrival to Mr. Sedley. After a surprisingly short wait, he opened his door with a broad smile and offered a warm handshake.

He requested coffee for us. Edna rushed to the office kitchen as a waiter would at a fancy restaurant.

Sitting down in the big chair in front of Mr. Sedley, I said, "This feels different, sir."

He wrinkled his brow. "What do you mean?"

"I don't know. Just a bit different."

Mr. Sedley was uncomfortable with that statement, squirming in his chair while thinking about a response. "What do you mean by *different*?"

I should have kept my mouth shut. My off-the-cuff statement sidetracked him.

"Nothing, sir."

"Are you talking about my son's indiscretion? He's a good man, works hard, and will be a fine attorney someday. But some things aren't a given and need to be learned."

His son? Was I hired because his son embarrassed the firm by tearing up my business card? That was it. My opportunity for further employment was due to the way I addressed the situation with his son. Mr. Sedley might be warming up, relaxing a bit, with the attitude of an employer more comfortable with an employee. No further comments about anything pertaining to his firm early on was the way to move up on his confidence rung.

"Sir, I can give you an update on my time at the Pothole."

"Have you seen Damon Slade?"

"No, sir."

"That's okay. Well, Mr. Zubell, I'll tell you this much: I heard from him. So, as far as I'm concerned, you did your job. I'll advance you another day's pay, okay? Would you say you're due for four days and one day traveling to Stuartville, plus expenses?"

"Sure. You got his attention? That's what you wanted?"

"Yes. You did what I asked. I'll take it from here. Coffee is on the way."

"Damon Slade never showed up at the Pothole."

"I'm glad he didn't."

"Really? Why was I there?"

"I don't wanna go into that."

Edna entered with the coffee mugs on a polished silver platter. Mr. Sedley nodded in appreciation. I took my coffee black; Mr. Sedley, two sugars and three creams.

"So no more waiting at the Pothole for Slade to show up?"

"No. No need to waste your time there. I'll keep you in mind if I need your services again. Do you play golf?"

"No, sir."

Mr. Sedley instructed Edna to give me one hundred dollars from petty cash. He downed a large gulp of coffee as a signal to leave soon.

"I appreciate your efforts. Are you finished with your coffee?" he said, extending his hand. I stood up but didn't leave. I had to know why. I could be bullheaded when frustration set in over unanswered questions and unfinished matters.

"Sir, may I be frank? I don't understand why you think I did my job. I delivered an envelope and sat at a bar waiting for what? Was that of value to you and your case?"

"What case? Oh, it doesn't matter now. I don't need your services any longer."

"Sir, you had enough confidence in me to follow through on two odd assignments. And that's good enough not to work for you any longer."

"Well, respect that I know what I'm doing. Anything further is not open to discussion."

"Slade didn't like the idea of you hiring me. I'm real curious why."

"I'm not going around and around with you discussing Damon Slade, Mr. Zubell."

"Just set my mind at ease—"

"Be careful, Mr. Zubell."

"Does this have anything to do with your brother, Billy Sedley?"

It was risky pushing Mr. Sedley for answers. I had nothing to lose now. Perhaps referencing his brother's death might demonstrate my ability to dig for information.

He returned to sit at his desk with a cold stare and no comment.

"I heard about your brother at the Pothole."

"What's your game, Zubell?" He was angry.

My attempt to demonstrate how I got information had backfired. "Sir—"

"Who told you about my brother?" He was angrier.

"I struck up a conversation with a member of your brother's church. A guy named Eddie Kelter."

"That's not your job."

"To be candid, sir, I had no idea what my job was, since I wasn't told anything."

He shouted, "Mister, you're in way over your head."

He lost his cool too fast. I struck a nerve.

"You have just lost favor with me." Noticeably, he grabbed control of his emotions, calming himself with ease as if dousing a flame. It was impressive. "Good day, Mr. Zubell."

Bad timing to mention his brother's death, when Mr. Sedley thought the handshake ended my temporary assignment. I touched an uncomfortable subject. Information was unnerving when I found out something he didn't want me to know. He then swiveled his chair and stared out his expansive window.

I wouldn't get another shot at employment here. I had little to lose now. "I don't need the money, sir. Just the work."

"Do you not understand what the expression 'good day' means, Mr. Zubell?"

"I understand, sir."

"Good day, Mr. Zubell."

"Mr. Sedley, thank you for the work. Can I use you as a reference?"

Turning around to face me, he said, "No. No, you can't."

"I don't understand, sir. You commended me on my efforts. But I can't even mention I worked for you?"

"No. It was confidential."

"I won't mention names or details. Just say I worked for your firm and did a good job."

"When was I vague? You won't mention me to anyone. I'll deny I ever met you. Edna will pay you on your way out. Please excuse yourself, Mr. Zubell."

I left. Edna looked perplexed when she handed me a plain white envelope. Right outside Mr. Sedley's firm, I ripped open the envelope to thumb through the cash. Cash meant there would be no record of my employment.

I had no access to find out what was behind the legal maneuverings between Claude Sedley and Damon Slade, and if his brother's death had anything to do with their entanglement. I had to get past my frustrations.

Driving back to the house, I had doubts about opening doors again for investigative work. I visited a dozen law firms in Charlotte to no avail. I found no enjoyment in searching for work, but I needed somewhere to go every day, which meant working for a boss. I questioned my mindset with an unfamiliar feeling—the anxiety of no job security—which led to sleepless nights. The curiosity of embarking on a new career met reality after only two weeks.

I entered the house grumbling about my predicament. On the floor next to Major Jack's chair were six empty beer bottles. He was staring out the window. Watching him sit comatose for hours was a stunning contrast to what he was before shrapnel took away his mobility. Full of energy, he matched every physical challenge with a bolder dare to top himself. And he was a natural leader. To his few close friends, he was that rare person who would never leave your side no matter what hell brought. It hurt to see him like this.

I went to the refrigerator for two beers and returned to the living room to sit on the sofa. To my surprise, Major Jack started a conversation after accepting a beer.

"What happened?"

"Sedley fired me."

"Figures. Where does that leave you now?"

"No clue."

"Face it, Zin. What do you really know about being an investigator? Aren't you sick of bosses?"

"Had bosses all my life."

"Forget working. You got money to burn through."

"Yeah, I could do that. But I just can't get over my hunches about Mr. Sedley and Slade. There is something going on."

"Of course. It's their business and none of yours," the major said.

"Why hire me and not use his staff?"

"'Cause they have work to do, and you don't. Anyway, he don't owe you an explanation."

"My instincts tell me it's bad."

"It's far outside anything you can find out about."

"I don't think he has opened up about Slade with anyone on his staff."

"How do you know that?"

"Told not to tell anyone when he sent me to Stuartville. He won't return my calls. No introductions to his staff. And he's pissed when I show up unannounced. Too much shunning for my liking. Makes me real curious to find out why."

"He used you but doesn't trust you."

"Yeah."

He tossed all the beer cans surrounding his chair over his head in the direction of the kitchen. I did the same with cans near me. Streaks of splattered beer across the living room made our house smell like a single guy's home.

"You ever feel like you wanna go back to the good ole days, when you could punch another guy at the NCO club just to burn off some things you're pissed about?" I said.

"All the time. But face it, we're just old dogs lying under the porch now."

We finished our beers and tossed the cans against the wall near us.

"I feel like a big ribeye and a bottle of Jack. You?" I said.

"You asking me on a frigging date?"

"Do you see anyone else around here to go out with?"

The major belched.

I farted.

He said, "I'm a fuckin' hard guy to put up with. You gotta be thinking you should've let the VA finish me off."

"No. I need you around to piss me off."

I got us two more beers—his med of choice and my pleasure—which were our stimulus each day. I was in the mood to get drunk. The major was always in that mood.

"You think you'd lose the security deposit with my brains staining this shitty furniture?"

"I sure wouldn't clean it up."

"Wouldn't expect you to."

Reaching for dark humor was a good sign. I played along; I loved it. It was his fallback when he struggled to block his depression, which ate up his waking hours.

"You're so out of practice you'd miss your head at close range anyway," I said.

I caught a faint smile cracking through the glare he held on to for too long. The grin went away as fast as it appeared.

"It's fucking hard for me to be civil."

"Roger that."

The major was silent, thinking about a serious subject, with a disturbed frown, then he said, "I can't even concentrate enough to jerk off anymore."

"Don't expect me to help you out there."

"Don't know, Zin."

"Don't know what?"

"If I wanna keep going."

"C'mon, Jack, you still got a lot of fight in you."

"You don't know the fucking pain I live with."

"No, I don't. But I can't keep feeling bad for you all the time."

"Yeah."

Major Jack reached into his jeans for a folded piece of notebook paper. He read aloud, "Last Will of Jack Klinkscales. Zinny Zubell gets everything I have. Signed and sealed." He extended his arm so I could read his signature, the date, followed by his military rank and social security number. "I wrote my will the day you took me out of the VA."

I nodded my approval, even though a simple will was troubling. The major never planned, always lived full bore for the present. Showing me his will wasn't a plea for attention. Not his style. How could I boost his spirit to face tomorrow? Beers.

"I'm not going to date you," he said.

Major Jack, the only person whom I could ask out, turned me down.

CHAPTER 5

It was frustrating not knowing why I only delivered a document and nothing else. Mr. Sedley claimed confidentiality for not giving up the details about his dealings with Damon Slade. I had no idea how to untangle the connections between him and the Sedley brothers. So, with nothing else to occupy my time, I warmed up my curiosity and decided to press on in my search for answers, starting with more beers at the Pothole. Billy Sedley's connection to the drunks at the Pothole intrigued me.

Major Jack returned to the living room at a stride he couldn't keep up. He lost his balance, fell against the wall, and slid to the wooden floor. I didn't help him up. He hated being an invalid. He stayed on the floor, then cursed at his pratfall while crabbing his way to his chair. "Never fell when I was drunk."

Encouraging to see him not take himself seriously. It was time to announce my plan to get involved with Slade and Sedley again.

"Going to the Pothole again."

Major Jack laid his head back and closed his eyes. "This ain't gonna end well."

"Probably right."

"Nosing around in someone else's problems."

"I'm going back 'cause I got no feel for what's really going on."

"And what happens when you act like an asshole around drunks?"

"Get my head busted."

"And that's what you want?"

"I'll back off before it gets that far."

"Nobody wants you involved."

"I gotta know why I was hired."

"That guy hired you to see if you were dumb enough to do it. Accept it."

"Don't think that's right."

"Nobody's got your back. That's when bad shit happens." Major Jack summed up the situation well.

"I'll face it."

"Like when I climbed on the tank."

He moaned like a wave of pain shot through his body, draining away the conversational tone, replacing it with a depressive grimace. He never reflected on his injury, never thought he was brave, never spoke of being awarded the Silver Star. He'd sink into a dark place if I mentioned that dreadful day.

I stopped asking if he took his pain meds. On occasion, I checked the pill bottle. No need for a refill. He never spoke about his pain in depth. Hardly complaining about his pain was his way of proving how tough he could be for my benefit. He was a soldier's soldier. I wondered how I would manage the pain he endured every day. Badly, I imagined.

Major Jack expected to accompany me to the bar for the fisticuffs. He wanted to play. His excitement was short-lived. He raged when I refused to take him. I couldn't convince him that I was going there under a white flag.

He fumed. "It fuckin' sucks to be me."

"I can't risk it today. Just in case I need to leave in a hurry."

"You're gonna need me sometime, and I won't be around."

"Probably right. But not this time."

I left the house listening to continuous cursing about the various flaws in my character. It was like I invited my drill sergeant from basic training to stop by for a dressing down.

———

The Pothole was like finding rats in the basement. I pulled into the bar at happy hour on a Friday afternoon. The vehicles in the parking lot were hardly flashy, even when new.

This bar was where laborers numbed themselves at the end of the week. Lugs and a middle-aged, hard-looking woman with ample exposed flesh were behind the bar. I sat sideways at the far end of the bar counter with my back resting against the wall. The woman bartender got me a beer. Then Lugs pointed his finger in the shape of a pistol. I ignored the threat and waited to see if he'd attempt to force me out of the bar. He didn't.

Two beers later, I reminded myself of a recon rule of thumb: when you're tired of waiting, wait, and watch a while longer. Timing was right for that to come into play. Standing up by my stool to stretch, I saw Damon Slade enter the bar in a T-shirt, jeans, and work boots. He looked more like a construction boss in a foul mood and less like a ladies' clothes salesman. He walked right up to Lugs. They locked into a heated conversation, with Slade questioning him in the same way an angry boss would address an employee who screwed up. I sat down and leaned toward them to overhear what Slade was saying to Lugs. His tone was angry, the volume low. Still, I picked up words here and there, such as, "Claude Sedley . . . Silver . . . and Eddie . . . shit hitting the fan . . ." Lugs glanced around to see me tuning in to their conversation. He pointed for Slade's benefit, who pivoted to face me with a tiger's stare.

Lugs motioned for the woman bartender to deliver a message. "Lugs wants you gone," she said. Her voice was like a sledgehammer against concrete.

"That's lousy customer service."

Outmanned two to one. I reached into my wallet to drop four dollars on the counter. Slade scowled and approached me, which I should have expected. I came here looking for answers but found trouble, like Major Jack said. But I wouldn't back down. I walked toward Slade and set my jaw for whatever was about to happen.

Neither of us noticed Eddie entering the bar. He butted in on our inevitable confrontation, shouting, "Slade, yeah, you—Slade. You got—you got problems with Silver—got problems with me."

His demands halted Slade's approach. Everybody turned around to gawk at Eddie, who had the look of someone anticipating a dentist's drill without any painkillers. He stayed near the front door. Slade widened his eyes to confront Eddie.

"Where's Silver?" Slade said over the other patrons' rumblings.

Eddie must have anticipated trouble. He jerked both arms behind his back and came around with a .22-caliber pistol in his right hand. He pointed it at Slade's head. Slade halted in midstride and put his arms up. Out of the corner of my eye, I saw Lugs sidle over and reach under the bar counter.

"Back off, fuck ya, back off, asshole," Eddie said. "Yeah—yeah, that's right. My way now. And ya ain't gonna—ain't gonna hurt Silver no more, asshole."

"All right, Eddie. All right, man. I'm cool. You stay cool," said Slade. A surprisingly calm tone for someone with a pistol aimed between his eyebrows.

Patrons scattered to the far corners of the bar. I noticed Eddie's pistol hand shaking. Not a good sign. His weapon could discharge with an unexpected twitch.

"Tell me—tell me—yeah, where's Mosie? I mean it, asshole."

"I've told you over and over. I don't know. Think about it, Eddie: Mosie said she wanted a new life someplace else. Silver ain't worried about her. Why you being so crazy and worrying so much? Put the gun away, and we'll talk this over, man-to-man, okay?"

"Lies—lies—lies. All you assholes lie. I won't be—won't be scared off no more."

"I just wanna talk with Silver. That's all, son," Slade said.

"No. You hurt her."

Slade took one small step closer to Eddie. He read his fear and gambled on Eddie's reluctance to pull the trigger. His cool demeanor facing a pistol was impressive.

"Ya know, Silver's coming back to me, Eddie. Ya know that. You're a man. Ya know what you gotta do sometimes when your woman gets out of line."

"Where's Mosie? Where's she?" Eddie stood his ground.

I respected his dogged devotion to his mother but extracting information this way was stupid. If pressed to the point of being afraid for his life, Eddie might shoot Slade out of fear for his safety. He lowered his aim to his chest, signaling he had serious intentions and couldn't miss his target at that range.

I stepped toward Eddie. He kept his focus on Slade.

"Silver pissed me off. Okay, I bruised her up a bit. I heard your old man slapped you and her and Mosie around a lot. So gimme the gun. I don't have a problem with you, man."

"Put it down, Kelter," Lugs said. "You fucked up as usual."

Lugs aimed a twelve-gauge shotgun at Eddie. A half dozen patrons scurried out the door before the showdown turned bloody; several guys huddled under the tables in their booths; other drinkers in the far corners rushed to the back hallway leading to the bathrooms.

"You ain't gonna shoot me," Slade said. "Put the gun away, or you won't like what I do. You don't want that, Eddie."

By doing nothing, I was in the line of fire for a stray bullet. I decided to defuse the standoff. Army sergeants rarely backed away from conflicts; it was how we earned our stripes. I stepped in front of Slade to be Eddie's target.

"Ease up, Eddie. Walk backward out the door. I'll stay in front of Slade all the way," I said.

I motioned with an air push to shepherd Eddie in the direction of the door. Eddie ignored me and fixed his eyes on Slade. I raised my voice to the barking level of a sergeant to recruits. "Back down, Eddie. Back down." I moved my head up and down in a steady, reassuring way to reinforce my directive while I advanced toward him. I got Eddie's attention, even though he appeared unfazed by the recklessness of his actions. He backed up but didn't drop his aim on Slade.

"Listen up, Eddie. Your crazy shit is why you piss us off. Silver is my responsibility now. Ya hear me? Mine. She's mine," Slade said.

Eddie followed my continuous air pushing to the bar door. He aimed his pistol over my shoulder when his left foot reached the door. I grabbed his left arm to guide him outside, allowing the creaky door to shut behind us. Eddie pushed me away.

"What's—what's your deal, man? Why're you—you in my face, huh, asshole?"

He dropped his .22 to his side. I gripped his pistol-toting arm, pulled him in a fast walk to his Mustang, and forced him into the driver's seat.

Leaning down to yell at him, I said, "Lugs could've shot you, Eddie. Had reason. And I'll bet the police are on their way. Put the pistol on your seat. Wait for them to show up. I'll wait with you."

As soon as I stepped away from his window, Eddie started his Mustang, backed up, almost hitting me with his rear bumper, then sped away. I rushed to my truck to follow him down the street at ten miles per hour over the speed limit.

Eddie led me on a weaving journey through the city—through neighborhoods, backstreets, then back through more neighborhoods, all around a shopping center parking lot, then back into the city. I honked at him many times, which only encouraged him to be more of a jerk. After thirty minutes of wasted driving, I sped around him, ignoring his honks, and drove to a restaurant called the City J Restaurant. I pulled into the parking lot with Eddie right behind me. He laughed getting out of his Mustang.

I walked inside with Eddie close behind me. The midsize restaurant invested in warm, fifties-style decor for casual diners. We sat down at a booth near the front register. Eddie was still smiling as wide as his mouth could stretch, gloating about his manly stunt.

"Eddie, being a jerk just ended my willingness to help you."

"Never wanted it. Nothin' from the likes of you. Yeah, that's right, never wanted your help."

"Got it."

A freckled waitress forced a smile, then said, as if waiting on tables was the last thing she wanted to do, "What're you guys drinking?"

"Give us a minute, ma'am."

She walked away shaking her head, not pleased with more steps on her rounds.

"I'm gonna cover my ass."

I got up from the table and went outside to a pay phone in the covered entrance to the restaurant. I inserted a dime, dialed the operator, and asked for the police.

"Is this an emergency?" said the police dispatcher.

"No, sir. But I have a question. Did anyone call in an incident at a bar called the Pothole?"

"What kind of incident?"

"A guy pulled a pistol and made threatening gestures."

"Hold please, sir."

After a short wait, the officer came back on the line. "There was a call about a man with a gun at the Pothole. What do you know about this incident?"

"I'm with the guy who pulled the pistol at the Pothole. His name is Eddie Kelter. He's with me at the City J Restaurant on North Tryon Street."

"Hold please, sir."

Another policeman came on the phone with the tone of a man who was crossing off the days until his retirement. I could hear him shuffling papers as he said his name in a husky voice, "Cutter."

That attitude was familiar. Much like the army, paperwork wore out one's interest in the job long before their feet did.

"Who am I speaking with?" he said.

"Zinny Zubell."

"Mr. Zubell, what's your involvement with the incident at the Pothole?"

"I'm the guy who convinced Eddie Kelter to leave the Pothole."

"Are you a friend of his?"

"No, sir. I met him while on the job."

"What job?"

"Investigator for a law firm."

"Good for you." His sarcasm oozed out of phone. "CPD has sent patrolmen to the Pothole to investigate the incident."

"I'm with Eddie Kelter at the City J Restaurant on North Tryon right now."

"Okay. CPD appreciates your civic duty. You say this guy is with you right now?"

"Yes, sir."

"Is he still armed?"

"His .22 is in his car at the restaurant."

"Okay. I'll send a cruiser there for Mr. Kelter. Why don't you come along, just for grins, okay?" said Cutter. "Let me speak with Mr. Kelter."

"You have a problem with what I'm doing, sir?"

"Did I say anything like that?"

"Okay. I see him coming out right now."

Eddie exited the restaurant with a confused frown on his face. Seeing me on the phone, he said, "That—that your friend?"

"The police," I said.

Not believing me, he mocked me with a sneer, jerked the phone out of my hand, then said into the receiver, "Fuck ya."

The blood in Eddie's face drained away when he heard Cutter's voice. He got a dose of real police threats from a seasoned policeman. The fun was over. He hung up the phone with care as if he expected Cutter's teeth to bite him through the receiver. His lighthearted mood sank. "That—that—that was—was a real cop."

"I don't want Slade and Lugs reporting me to the police. My advice: Don't run, be respectful, cooperate. Tell them you had reason to fear for your safety after Slade beat up your sister. And for God's sake, apologize for cursing at the man. Say it was a big misunderstanding."

Eddie stood there, not saying a word. He shook his head from side to side in disbelief. He started pacing in small circles, avoiding eye contact. "Fuck! Fuck! Fuck!"

"I'll back up your story, Eddie."

He didn't answer.

"Do you want me to call Silver?"

No response. He wouldn't face me. He kept mumbling.

I stood with him by his Mustang. About ten minutes later, two squad cars with blaring sirens pulled into the City J Restaurant's parking lot. Four uniforms got out. A small gathering exited the restaurant to witness the scene. I motioned the police over to us. I pointed at Eddie for identification. Forming bookends around him, two officers guided him to the nearest squad car, pushed him facedown across the hood, frisked him, and asked about the weapon. I walked toward the uniforms to explain the situation. A patrolman escorted me to the back seat of the second squad car. Another officer went to Eddie's Mustang, where he found the .22 on the driver's seat. Eddie was incomprehensible because he was stuttering, spitting with his eyes wide open. They handcuffed him. He was in for an unpleasant stay with the police.

———

Down the hall on the second floor of police headquarters, my escort guided me to the detective squad room with straight rows of cluttered steel desks. At the fourth desk from the door, I read the nameplate: Stedman Cutter. I stepped up to face a man in his late fifties, with brown-and-white hair, attired in a white short-sleeved shirt too small for his round stomach and a brown tie best served tying up tomato plants. The officer left me alone with Detective Cutter.

"Sir? Detective Cutter?"

"Yeah," he mumbled like he did on the phone. It took him a long ten-count to glance up. "It's all about the paperwork, right?" I said.

"Who wants to know?"

"Zinny Zubell, the guy who turned in Eddie Kelter."

"Oh yeah, that's right. Sit." He looked me up and down. "You don't look like a guy who hangs out at a shithole like the Pothole."

"Investigating a guy who frequents the bar."

"Investigating what? Or who?"

"I'm not at liberty to say."

"Why not?"

"The attorney who hired me told me to keep my mouth shut."

"Figures. What can you tell me about this guy, Edward Kelter?" He looked down at the police report. "Pulled a pistol on one Damon Slade."

"He beat up Eddie's sister. And Eddie was afraid Slade would come after him as well. That's why he came to the bar to confront him."

"You said you couldn't tell me anything. Get your story straight, son."

"I'm still learning."

"Not too bright, huh? Is his sister filing charges against Slade?"

"Don't know."

"Since you're opening up, what else can you tell me that I need to know?"

"Eddie Kelter is looking for his mom, Mosie Kelter. Some mystery behind her sudden disappearance—"

"I don't know anything about that," Cutter interrupted. "What's your contact info in case we need to speak with you again?"

I put my business card on his desk with my handwritten phone number. I asked for a ride back to my truck. I waited about forty-five minutes, then called a cab.

———

The major and I spent the weekend drinking beer, eating frozen dinners, and watching too much television. We sparred over the pile of beer cans and half-eaten food trays lying around his chair that I refused to clean up. He was stubborn to the point of his area smelling like a garbage bin.

I left the house around ten that morning without telling him where I was heading. I went to the Charlotte police station on Third Street to find out about the charges against Eddie Kelter. The desk sergeant confirmed his arraignment was set for nine o'clock this morning. I walked to the Mecklenburg County Courthouse in hopes the wheels of justice were slow.

Two hours later Eddie Kelter appeared before the judge looking sleep deprived, unshaven, and his hair greasy and wet. His lips protruded out, pouting like a disciplined child, wearing an oversized orange jumpsuit labeled Mecklenburg County Jail. He kept his head bent in humiliation.

The round-faced, perfunctory, muttering judge waited for the district attorney to read the charges filed against Edward Kelter. His attorney, carrying at least a six-inch stack of legal folders under his left arm, stood with Eddie as the DA read the three charges filed against him. He greeted Eddie like he had just met him and knew as much about him as a retailer did about a new customer. The judge reviewed the paperwork briefly, then asked, "How do you plead, Mr. Kelter?"

"Not guilty, Your Honor," said his attorney in a seersucker suit.

"Bail recommendation?" the judge asked.

"The state recommends fifteen hundred dollars."

"So ordered. Bail set at fifteen hundred dollars."

A sheriff escorted Eddie back to jail. I introduced myself to Eddie's attorney, then inquired about paying the bail bond. He directed me downstairs to the court clerk for an interminable wait for the paperwork to arrive from the courtroom. Two hours later, after posting bond with a recommended bonding company, I met up with a sheriff's deputy escorting Eddie to the release station. He looked dazed. The deputy reached out with a bag of his few possessions. Eddie wouldn't take it, so I did. The deputy informed us Eddie's Mustang was in an impound lot. Information about retrieving the car was in the bag.

After departing the courthouse, Eddie angrily grabbed the bag. "Gimme my stuff."

"I posted your bond. You're welcome."

"Why, huh? Huh? Yeah, what's up with you, man? Huh? Huh? Why's— why's your lawyer coming after me? I owe folks. Right, but what the fuck! I'm good to pay up, ya know?"

"I don't know anything about that. That's not why I'm here—"

"Then what the fuck, man?"

"I got my reasons."

"Don't need it, don't want it, don't need it, asshole. Yeah, you got it?"

"It's stupid to turn down my help."

"You—you—you turned me in. Help me? You're—you're fuckin' crazy, man. Get away from me."

How desperate could I be to want to help an unappreciative jerk like Eddie Kelter? My interest in finding out more about Damon Slade was trumping any PI experience I gained from being around Eddie. But I was willing to help the guy despite his resistance.

"How about this, Eddie? I won't charge you to search for your mom. But I do expect payment for posting bond. Take me to Silver, and I'll give you a lift to the impound lot."

"No fuckin' way."

It started to rain hard. I jogged across the street to the parking deck next to the courthouse. Eddie followed me, cursing me and his lot in life. The expression on his face was easy to read: no one was willing to help him without a price. Getting drenched got him angrier. He stayed way behind me. I didn't unlock the passenger's door when he finally walked to my truck.

"You want a lift to your car? Then you gotta take me to Silver."

"She won't like you, man. Gettin' none of that. No way." He shook his head from side to side, slamming his fist against my truck door. "Okay. Gimme a lift. Tryon Suites."

He gave me confusing directions on too many backstreets to be the best route to the Tryon Suites. He needed time to be himself. I heard him snicker after he told me to turn left at an intersection we passed through earlier. After a few more miles of circular driving, I turned into an industrial parking lot, stopped my truck, and reached across the seat to grab Eddie by his T-shirt. He had nauseating breath.

"Get out!" I shouted.

"No."

"Give me the address now, or I'll kick you out."

"You won't."

I hurried around to the passenger-side door, tugged him from the seat, then shoved him to the concrete with every intention of leaving him there. I worked slowly around my truck to the driver's side. I meant what I said. I started my truck and backed out of the parking space.

"C'mon, man, c'mon," he shouted as he slammed the back panel of my truck. "Okay, okay."

"One more chance, asshole. I mean it."

———

The Tryon Suites was a weatherworn one-story building with a crumbling exterior. A traveling salesman's motel twenty years ago, it was now a rest stop for people with limited resources and an eyesore to the Western Electric plant nearby. The police had to frequent the dump weekly. I asked Eddie for the room number, and he mumbled, "Seventy-nine." Weaving around the broken pavement on the back wing of the motel facing the rear of a distributor's warehouse was the room with a loose brad hanging on the door. I stood next to Eddie while he knocked on the locked door. Silver yelled out from inside the room, "Go away."

"It's Eddie. It's Eddie."

Silver opened the door wearing a short, tight T-shirt, cutoff jeans, white socks, and her hair in a ponytail. Silver was irate. The beating she endured— her face bruised, her right eye swollen and black, bruise marks on both arms where Slade grabbed her—was obvious in daylight. She raged at Eddie's bowed head.

"What happened to you? This place stinks. I've been eating candy bars and McDonald's for days. And some asshole banged on my door all last night."

Still outside the room, Eddie sheepishly looked up into her eyes. She blasted him again. "Have you been out drinking all this time?"

"Jail."

"For what? What'd you do?"

I responded for him. "He pointed a pistol at Slade at the Pothole."

She screamed as if attacked. "Jesus Christ, Eddie! He's gonna kill me because you did that. How stupid can you be! He'll really kill me this time." She lunged forward and slapped his face hard. He took it without pushback.

In the worst way, Eddie wanted to slug me for ratting him out, but he restrained himself. Next he stomped across the motel room, isolated himself in the bathroom, yelled like a yelping hound, and slammed his fist repeatedly against the bathroom door.

She faced me. "Are you a cop?"

"No."

"Are you one of Eddie's drinking buddies? I ain't gonna let any of you grease monkeys get drunk around me anymore. One of 'em tried to force me to have sex. I bit him hard and kicked him in the balls."

"No. It's not like that. I was there at the Pothole and stepped in to prevent a shooting. And I bailed him out today."

"Mister, I don't have the money to pay you back right now."

"I didn't help Eddie for money. Just real curious why your mom disappeared. I'm offering my help. You see, Silver, I'm uh . . . I'm uh . . . kinda an investigator."

"You look familiar, mister. But I don't know why. I can't deal with all this. Not now. Not now. I'm too scared to think straight. We don't have the money for that kind of help." Then she erupted with out-of-control shouting. "Wait a minute. What did Eddie offer you? I won't do any favors for him. You hear me, mister?"

"No, no, no. Nothing like that. I wanna help you guys find your mom."

"Why, mister? She don't wanna be found."

"Eddie thinks differently."

"He's an idiot."

"Eddie thinks Slade knows something."

"He don't."

"Let me find that out. And, also, I don't like the way Slade treats you."

"You think I do!"

Without thinking, I said, "I saw what he did to you in Stuartville."

Her reaction was immediate. "Oh my God. I remember you now. You're the guy Damon showed my poster to. Oh my God, you're stalking me. I got beat up because of all that. Stay the fuck away from us, mister."

Silver slammed the door. She shouted at Eddie, "See what you've done. You brought this guy into our life. Slade will kill both of us, Eddie. You stupid idiot."

Subtlety was never my strong suit. Another misstep in my on-the-job training. I went into my wallet to slide two business cards under the door. Leaning close to the door, I said, "You got me all wrong. I'm only here to help. Call me if I can help you guys."

"Go away, mister."

I waited outside their room as I heard Silver shouting at Eddie to come out of the bathroom.

Lost another job. I couldn't give away my services.

CHAPTER 6

Sports, weather, or the news never interested the major. His lack of interest in anything I said about sports, weather, or the news would eventually lead to a pointless argument. That was his overpowering mood. He sat in his chair all day and night. He rarely slept in his bedroom. The major's body odor was spreading across the living room to where I avoided the sofa. I told him to shower; he said he couldn't stand up that long. He could. He was being stubborn just to aggravate me. And listless, just sitting around swilling beer and eating junk food.

To get away, I drove to the Pothole at happy hour for the next few afternoons. Not to confront Slade or Lugs. Not to go into the bar but to do something. I waited in my truck in the parking lot with my driver-side window open and watched the drinkers coming and going. Every fifteen minutes or so, I got out and walked around the lot to sort-of exercise. I was there for no other reason than to have somewhere to be, pretending to work for a client.

At dusk on the third afternoon, two men in business suits came to the Pothole in a new Buick LeSabre, parked beside my truck, got out without paying me any attention, and went inside. It was odd seeing country-club types entering a sleazy bar. I was intrigued, but not enough to check out their story.

I waited and watched like a bored scout. No more than fifteen minutes later, Slade, in jeans and a golf shirt, walked out of the bar with the suits. None of them appeared to be in good spirits. Slade had a pained expression, stared down at the gravel lot, and didn't notice my focused attention on the approaching group.

"Damon, do you still think it's wise to be in business with Lugs?" said the suit to Slade's left. He spoke with no regard to whom might be listening.

"He's my friend and partner. It's legit, guys," Slade said curtly.

"Okay, Damon. Don't get upset," said the other suit. He reached for Slade's arm to face him before the group arrived at the Buick. No one noticed my prying ears.

"Listen, Damon, we set up this meeting to clear the air with Blaine and Bonnie Ridge. Get ahead of her accusations about you. Just try your best to stay calm," said the suit who halted him.

"How do I do that? I got a mind to take her to court."

"Just hear them out. Blaine believes Bonnie has lost her mind since the accident. Don't bring this up, but he's seriously thinking about having her committed for evaluation," said the suit to Slade's left.

"She needs to shut up. Or a lawsuit will do it," said Slade.

I listened with my left ear outside the truck window. Slade was the first to see me.

"There he is." All three glared at me as if I were a serious problem. Slade pulled the suits close so he could whisper something out of earshot. They agreed and made pointed hand gestures in my direction. Slade spoke up. "He's Claude Sedley's goon with some weird name."

Like guards in a watchtower, the suits engaged in a staring contest between us that made for an uneasy standoff. I leaned on my side to remove my wallet, pulled out my business card, then reached out the window to extend my card-carrying hand. "Here you go, guys. I wouldn't want you to misspell my name."

The older man took my card. The two suits looked at each other as if their thoughts were a collective mind. The man with my card shook his head up and down, mumbling, "Another one."

The younger suit walked to the driver's seat; Slade, the passenger's side; the other man to the back seat. They departed without further eye contact. Slade made men I had never seen before pay attention to my pursuit of his activities.

Another one? What was he talking about? A mysterious statement from someone I had no dealings with. Another reason to unravel what was going on between Sedley and Slade.

There was no reason to stay at the Pothole. Heading home, my thoughts danced around Slade and his escorts heading to a meeting about accusations he adamantly denied.

———

Losing a night's sleep was of no consequence. In the quiet of the night, I listened to the major dealing with the loneliness of his pain. In those hours, he confronted the pain without notice. No pretending he inured the pain. I often heard him moan. He tried his best to grumble as quietly as he could. But tonight he screamed out—a painful scream I remembered too well from 'Nam. I got up to see what I could do for him.

"Anything I can do?" I asked, bending over his chair.

He reacted with a swift roundhouse fist against my sternum. I backed up. The major needed no comforting hand, just a release. I obliged. He didn't apologize or ask for anything. I went back to bed.

Before sunrise I woke up thinking about my former girlfriend, Sally Aberdeen. The best two years of my army career were when she and I served together at Fort Bragg before my third tour in 'Nam. Sally wasn't like my ex-wife, Jeannie. She was an athletic, spit-and-polish, hard-running first sergeant who could match wits with any bull noncoms while still maintaining her femininity. When I returned to the States after my third tour, we reunited at the Pentagon on General Haywood's staff. Sally approached me early on in my reentry to single life about no-strings-attached dating, at least until my rebound love showed up, she said.

I never believed a woman who offered uncommitted dating. Despite reiterating everything was okay, I kept Sally at an emotional distance, following my pattern of being casual about a commitment as she warmed up to being a couple. She got cold while I moved around her in my self-centered world. She said that infamous statement—we should see other people. My lack of understanding relationships with women was vast.

I screwed up. I backed up on my commitment to Sally to strip my reverse gear. I never allowed myself to appreciate how much I needed, wanted her. When she said we should start seeing others, I sulked and gave up on the relationship. She moved on to pursue a behind-the-scenes affair with General Haywood. He was using her to fulfill a lust I understood.

Our friendship continued, without a physical aspect, but my heart pined for her. Sally was the woman I never realized how much I could love. I fell for the right woman after she was out of my arms.

At the alarming hour of five thirty in the morning, I called her. She answered on the third ring with a sleepy voice. "Hello?"

"Sal, it's me."

"Zin? What's wrong? Where're you?"

"In Charlotte."

"Why'd you leave Washington so fast? And didn't tell me where you were going."

"I just couldn't."

"Why Charlotte?"

"It's close to Major Jack."

"How's he?"

"A real pain in the ass."

"Good. He's doing better. How often do you see him?"

"He's living with me."

"Hmm. Doesn't sound like something you'd do."

"After your boyfriend fired me, I decided to do some good for somebody. The major was in a bad state at the VA."

"I'm proud of you for helping Jack. But you got to know the general had no choice, Zin."

"Yes, he did."

"I'm not gonna argue with you. I can't change what's been done." She cleared her throat before changing the subject. "So tell me why you left without saying goodbye."

"Avoid the temptation of slugging your boyfriend."

"Don't say things like that, Sergeant Major. Believe me, he feels awful about what he had to do. Senior staff had to be retired after 'Nam. He hasn't slept well since the RIFs."

"He's sleeping at your place now, huh?"

"Don't ask me about that."

"I still think about us."

"Don't, Zin. You know that isn't a part of us anymore. Tell me that you're okay."

"I'm okay."

"Call me later, okay?"

"You know he'll never leave his wife. It'll hurt any promotion he might be up for."

"Zin, please."

"You deserve better than a married man."

"I don't wanna hang up on you, but I will. You're no shining star when it comes to relationships. Find a woman who'll do what you like. She's out there. You're one of my best friends, but don't confuse love with lust. And don't call me if all you wanna do is make me feel bad."

"One more thing, Sal. It wasn't me who spread rumors about you and the general."

"Take care, Zin." She hung up.

Later that morning, Major Jack was still in his chair when I returned to the house with coffee and sausage biscuits from a nearby restaurant. I was beyond asking him what he was planning to do today. I had a thought. I mistakenly shared it with him.

"You think physical therapy would help? Maybe the VA will pay—"

"It fuckin' sucks that my feet won't ever get better. I can't push myself to get better."

Admitting his injuries were irreparable crushed any hope he had for a better day. No reason to comment. I sat down on the sofa to read the *Charlotte Observer* that I picked up outside the restaurant. I turned to the local section. An article caught my attention:

Body found in sunken car.

A dive team, examining the structural base of the bridge crossing Mountain Island Lake, found a decomposed body in a sunken car under the bridge. The discovery comes amid the charged debate concerning Governor Reynolds's plans for bridge improvements.

Identification of the body is pending an autopsy by the state medical examiner.

I stopped reading. My imagination jumped to a what-if scenario. Could the body be Eddie's mother? It was implausible to come to that conclusion with nothing to go on. But I was interested enough to phone the Tryon Suites. The phone rang six times before a grumpy man answered. I asked for room seventy-nine. No one answered the phone in the room.

———

The rest of the morning I thought about job searching, seeking a position from investigation firms in the yellow pages and revisiting law firms that accepted my business card. But I wasted too much time thinking about following through with the plan than doing something with a plan in mind. I ended up doing nothing—didn't even open the yellow pages. Instead, I enjoyed an afternoon of beers and salted peanuts.

I was surprised when the phone rang after five.

"Is this the not-too-bright investigator, Zinny Zubell? This is Detective Cutter."

I enjoyed his sarcastic tone. "Surprised hearing from you, sir."

"I wanna talk to your boy, Eddie Kelter. He's a no-show at work, and he lives where he works. What a dump."

"Where's that, Detective?"

"The W and J Wreck House. You're lousy at investigating. You have any idea where we can find him?"

"I took him to the Tryon Suites on North Tryon, room seventy-nine, after the bail hearing."

"What's he doing there?"

"Hiding with his sister, Silver, from Damon Slade."

"Why're they hiding?"

"Like I told you—he's afraid of what Slade would do to him and his sister. Ya know, speaking of Eddie Kelter, I read in the morning paper about a woman found in her car in Mountain Island Lake. I was wondering if the woman was Eddie's mom."

"What's your interest in that?"

"That's why Eddie pulled the .22 on Slade."

"What's her name?"

"He called her Mosie. Mosie Kelter."

Silence on his end. The delay had to be Cutter weighing what to tell me. "Well, I'll tell you this much. The license plate on the car was titled to Margaret Louise Kelter."

Devastating news for Eddie and Silver. He put up with beatings in pursuit of his mom's disappearance. And felony charges for forcing his concern at gunpoint.

"Thanks for sharing, Detective."

"That wasn't sharing, son. Public info. You know they're at the Tryon Suites?"

"I called the Tryon Suites earlier today asking for Eddie. The motel manager said they checked out."

"Why're you getting involved?"

"Like I told ya, I'm doing some investigating for an attorney—"

"Well, good luck with that."

Detective Cutter hung up. My interest level from a simple delivery to Damon Slade to a woman found at the bottom of a lake was heating up.

———

There was no follow-up article in the *Charlotte Observer* the next morning about Mosie's car in Mountain Island Lake. I opted to return to the Pothole later that afternoon without telling Major Jack where I was going.

Lugs had parked his big butt on a stool behind the bar looking at *Penthouse* magazine. I had the *Charlotte Observer* in my hand. Lugs had an immediate reaction to my presence, pointing at the door. "Fuck off! You ain't drinkin' here."

I approached him anyway. "Seen this article?" I held up the local section of yesterday's paper with my index finger on the article about the car found in Mountain Island Lake.

Lugs squinted to read the byline. "So?"

"Cops told me it's Eddie Kelter's mom in the lake."

I watched for his response. I wanted an instantaneous truthful reaction to the news. A nonmedicinal truth serum. I expected surprise, but he seemed unmoved by the article from all I could tell. He looked up with hardened eyes.

"I hear a nobody running his mouth in my bar. And that nobody better get outta here."

No reason to agitate a guy looking for a fight. I left.

———

Back at home, Major Jack had a disgusted look on his face after I told him about the brief encounter with Lugs.

"You really want your teeth knocked out, right?"

"Eddie believes there's a connection between Slade and Lugs and his mom's disappearance. And I'm beginning to wonder about that."

"The only connection is Lugs's fist to your teeth."

"I trust my instincts."

"You and that idiot on the same page? That's not onto something. That's sticking your nose where it don't belong."

"I'm within the law, Jack. If I find anything, I'll go to the cops. That's not sticking my nose where it don't belong."

"You'll keep turning over rocks until you find trouble."

"Yep."

"Fucking A."

"You up for a ride tonight?"

———

A high level of curiosity lured me to set up an observation post at the W and J Wreck House. I drove there with Major Jack to check on the comings and goings of Eddie and Silver Kelter. There was value practicing the patience of watching and waiting for something to happen.

The W and J Wreck House, an auto repair business off South Boulevard, was in a business district of warehouses, paint stores, lumberyards, and small strip malls. The yard on the side of the shop was a refuge for worn-out vehicles; a chain-link fence surrounded the establishment. Overnight lights were on in the first-floor office. An outside stairwell led to the second-story door, where I assumed Eddie lived. There were no lights on.

I parked on a side street with a view of the second story. Checking around on the quiet street, I noticed a white '62 Cadillac convertible parked about thirty yards behind us on the same side of the street. *Was there someone in the car?*

"Let me get this straight," Major Jack said. "We're here to wait for what?"

"To see who shows up."

"Why?"

"Eddie could be in trouble."

"How do you know that?"

"A hunch."

"Man, you have a real boner for that girl."

"No. But she's real cute."

"You got no life. 'Course, neither do I. Here we are, doing nothing."

A short while later, the Cadillac's headlights came on; the car headed toward us at no more than five miles per hour. When the car stopped at my open window, I peered into the open passenger-side window at Damon Slade.

"Had an idea you'd show up. Still working for Sedley, huh? A little advice, shithead: Stay outta my business. I'm warning you," Slade said, then drove off.

Slade was on the hunt for them. That was bad news.

———

I kept up my vigil the next night at the W and J Wreck House without Major Jack. I arrived around dusk. Earlier, at dinner, I read in the *Charlotte News* that the state examiner's office had identified the skeleton in Mountain Island Lake without releasing a name, pending notification of next of kin.

An hour and a half after arriving at my watch, Silver drove up in Eddie's Mustang, followed by Slade in his white Cadillac. Eddie dashed out of the passenger's side to open the fence. He had on dress slacks and a white shirt, Sunday church clothes for a man who got dirty for a living. I had a brief opportunity to waylay him before he was inside the fence. I called out to him as I got out of my truck.

"Eddie, you all right?"

Astonished, Eddie fumbled his keys, like a worm on hot concrete, while struggling to insert the key in the fence lock. I jogged to him. The closer I got, the more difficulty he had with the lock. He sputtered curse words and slammed his fist into the steel mesh fence.

"Eddie, what's going on?"

I bent down to see Silver behind the wheel of the Mustang. "I'm sorry for your loss, Silver."

"Mister, we don't want trouble. I know Eddie owes you money, but this ain't the right time." Her eyes were puffy, her black eye shadow running about an inch down her face. Despite her best efforts, the bruises and black eye from Slade's beating were visible.

"Silver, you need help?"

"Leave us be. I don't wanna get hurt this bad again."

Eddie unlocked the fence and stepped behind the gate, where he felt safe enough to yell, "Asshole, you're—you're making things worse. Go away."

"How, Eddie?"

I turned back to Silver, who appeared to retreat into a dark place. She peered over her shoulder in the direction of the Cadillac. She was weighing her concerns, I assumed, frantically thinking how to avoid being prey to violence again, exposing her fear of the man in the white Cadillac.

"Hey, you," Slade said. He came toward me with the steady confidence of a cop after a traffic stop. He summoned me with his forefinger. "Come here, you."

I didn't move.

"Okay, let me lay it out for you," he said in my face. "You're harassing these people. And in my shit a lot."

"Got plenty of problems with a guy who beats up a woman."

"Get the fuck outta here."

"You're making it worse, mister. Please leave," Silver said.

"Cops can stop the worst, Silver," I said.

Eddie opened the gate for Silver to drive the Mustang to the safety of the W and J Wreck House. He shouted at me, "Get! Get!"

Even closer in my face, Slade said, "You can probably handle yourself, so you get a pass. For now. I gotta look pretty for the funeral at three on Thursday at the Endover Towers."

I maintained eye contact with Slade, saying nothing. Neither of us seemed juiced for a dustup. Just hatred boiled down to a high-handed staring contest.

"He's serious, mister. Damon can advance you the money Eddie owes," Silver said, watching us stand toe-to-toe.

"I'm not giving him shit. He bailed out Eddie—that's on him. I've done enough paying for Mosie's funeral."

Slade backed away and headed for his Cadillac. The tension de-escalated faster than I imagined. Eddie hustled to lock the fence as Silver parked his Mustang next to the stairwell, and Slade parked next to her. Silver held Eddie's hand as they climbed to his second-story living quarters. Slade followed close behind.

Slade's money brought them back together. What intrigued me was Slade telling me the time and place for Mosie's funeral. He must assume I'd show up. He was right.

CHAPTER 7

Days later the follow-up story in the local section of the *Charlotte Observer* read: "The coroner's autopsy on the woman found in her car in Mountain Island Lake concluded her death was an accidental drowning."

Accidental drowning. That should put to rest any suspicion Eddie had about his mom's mysterious disappearance. What stirred up Slade's anger? The optics of his grievances made me believe there was more to his anger than a legal or money dispute. There was no reason to pursue answers. Slade warned me not to go to Mosie Kelter's funeral. It would be smart to stay away from everyone involved with Damon Slade.

———

I dressed in my plaid blazer, white shirt, and service khakis to attend Mosie's funeral. Major Jack insisted on going with me, even dressing in his wrinkled white shirt and service khakis. I had doubts about his interest in attending a funeral. He talked more than usual to convince me that he would be civil and respectful at the solemn rite. I wanted to believe him. He even agreed to use his crutches.

On Thursday, at 1500, the parking lot at the Endover Towers was full of cars. A funeral driver parked a black Cadillac limousine at the sidewalk leading to the entrance of the building. The ten-story building on South Boulevard had the design of a college dormitory. The location on a busy four-lane street—stuck among churches, small retail stores, and commercial buildings—made me think this facility was for public housing for the elderly. An unusual site to hold a funeral.

We planned to arrive after the funeral had started on purpose, wanting to sit in the back to be the first out of the building. There I could observe the interactions of the attendees as they filed out, especially Slade, Eddie, Silver, and Lugs.

After we parked at the back of the lot, we were surprised to see groups of couples exiting the building. Men in suits and women in understated dresses. The funeral crowd. Major Jack and I looked at each other.

He said, "I thought you said three?"

"That's what Slade said."

We went toward the first couple approaching us. I stepped ahead to ask, "Was that Mosie Kelter's funeral?"

"Yes," the man said.

"I was told it was at three."

"No. Two. It was a beautiful service for a sweet lady."

Slade's purposeful deception. I headed to the building, nodding at the passing couples like I was the friendly type. Major Jack, using his crutches, trudged behind me. I traipsed around the two dozen or so couples lingering after the service to chat up one another. On the sidewalk outside the front door, I saw the two guys who escorted Slade and Lugs out of the Pothole. They noticed me at about the same time I saw them. The older of the two men came forward with a purpose in mind. He never broke eye contact.

"Sir," he slowly approached me, "how can I help you?" The intent behind his words was the opposite of friendly.

"We're here to pay our respects. That's all."

I looked away from his stare to avoid even a hint of a confrontation. He backed away to walk with an affable group strolling to their cars. I scanned the crowd for Slade or Eddie or Silver. I wondered if they waited for the crowd to disperse before exiting the building.

Major Jack walked up behind me. "Well, a waste of time. I gotta go to the head, Zin." He reassured me with a head shake and an agreeable grin. He slapped me on the back. "I won't be long."

"Can't it wait?"

He shook his head with the honesty of a teenager promising to be home before midnight.

"We should get outta here. Don't be long."

Major Jack took longer than he should to return from the bathroom. I went to the door to the building to wait for him after greeting the last of the dispersing couples, who in turn were courteous. Eddie Kelter came outside with a teary face, walking slowly with two men in white shirts, khakis, and no neckties. As he passed me, I said, "Sorry for your loss, Eddie." He ignored me. One man had his arm around Eddie's shoulder as they headed for the limo. Peering down the straight hallway, I saw Slade guiding Silver by the back of her arm toward the exit. She looked more stunned—a cry for help or just overcome with grief.

Slade kept moving Silver until they were about fifteen feet away. I gestured to her with a halfhearted wave. Slade angled her out the door, away from me, then whispered something I couldn't make out.

I looked all around for Major Jack. He was nowhere in sight. I turned around to find Slade only a few feet from my face. Silver remained where he left her. This was my cue to turn away, search for the major, and avoid trouble. But Slade grabbed my arm, yanking me closer to him. A confrontation I never believed possible at a funeral was unfolding.

"Hey, I told you not to come."

"I don't want trouble, Slade, so hands off me."

He tightened his grip. "What's eating your bones, huh? Claude Sedley's got you all jacked up for a fight."

He poked his left index finger hard against my chest. I slapped his hand away, trying to wrestle his grip off my arm. He tightened it.

"It's a funeral, Slade. What's your problem?"

"Me and the church elders are getting tired of you, and we're gonna do something about it." He again poked his finger against my chest. "You want money? Here you go."

Slade reached into his left pants pocket for a handful of bills, tossed them in my face, and laughed with dismissive ridicule at the demeaning act. He relaxed his grip on my arm, so I jerked it downward and caught him off guard. He released his grip, struggling to maintain his balance. After regaining control, Slade shoved me, and I almost fell over. My frustration built up quicker than I could control. My fist landed right below Slade's left eye and nose, staggering him. My right hand stung from the force of the blow. Slade fell. He stayed on the ground with a stream of blood running from his nose.

"You fucked up now!" Slade shouted, checking his hand for blood.

It was a given that I should know how to respond with more restraint to a deliberate confrontation. I then noticed the slight smile on Slade's face. I should have walked away. Slade wanted me to slug him. I was set up, and he'd file charges against me.

Silver rushed to Slade's aid, knelt beside him, but he pushed her away. He stayed on the ground and rolled on his side to rub his jaw. He stunned me when his wrath erupted at Silver.

"For your fuckin' sake, you better not be friendly with this guy."

"Damon, I didn't do anything. Why're you mad at me?"

Slade labored to stand up. "You need another lesson, missy." He grabbed Silver's right arm to pull her in the building. She resisted like a hellcat. I stood there. *Get involved?*

"Zinny! Zinny!" I heard the major shouting behind the building. I jogged across the grass to see Major Jack using his crutches to exit the back side of the building at a faster pace than normal. He sounded excited, alarmed. I stopped running, glanced over my shoulder at the entrance to Endover Towers, but Slade and Silver never came out. The major beckoned me with his right crutch to pick him up. With a difficult decision at hand, I chose loyalty to the major over intervening in a domestic situation. I hustled to my truck, circled the parking lot, made a left turn on South Boulevard, then a U-turn to pick up the major.

I watched him pull and twist his legs to climb into my truck.

"What's wrong?"

"I tagged Lugs with my crutches."

"You did what?" I was surprised he did that.

"Yeah, I got him good in his balls after he slapped me like a girl."

With cars stopped and honking behind me, I drove on. "Well, there's a coincidence. I slugged Slade."

"That's not like you. He deserved it, right?"

His delight at my overreaction convinced me that we had to talk. Blocks away, I spotted a Toddle House restaurant. I parked in a space near the front entrance to give Major Jack fewer steps to walk inside.

"Jack, we're outta control. I stepped on the gas too soon for a new career. Look where we are."

"We don't adjust well."

"And I dragged you along to add to my issues."

"What I do best." The major smiled.

"They'll file charges."

"You don't know that."

"Slade said it without saying the words."

"My God, a marine can't take a punch every now and again?"

"He set me up to do what he wanted. Now he has the upper hand."

We ordered the house special: hamburger steak with gravy, mashed potatoes, green beans, and sweet tea. After eating without talking, I decided to get in front of whatever Slade and Lugs decided to do. I was convinced that was the right play. The major disagreed with my decision with a persistent, "No, no, no."

"If we explain our side first, maybe we'll get a break from the authorities. Come clean first about the circumstances."

"I don't see any reason to do that. What if Slade doesn't go to the cops. We confessed to an assault the cops don't know about. Huh? That's stupid, right?"

—

I dropped off the major in front of the Charlotte police station and circled around the block for a public parking garage. The major, to his obvious disgust, had done too much walking today. He was upset about being here to the point of refusing to ride in the elevator to the second floor of the police station. Climbing the stairs, he lost his balance and fell backward, clutching his crutches and not the railing. Fortunately, I was holding the support railing and able to block his fall.

"Bad idea, Zin. Remind me to tell you so over and over."

Detectives ignored us as we walked into their squad room. Cutter, however, leaned back in his chair and locked his hands behind his head, clearly irritated by an interruption from his paperwork. "What do we have here?"

"We're here to talk about an incident involving us, Detective."

No invitation to sit in the chairs in front of his desk. He shook his head as if he were dealing with starstruck wannabe cops.

"What does that mean?" He avoided eye contact.

"Sir, there might be reports of incidents involving us."

"Son, I don't have time for games, and I'm not looking for more work. Good day."

"Make a note, sir. We tried to cooperate."

He tossed the pencil balanced between his right ear and scalp across the room. "Goddamn it. What kinda incident?"

"At Mosie Kelter's funeral."

"A funeral? What the fuck happened at a funeral?" Cutter shook his head, released a disgusted sigh, then leaned forward in his chair. "Okay, talk."

"Damon Slade poked and shoved me for no reason at the Endover Towers. So I slugged him. And Major Klinkscales defended himself after he was slapped by Lugs."

"Poked? Did you just say poked? And slapped? At a funeral? Who's Lugs? I've heard too many stories about wild shenanigans, but poked! That's another winner. This is what I have to put up with for a measly paycheck."

"Let's go, Jack. You were right."

"Sit. I'll check this out."

Cutter picked up his phone and asked a dispatcher about a police report involving an assault at Endover Towers. He waited for a minute before saying, "I see. Thanks." Cutter hung up the phone. "Hmm. Well, well, well. Seems there are folks who have issues with you boys. And our patrolmen are on-site taking statements about an assault. My, my, my. And here you are. And just for the record, it don't matter that you came before we found ya."

No favorable check marks for cooperation.

"Your friend doesn't say much, does he?" Cutter said to Major Jack.

"What's the point? I'm here," said the major with a sarcastic tone.

"What attitude are you boys going with?"

"We're in-line, sir," I said.

"Good. Tell me this: You think PIs should go around slugging folks?"

"No. We're gonna be here awhile, right?"

"Looks like it, gentlemen. Let's see what's in the reports."

"Probably best we talk to a lawyer," I said.

Cutter fixed his stare on Major Jack, who hopefully knew saying nothing was the right move.

"What's your beef with those people?"

"It's best we don't say anything else," I said.

"All right. All right. Welcome to our world." The satisfaction he felt was evident in his alert green eyes.

I struggled to stay calm. The thought of confinement made me crazy; the anxiety brought waves of anger. I flashed back to a challenging exercise at a mock prisoner-of-war camp during special forces training for 'Nam. The mental abuse of confinement was much more difficult than any physical harassment. There was no way to build up enough fortitude to deal with it, yet I remembered useful advice from an instructor: "Let your anger get you through it. Get angry; stay angry."

Cutter made a call to alert the cruiser we were already at the station. He turned to his right to type a report while asking pertinent questions to our arrest. "Hire a good attorney who pleads you down to whatever the system calls for. The judge will laugh when he sees the word *poked*. But tonight you're with us."

Cutter marched us downstairs at a gait the major couldn't keep up. He refused any assistance. The jail atmosphere was stale, as it was cleaned with dirty mops and ammonia water. A uniformed woman fingerprinted and photographed us. Our clothes and possessions taken, we changed into orange jumpsuits; then we were escorted upstairs to a holding cell. Before leaving us with a perfunctory jailer in a brown Mecklenburg County sheriff's uniform, Cutter said, "Sweet dreams, boys." Turning to the jailer, he said, "Bunk them together."

"I wanna call my lawyer," I said.

"One phone call before lockup," said the jailer.

The jailer walked me to a row of phones with the warning of a local call only. I dialed the only phone number I had memorized: Mr. Sedley's law firm. I was concerned my after-hours call would go unanswered. After six rings, a female voice other than the receptionist's said, "Sedley, Cannon."

"Claude Sedley, please."

"Hold, please."

The jailer grew impatient when I wasn't talking. After an uneasy minute passed, I heard, "This is Chip Sedley. How can I help you?"

"This is Zinny Zubell."

"Well, hello. I can't tell you how much mileage I've gotten out of your ten-cards-for-a-dime story." Mr. Sedley's son, the young man I insulted with my dad's ploy, answered my call.

What else could go wrong today?

"Glad you didn't take offense, sir."

Chip said, "So Dad's gone home. I understand you're working with him on something. Do you want to leave him a message?"

"Do you have a good criminal defense attorney at your firm?"

"The best. Lew Ableman. Why?"

"I need to hire him."

The jailer said, "Hurry up. I ain't got all day." The jailer approached to place his finger near the disconnect button. "One minute, and you're done."

"Who's the client?" Chip said.

"Me. I'm in custody. I'll pay the going rate."

"All right. Don't talk to anyone without him present."

The impatient jailer demanded I hang up the phone. He walked Major Jack and me to the city jail, adjacent to police headquarters. I assisted the major despite the jailer's belief he was faking his injury.

The mental anguish of sitting in a jail cell after years of rigid structure and disciplined duty was torturous. Even the major, who found pleasure on the edge of disobedience, seemed disturbed by the predicament. There was a little space to pace. And talking would lead to an argument that might get us separated. Nothing served staring at each other either. Lying on the uncomfortable cots was our pastime. Only an occasional "fuck" broke the silence.

After what seemed like an hour, the major said, "Figures."

"What?"

"We're upside down. Yeah, no career, no family, no purpose. Nothing."

"We shoulda fucked up doing the right things. Not the wrong things."

"Roger that," he said. "Still, I'm glad I crushed Lugs's nuts."

"Yeah, slugging Slade felt good."

"No doubt."

We shut down the conversation, tried to rest, but neither of us went to sleep. I glanced at him many times; his eyes were open. We shared no thoughts. And I stayed in a state of relentless concern. The walls of the cell inched closer hour by hour.

———

In the middle of the night, with no sleep upcoming, I turned to the major and said, "You awake?"

"No."

I grinned in the dark. "Ya know . . ."

"Ya know what?"

"Those guys, Slade and Lugs, are bad guys. My instincts are right. I just—I just wanted to expose them."

"How'd that work out?"

"We're in jail."

"Yeah, so let's review: it's been fucked up from the beginning," he said.

"Hard to argue with that lying in a cell."

"Listen, Zin. Those guys are real assholes. I get that. But from the beginning, you were only a delivery boy and couldn't leave well enough alone, with nothing to gain and everything to lose."

"And what kinda play involves slamming crutches in a guy's nuts?"

"I guess civilians don't put up with that kinda horseplay."

"Yeah. I'm more to blame."

"Accepted."

"Jack, we were stupid."

"That's what we are right now," he said, sitting up.

I sat up. "Hard to see a clean way outta this."

"We'll see how it turns out."

"Maybe we can plea the charges down, but there's still a criminal record."

"We'll adjust in time."

"Oh, really? How?" I asked.

"You're more depressing than me, Zin. And that's fuckin' impossible."

He laid back down. I did as well. I made a mental note that he tried to cheer me up.

The stark light outside our cell was a constant reminder we had gifted the upper hand to people who wanted us to be where we were. Sitting on the edge of my cot, I had ample time to reflect on my actions. My standard operating procedure was duty first, duty strong. But this time I didn't have experience to rely on and didn't know the game nor the players. I had to change my approach, and fast. Or get out.

CHAPTER 8

The next morning a jailer took me to a visiting room to meet with Ableman. He was a slump-shouldered, balding, middle-aged man with a gravelly voice in a gray suit apt for an expensive lawyer. His furrowed, contemplative stare impressed me as a serious man who would be no fun at a dinner party. I liked that about him.

"Mr. Zubell, I'm Lew Ableman. Chip Sedley said you asked for counsel. Is that correct?"

"Yes, sir. Thank you."

"Okay. I read the charges. Let me hear your side of what happened. But first make note: always tell me the truth."

"Yes, sir. I attended a funeral for a woman who drowned in Mountain Island Lake—"

"I remember reading about that."

"Yes, sir. Well, this guy who's pressing charges, Damon Slade, goes out with her daughter. He confronted me at the funeral, started threatening me, poked me hard in the chest repeatedly, then shoved me. I overacted and slugged him."

"Why would he provoke you like that?"

"Claude Sedley Senior hired me to deliver some papers to Damon Slade in Stuartville. I gave him a sealed envelope for his eyes only. He got angry at me and Mr. Sedley before he even opened it. We've had issues ever since."

"Issues? What kind of issues?"

"Hatred, basically."

"No other physical confrontation, right?"

"No, sir."

"Did Claude tell you anything about the contents?"

"No, sir. I assumed it was confidential."

"How long have you known Claude?"

"A few weeks."

"Really? Hmm. How'd you meet him?"

"Walked into your firm and asked for work."

"Do you need work that badly?"

"No, sir. I'm a retired army sergeant major. I was just looking for work as an investigator to get my foot in the door."

"Not anymore. This just doesn't sound like something Claude would do. Hire someone he doesn't know on the spot. Are you still working for him?"

"No, sir. That's why I'm so curious why he hired me."

"Did you have any other dealings with Damon Slade?"

"Mr. Sedley paid me to watch for Slade at a dive called the Pothole."

"Why?"

"He never said."

"That's really odd." After he said that, his body language told me that he regretted being so honest.

"Well, then Mr. Sedley got furious with me and fired me when I told him that I had heard about his brother's suicide at the Pothole."

His reaction was an uncomfortable shift in his chair without telling me why he appeared concerned.

"Seems, sir, I've pissed off Slade and Mr. Sedley, and I don't know why. Can you shed any light on your firm's dealings with Damon Slade?"

"No."

"He paid me in cash."

"That doesn't sound like something Claude would do either. Well, anyway, I've got to be in court shortly. I'll do my best to get you released on personal recognizance."

"And my friend Major Jack Klinkscales."

Taken aback, he crossed his arms with a confused frown. "What're you talking about? I know nothing about your friend."

Did I mention Major Jack when I spoke with Chip Sedley?

"He's in the cell with me. He's charged with assaulting Slade's friend."

"When?"

"At the funeral."

"I don't understand. Was this a brawl? Why wasn't I told about this."

"No, sir, no brawl. Major Jack was assaulted first by the owner of the Pothole—"

"Well, this is a real cluster. We'll go over more details later. Can you post bail if need be?"

"Yes, sir."

"Major, huh? I'm surprised you guys didn't know better."

"Agreed, sir. No excuse."

Ableman shook his head with obvious doubts about representing us. Our actions sounded even worse when I explained them aloud. He could assume I was reckless. He thumbed through a folder he had in his over-stuffed leather briefcase. After perusing paperwork with a quick scan, he resumed an attentive posture, arms on the table, head forward, frowning. "Hmm. Anything else?"

"Maybe Mr. Sedley can shed some light on all the intrigue—"

"Don't concern yourself with intrigue. Stay away from Damon Slade."

He took off his half-frame reading glasses and dropped them on his folders. "Did you say anything to the police without me present?"

"Yes, sir. I said I slugged Slade."

"That doesn't help. Did you tell them that after they recited your rights?"

"Before."

"Okay. All right. All right. Don't talk to anyone without me present from now on."

"Yes, sir. I owe Mr. Sedley an explanation."

"No. Don't. He said don't call him—in a very unprofessional way. I'll see you at the preliminary hearing."

He left the conference room without shaking my hand. Since moving to Charlotte, my life had been more steps down, none up.

———

The preliminary hearing was at one o'clock. I was sleep deprived, weary, my steps laborious, having spent much of the morning pacing in my cell. Major Jack grew impatient with my annoying restlessness. He f-bombed me. I ignored him.

Two deputies escorted me in the orange jumpsuit to the courtroom to stand beside Ableman, who was reviewing a stack of folders. He whispered advice as we stood together at the defense table. "Don't say anything until the judge asks for your plea. Patience. The system works at a turtle's pace."

He then described the overweight judge who would preside over the hearing: "A cop with a gavel." But he assured me that he had ample experience trying cases before the judge and was confident in his ability to assist Major Jack and me.

The court clerk called the next case before the judge. "Case number four three four five nine dash ten, *State of North Carolina versus George Zachary Zubell*. Charges are second-degree assault and battery, trespassing, and communicating threats."

The clerk handed the folder to the judge. He looked up. "I see you're represented by Counselor Ableman, Mr. Zubell."

"Yes, Your Honor. I'm representing Mr. Zubell."

The judge said in a low voice, "How do you plead, Mr. Zubell?"

"Not guilty, Your Honor."

The assistant DA—a tall, suited, thirtyish woman whose voice matched that of a baritone—appeared to be reading the file for the first time. "Your Honor, the state recommends bail be set at fifteen hundred dollars."

Ableman requested release on personal recognizance based on my years of military service. The judge interrupted his plea midsentence. "That's a fair bail. Let's move along, Counselor. So ordered."

An hour and a half later, I paid the bond with the cash I had in my wallet. Ableman told me bail was round one in a lengthy process to clear the charges. He also advised me not to return to the courtroom for Major Jack's hearing. The same judge would preside over his case.

After waiting another hour and a half, I posted the same bond for the major. When we returned home, neither of us were in the mood to talk about anything. Major Jack went to his bedroom to sleep. Restless anger wired me to pace around the living room. Against his advice to avoid any contact with the firm, I decided to pay an unannounced visit to Mr. Sedley tomorrow. He was due an opportunity to vent. I was too.

Around 1100, outside Mr. Sedley's office building, I stopped before entering to go over the precise wording of my apology for assaulting Slade. At the ornamental steel-and-glass doors, I saw four men in suits escorting a woman in a wheelchair. The men formed a huddle around the woman, holding a group discussion. One man—a square-jawed, husky man—peered at the pedestrians who had to walk around their group positioned in the middle of the sidewalk. He recognized me, and I remembered him and another man at Mosie Kelter's funeral. He glanced back at the group and interrupted the guy speaking to say something. The group stared at me, with two other men saying something indistinguishable. My presence bothered them.

I stared at the tearful woman in the wheelchair. She had cheerleader good looks, small in stature, but breakable, with thin legs positioned tightly together. Her bearing was that of a child coerced into jumping off the high diving board. Panic stricken, she wheeled around to head back to the building. Two guys in the group prevented her from advancing or retreating. She looked up at her blockers with a silent plea for help.

One man in the group separated himself to approach me. With an athletic build, and handsome by male standards, I typecast him as a former college fraternity president and "Most Likely to Succeed" in high school. Taken aback by his aggressive glare, I wanted no trouble in a chance encounter with people I had no interest in ever seeing again.

"Mister. Yeah, you. Stay away from my wife. You and Claude Sedley."

Another man from the group—one of the suits I recognized at the Pothole—came forward to set up a double-team. Testosterone-blessed, well-dressed civilians.

The man from the Pothole, in support of his younger peer, threatened, "We're serious. Stay away from Bonnie Ridge."

Bonnie Ridge? I remembered a conversation outside the Pothole between Slade and the suits from the church about a meeting to clear the air with a woman and another guy. Could that be Bonnie Ridge? How did that meeting have anything to do with me? Another reason to get answers from Mr. Sedley.

"Have a good day, gentlemen," I said to the men standing nearly shoulder to shoulder in front of me. I walked right between these guys, moving them farther apart with my outstretched hands. To their credit, there was no resistance.

When I reached the door to the building, the handsome man said,

"Bonnie doesn't need to hear more lies from you two."

Lies?

The woman made another attempt to maneuver away from the group. Failing that, she gave in to the futility of her efforts to flee, dropped her head, and covered her face with her hands. "I'm so sorry, Blaine," the woman cried out to the handsome man. "I'm sorry. I'm sorry."

"Ma'am, you okay?" I asked.

"We know what you're doing. We'll file a restraining order, if need be," said another suit in the group.

Blaine bent down to Bonnie to admonish her. "Why in the world would you trust those guys? They don't have your best interest in mind, Bonnie. We'll decide what's best for you. Hear me?"

I had heard enough. I entered the building. No one followed me. At Mr. Sedley's floor, I walked right past Mary Lou without saying hello, marched down the hallway, and stopped at Edna's desk.

"Is he in?"

"Sir, he's not available right now."

"I'm going in."

Edna stood up to show her disapproval of my impertinence. Despite her denial of entry, I opened Mr. Sedley's door and stepped inside. There I found him without his dark suit coat on and actual papers on his desk. And perturbed to see me.

"What're you doing here? Edna?"

Edna stepped into his office. "I told him not to come in, Mr. Sedley. But he came in anyway." She swayed from side to side in anticipation of a rebuke.

"I was just threatened with a restraining order outside your building by people I don't know. It's time for some answers, sir."

"What do you want me to do, Mr. Sedley?" Edna said as if her job was on the line.

"Leave us." He motioned her away with a wave of his hand. "So, Mr. Zubell, you think you can come in here whenever you want. I had concerns about trusting you. Now I see I was right."

"I came here to talk about my mistake—"

"Mistake? What you did wasn't a clerical error. You got arrested when I explicitly said to avoid anything like that." He took a moment to reorganize the papers on his desk. When nervous, he stroked his face like he was wiping off sweat, which he had none. "I made the initial mistake of trusting you. Why didn't you leave well enough alone?"

"Unanswered questions, sir. I wanted to find out what's going on."

"Why was that your business?"

I expected his grumbles. "It wasn't. But I made it my business. I thought there was way too much going on."

"You weren't paid to question anything. Now I have to get involved." Mr. Sedley struggled to control his impassioned voice.

I could see he was angry enough to scream—a disparate feeling from a man too careful to expose his true feelings to anyone. He was right. I went out on my own for answers without his knowledge or approval. I still had another question to unravel: Why did he say he had to get involved?

"I don't understand, sir. You don't have to be involved. It's my problem."

"No, it's not!" he shouted. "Now it's no longer about you working for me in confidence. You exposed me, Mr. Zubell." His glare was ferocious.

"Okay, okay, Mr. Sedley, you're right. But I have a right to know why those men threatened me with a restraining order."

Mr. Sedley held on tightly to his entanglement with Slade. He sighed at least three times, rubbed his forehead, and removed his reading glasses. I had doubts he would reveal the reason behind the threat, but I had to ask again. "Sir?"

I witnessed his mental plotting a strategy to move beyond emotion. As his jigsaw pieces meshed, his directive would be clear, concise, and pointed away from his involvement with me. After processing his thoughts, his eyes appeared satisfied.

"Leave Damon Slade alone. And stay away from everyone with that church. No reason whatsoever to be around them. Do we understand one another? Can I trust you to do that?"

"Okay. But I still don't get why they're angry at me."

"You keep your word, and here's what I'll do: Lew will work pro bono to represent you. This offer ends if we hear you have any further interactions with Damon Slade or anyone involved with him. Do we have an understanding?"

"What's pro bono, sir?"

"You won't be charged for our work. That's my only offer, if you cooperate."

To get me untangled was worth more than I realized—too lucrative an offer to turn down. I nodded approval. A verbal understanding, but no handshake. He turned away to review a folder on his credenza. I walked out of his office, looking away from Edna's glare.

He offered something I appreciated—free legal work in exchange for not digging deeper into Damon Slade's activities—without satisfying my curiosity why he withheld the reason behind the threat of a restraining order. I was conflicted. I wouldn't quit looking for answers. Subtlety, of course. One might easily conclude I was stubborn.

———

I woke up Major Jack for an early dinner at Anderson's restaurant, where locals gathered across from Presbyterian Hospital. Being close to a medical facility brought back painful memories for the major, but he was talkative tonight and in less pain walking from the parking lot to the restaurant.

"Zin, I don't regret what I did to that asshole Lugs."

"You may if you end up spending time behind bars."

"Perhaps if I pretend to be crazy—"

"Pretend?"

"Okay. Point taken. Let's get outta this town soon."

"Best to lay low and clear up our legal problems first."

"That could take some time."

"Maybe. You up for a road trip?"

"Where?"

"I was thinking about seeing Sally."

"No. Bad shit there. Anyway, why go there? Seeing the general with his girl toy would be more than you could handle."

"Don't say that about Sally."

"She should know she can't fuck her way to sergeant major."

I reached across the table to grab Major Jack's shirt and pulled him to my face. "Don't ever say that about her again." I pushed him back to the booth seat.

My feelings for Sally were open wounds. But the major had no qualms about stomping on feelings I held on to like a life preserver. Harsh opinions cost him girlfriends and friendships. He had no regard for discretion. Told often, his ill-timed candor had limited his opportunity for advancement in rank.

"It's the truth, Zin. I'd do what she's doing if it meant advancement."

I wanted to slug him in the worst way, but he knew I wouldn't do it in a public place. I looked away to avoid igniting any more of my anger. "What you think and what you say should be on the same page."

"I don't care."

The tides of our civility would come and go when we spent this much time together. Unproductive time brought out the worst in us both. Silence was the best way to balance our clashes.

CHAPTER 9

M r. Sedley confused me. He was cautious about trusting me at first, understandable; then glad-handing about my successful envelope delivery, understandable; then angry about me learning of his brother's death. His duplicitous shifts in attitude convinced me that his dealings with Slade were more personal than client based. More reason to find out why.

Major Jack's crude comments about Sally agitated me all day. I needed a break. I followed through on a questionable decision to drive to the W and J Wreck House. Any face-to-face involvement with the Kelters and Slade could endanger the pro bono offer. But no matter. I was going anyway. I left after dark. I watched their apartment from my truck parked on the street.

The second-floor lights were on, and the front gate was open. Eddie's Mustang was parked along the side of the building. Sitting, waiting, and watching was near the top of my understanding of an investigator's job. I was a practicing intern.

Checking my watch made the waiting interminable. I took my watch off and put it in my pocket. About an hour later, Eddie, still wearing his greasy overalls, staggered out and headed down the stairs. He was unsteady on the steps, and he moved slowly, holding on to the handrail with his left hand. I squinted. *Is that a pistol in his right hand?* When he almost lost his balance on the steps, he braced himself against the building wall. I saw the pistol in his hand. Drunk and armed was a bad cocktail.

Eddie sped out of the W and J Wreck House, screeching his tires. He ran a red light at the nearby intersection, causing a driver to slam on the brakes to avoid a collision. I made a hasty decision to follow him. Turning the truck key, I heard only *click, click, click*. I had problems with the solenoid switch. Eddie turned right at the next intersection, then drove out of sight. My truck started on the third try. It was fortuitous not to pursue further trouble.

A conflict Eddie would regret awaited him.

———

I was restless all night thinking about yesterday's events. And concerned about Eddie. Night sweats had me sitting up on the edge of the bed, resting my head in my hands. Tonight the major moaned, grunted, and cursed as he wrestled with the demons of relentless pain.

At dawn I wanted to talk with someone, but not Major Jack.

"Sally?"

Her raspy voice said, "Huh? Zin? What's wrong? Why you calling so early?"

"I always liked your wake-up voice."

She took a moment to clear her throat before talking again. "That's weird, Zin. What's up? What're you guys doing in Charlotte?"

"I did some investigative work for an attorney."

"How exciting for you. Call me later and tell me all about it, okay?"

"Several brief assignments for the guy, then fired without cause. That's twice in a month. I'm getting a bit sensitive about that."

"You'll find something to do."

"Yeah, but you see, I stayed after the guy after being told not to."

"Sounds like you."

"He's a bad guy, Sal. I trust my instincts. He's involved with some bad stuff."

"But that's not your problem, is it?"

"Sal, I got pissed off, punched the guy, got arrested. And Jack did the same to his friend."

"What? Are you serious? What're you guys doing acting like drunken grunts? No excuse for grown men acting like that."

"Agreed."

"No excuse, Sergeant Major."

"The law firm I worked for hooked us up with a criminal lawyer who I'm told is really good. We'll be all right, I think."

"Get your act together, Sergeant Major. You don't want me to come down there and kick your ass."

"Yes, I do."

"I'm really surprised you'd be that stupid, Zin."

"Is the general there with you?"

"None of your business."

"I just realized something. Talking to you is harder than I thought." *I missed her more than I could handle right now.* "Take care, Sal." I hung up.

———

At 0900, I woke up Major Jack for a cup of coffee. He appeared upset, squirming in his chair as if no position were comfortable. His disturbed mumbles told me that he was in a mood to argue and complain.

"Zin, I was a good soldier."

"Soldiers wanted to serve with you."

"But I acted like I was invincible getting on top of that tank like some goddamn movie soldier."

"Bad things happen in war."

I had no desire to rehash the incident. I drank my coffee, trying to think of something to take his mind off where the conversation was heading.

After a few silent moments, he said, "I dreamed about our friends, Zin. I can't shake the dream."

No reason to pretend I didn't know whom he was talking about; that's why he woke up in a mood. I had similar dreams on occasion. We won't ever find relief from those memories.

"Sometimes I dream they're staring at me—gray faces without expressions."

Remembering those guys—Mickey, Bongo, Badger, and their patrol—brought back horrors rooted in our subconscious. I relived the day our patrol exchanged gunfire with NVA troops at a top-secret base camp we set up for covert operations in Cambodia. Our mission dictated we abandon camp once exposed. We radioed special ops headquarters for a high-threat combat rescue. Within an hour, we escaped across a rice paddy, exchanging gunfire with the NVA, to the rescue LZ. We figured Mickey, Bongo, and Badger's patrol was making the same retreat from another direction, but they were nowhere in sight. No ten-fours over multiple walkie-talkie transmissions. We repeated the LZ coordinates over and over. Nothing but static.

Two Hueys, on approach to fly us back to special ops headquarters, opened fire with their M3 rocket launchers and M60 machine guns in the direction of NVA troops. As we boarded the gunship, rounds tore through the fuselage near us. The helo pilot, not our usual special ops rotorhead, shouted he had orders to lift off if we encountered gunfire. Both helos lifted off despite our pleas to wait a little longer for the other patrol. To no avail. We abandoned Mickey, Bongo, Badger, and others in Cambodia.

Major Jack and I organized an extraction team for a direct-action vertical insertion at the base camp at dusk. We knew the risk of returning for the team left behind in Cambodia. The commanding officer signed off on the mission without receiving General Haywood's approval. We struggled with the reality of leaving good men behind.

Master Warrant Officer Bike Crandell, the best helo pilot we knew, flew the lead Huey. Approaching the LZ, we expected intense gunfire. But after touchdown we only heard typical jungle sounds. The major and I led a patrol to the base camp with the anticipation of a surprise NVA attack. But nothing happened. No NVA troops. And no sign of the other patrol. Supplies ransacked. I transmitted on a walkie-talkie, risking exposure of our position at the camp. No response. We searched the immediate area for any sign of our men. Found nothing. We returned to the Huey believing their patrol was either captured or dead deeper in the jungle.

General Haywood wouldn't authorize more search and rescue operations into Cambodia. The bureaucratic denial of ever having a covert base in Cambodia sealed the fate of the patrol. That decision left an open wound that would never heal.

"That's why I did it," Major Jack said.

"Did what?"

"Why I got on that tank. I was fuckin' angry. I wanted to kill 'em all."

"That was all you on that tank."

"Well, I never saw you get pissed off at the bullshit the general laid on us."

"Duty first."

"Bullshit, Zin. Well, look what it got me."

"You've always been a cowboy in olive drab. But I share some of the blame. I should've stopped you."

"You couldn't. I outranked you."

"At the forward edge, no one outranks a sergeant major."

Major Jack winced. He twisted to a less painful position in his chair. "Sometimes I want the war out of my head. It fuckin' pisses me off thinking about it."

"Yeah. Seen it."

"Oh yeah? I'm so glad you weren't wounded." His sarcasm was as biting as a fresh jalapeño.

"Thankful every day."

We shared smiles. Our friendship lasted through the years based on unfiltered honesty. Never hold back. Say it, don't apologize, move on. This time my glib reply shut down any further war conversation. Typically, the major would start drinking beer and reminiscing about sex with former girlfriends. But today the major wasn't satisfied with daydreams. His troubled thoughts brought out an angry frown.

"I bring a lot of shit to your life. You'd be chasing tail if I wasn't an anchor."

"I volunteered."

"You know, I think too much about 'Nam."

"Understandable."

He pointed to his legs. "Hard not to."

"Yeah."

I witnessed too many soldiers suffer horrendous injuries. No way to perceive the pain they endured. Nothing's served commenting on the pain the major lived with each day.

After an uncomfortable pause, thinking about what words to say, the major sighed, closed his eyes, and spoke from the heart. "I should've been in one of those body bags, like our comrades."

"Yeah, well, I dig the graves, say a prayer, and move on. It would eat away my life if I dwelled too long there."

"Yeah. The mission—always for the mission. But good men died."

"Yeah, but we lived the soldier's way." I stopped for a moment, then said, "But I'll always remember. The ghosts never go away."

"Fuckin' A."

Major Jack reflected aloud about Vietnam. As for me, I bottled up my feelings in tight compartments that only seeped out when I was alone—my way of coping with the memories of soldiers lost and comrades deserted and left in the enemies' hands. Rationalizing how to move beyond those memories was impossible.

"I'm still thinking about driving to DC. You interested?" I asked.

"No."

"I need to say goodbye to friends and Sally."

"Why don't you just run right into that wall there? You'll get over that hurt quicker."

"Don't you wanna get outta here for a few days? You got nothing else going on—"

"It's what I do best now."

"Bullshit. You got a lot to offer—"

"Strike up the band; play the national anthem!" he yelled.

"The army was our life—"

"We're not chained together. Nothing's stopping you. Go. Go, goddamn it. Leave. Go."

Major Jack spewed out rage in machine-gun bursts. The military conditioned me to accept occasional tirades from officers. Even though I was a civilian now, free to speak my mind, I still found it difficult to release the governor and respond with equal anger to a ranking officer. I looked away.

He eased up on the hostile tone. "It'd be good to be alone for a while." The working departments of Major Jack's mind struggled at times to cooperate with each other but agreed about this: never go anywhere, and don't do anything.

———

Later that afternoon we saw an unmarked black sedan approaching our house. Police could announce their presence without a siren or flashing blue lights; just drive up in an ugly black Ford with no whitewalls. The sedan pulled into our driveway, and Detective Cutter and his younger partner got out. Cutter noted me with an insincere grin. I opened the front door before they got to our stoop.

"Gentlemen," I said.

"You boys look like laziness appeals to you," Cutter said.

"What do we owe the pleasure, Detective Cutter?"

"Had to find out if private dicks lived in better neighborhoods than us public servants." He looked over his shoulder at our neighborhood. "Nope, you don't. You think you're gonna get rich taking pictures of middle-aged men screwing their secretaries?"

"Never got rich in the army. Why expect money now?"

"Invite us in. Oh, this is my partner, Detective Pitman."

I stepped aside to allow them to enter. Pitman searched our living room with attentive eyes. Cutter shined his flashlight eyes on us.

"Your furniture looks worse than the neighborhood," Cutter said.

"Rented."

Cutter eyed Major Jack in his jeans and wrinkled T-shirt, sitting motionless in his chair. Both men viewed our quarters like real estate agents in the wrong neighborhood. Cutter glanced about with a scowl—a beacon of disturbing questions on his mind—but went no farther into our house. He mumbled something. I enjoyed the man's grouchy manner. It reminded me of the banter between fellow sergeants on Friday nights at the NCO clubs in the army. Sergeants respected each other enough never to say a kind word or be pleasant.

Pitman walked to the two duffel bags on the floor beside the sofa. He bent down to lift them up, then set them back down without examining the contents. "Going someplace?"

"The major lives out of his duffel."

"You boys planning on heading somewhere?" said Pitman.

"Maybe."

"It don't look good leaving the area after just being arrested," said Cutter.

"Just me, not the major."

"Like I said, it don't look good. But I can't stop you."

"What're you looking for, Detective?" I asked. Empty beer bottles and heavy-duty bathtub rings were all they would find in our house.

"In due time, son. In due time," Cutter said, with his glances playing tennis between Major Jack and me. He had concerns about something he wasn't willing to share with us now. He skulked in a complete circle around the room, then ended up standing over Major Jack.

"A sergeant and a major living together? Wouldn't happen when I was in the service."

"I'm impressed you can still remember the First World War," said Major Jack.

Cutter laughed mockingly, sneering at Major Jack. "Your boyfriend has a mouth. I'm gonna remember that. Why're you leaving now?"

"Ya know what it's like to miss a friend," I said.

"Have you boys seen Edward Kelter lately?" Cutter asked.

A barking dog had more tact than a cop bearing bad news. Something happened to Eddie, and what I knew about it was the reason for their visit. This was a police inquiry.

"Why?" I asked.

"Well, boys, would it surprise you to hear he's dead?"

Eddie ran right at the grim reaper. Drunk and flashing a pistol was the way to be at death's access point.

"How did he die?" I asked.

"It wasn't pretty."

"Never is."

"Suppose you boys wanna tell me where you were between midnight and three this morning?"

"Right here, asleep," I said.

"I haven't figured you boys out yet, but I'm gonna, sooner or later," said Cutter.

"We're not up to anything, Detective."

"Tell me the last time you saw him," said Cutter.

"Last night."

"Really? Last night?" said Pitman.

"I drove to the W and J Wreck House around seven."

"Why?" said Cutter.

"To check on Eddie. I never got out of my truck. I saw him drive away from the shop in a real hurry."

"You went there but never got out of your truck. Why were you there, then?" said Pitman.

"I was concerned about him since his mom's funeral."

"Why're you so concerned about him? What's he to you?" Cutter said.

"He told me at the Pothole he was real concerned about his mom's disappearance. I was looking for work as an investigator. I thought I could help him find out what happened."

Cutter frowned, said, "His mom? Margaret Kelter? The woman divers found in Mountain Island Lake?"

I nodded.

"Her death was accidental. Why go messing around in that shit? You looking to bill people for doing shit?" He sighed, then said with some hesitation, "We found Edward Kelter burned to death in a Mustang over on Old Dowd Road last night. Someone sure wanted us to think it was an accident. But our boys think the way it burned was no accident."

Cutter and Pitman studied my reaction to the grim news. I just shook my head from side to side. Pitman looked around our living room and checked behind the cushions. We all watched him open our living-room closet to find it empty. He then headed for the bedrooms.

"You boys got any idea what he was doing out there late at night?" Cutter said.

"No idea," I said.

"Does this guy ever say anything?" Cutter pointed at the major.

"Nope," said Major Jack.

"What else do you know about Edward Kelter? You bailed him out of jail. Why'd you do that?"

"Because I had the money, and he didn't. And like I said, I thought I could help him find his mother. Good experience for a green investigator."

"He sure could've used your cheap protection last night. How'd you meet Edward Kelter?"

"Like I said, at a bar called the Pothole. Eddie hung out there because he drank a lot."

"You didn't just happen to meet him at that bar, right? There's more to it than that," said Cutter.

"I was working for an attorney when we met."

"Doing what?"

"I can't say."

"What was this attorney's interest in you talking to Kelter?"

"No interest. He paid me to look out for another guy."

"Who?"

"Can't say."

"Really? An attorney paid you to hang out at a bar. I'm quitting today and working for that guy." Cutter smiled, pleased with himself. "Really, Zubell? Sounds like a crock of shit. What's this attorney's name?"

"He told me the work was confidential and not to discuss it with anyone."

"I don't give a goddamn what some lawyer thinks is privileged or not. If you know something about Edward Kelter's death, you better come clean. Way over your head, son. This is serious shit."

"I have no idea what happened to him, Detective."

Pitman returned to our living room after a walk-through of our house. He shook his head to Cutter. Nothing incriminated us.

Cutter tightened his jaw but restrained himself. He stepped forward and dug into my eyes, probing for lies. I allowed him to read my blank expression. After a few tense moments, he stepped back, satisfied for some reason.

"We're gonna find out what happened. So where are your toys, boys?"

"Toys?" I said, knowing full well what he meant.

"You army guys gotta have lots of guns."

"There're no weapons in the house."

Cutter shook his head in disgust. He waved his hand for Pitman to head for the door. "I don't know what's going on. I'd hate to find out you boys were involved with something I don't like."

At the front door, Cutter stepped aside to let Pitman exit. He turned back to question me one more time. "Impress me with your investigative skill. Where can we find any kin to Edward Kelter?"

"Silver Kelter, his sister, is Damon Slade's girlfriend."

"Damon Slade. The guy you slugged. Interesting."

"Detective?" I asked.

"What?"

"Are you guys gonna investigate how Margaret Kelter got in the lake?"

"Why? Why do you care?"

"'Cause it's real curious how she wound up there."

Cutter scowled like a parent at their child's interest in an unacceptable lifestyle. He had no patience with my interest in her accidental death. I was annoyingly inquisitive.

"Since you like playing cop, I'll tell you this much: Coroner found a broken arm, hip, and leg. All on her left side. So that's why she couldn't get outta her car. But there was something strange about the accident. The driver's door crushed in. Really crushed in. Hard to figure how that happened without more damage to the rest of the car."

My curiosity leaped to a higher level. "That should be enough to open an investigation. Possible she was forced into the lake?"

"Zubell, go to the police academy and get a badge and take up dead-end casework," Cutter said, exasperated now, unwilling to discuss the matter any further.

On his way out the door, he said, "Be available, guys."

Major Jack raised his middle finger high at the departing police. His disrespectful gesture went unnoticed.

"They're just doing their jobs, Jack."

"They got no respect for us. They get that in return."

The news of Eddie's death affected me. His persistence on his mom's behalf moved me to offer my help. He reminded me of some raw recruits with issues whom I unfolded and molded into good soldiers, some of whom were now buried at Arlington. I cared about them staying alive and surviving the war.

I hardly knew Eddie. He was difficult to be around. His personality evoked strong reactions from even tolerant people. But never enough for a fiery death. Burning him up in his Mustang was a depraved act. Someone wanted to bleach their soul of any decency by killing an innocent man. Two men came to mind.

And what about Silver Kelter? She was alone now, living with a man who was abusive, at the least. A pretty face could bring on more options for a better life, or invite unwarranted adversity with the added challenge of codependence for survival.

———

The army prepared me to expect harsh, unimaginable cruelty in combat. I never imagined being privy to killings doing a snoop job for a law firm.

Major Jack broke up my thoughts. "Zin, you're in a dangerous situation. You see that now, don't you?"

"Clear."

Going to my bedroom, my duffel bags weren't unzipped. The clothes on the floor were where I left them. Pitman was curious, but not enough to scatter my possessions for a more detailed examination.

Major Jack said from the living room, "How come the cops didn't find your .45?"

"I said no weapons in the house. It's in the truck."

"Good move. Lying to the cops."

———

We had a few quiet hours before the phone rang. Edna called, sounding irked. "Mr. Sedley asked if you're available tonight to meet with Pastor Crigler of the Church of the Holy Spirit."

"Who?"

"The pastor who replaced Mr. Sedley's brother."

"Why would I wanna meet with him?"

"I was told to ask about your availability. Mr. Sedley says it's important. Important to him means you should do it. I'll tell him yes?"

"I don't wanna be party to any meetings."

"He'll pick you up at six." Edna was demanding, as ordered.

I reluctantly gave her directions to my house. Mr. Sedley pulled me back into his quagmire after I thought he had cleaned me off his busy plate. I had a strong sense this meeting was an ambush to blame me for stepping beyond his directive.

I called the firm to ask for Ableman's office. His secretary took my name and number for a return call. He was in court.

CHAPTER 10

An hour later, that same afternoon, Ableman called back. "I don't know anything about the meeting tonight, Zinny."

"I thought he had no interest in being involved with me."

"All Claude said was he set up a meeting to straighten out some misunderstandings—"

"What misunderstandings, sir?"

"You know as much as I do, Zinny."

"Why won't someone level with me?"

"Maybe you'll find out tonight. I'm in the dark just as much as you are. If anyone brings up the assault charge, don't say a word and admit to nothing. Claude will know the right course of action, okay?"

"Why aren't you going?"

"I wasn't asked to."

"You're still my lawyer?"

"Yes. Listen, he's . . . I don't know anything. Go with Claude and find out for yourself."

———

Around 1730 the major and I were eating McDonald's hamburgers at home when demanding knocks on our front door surprised us. The pounding wasn't neighbors inviting us to a barbecue. The hard knocking was continuous.

"We don't know a soul in this town, but we keep getting company," Major Jack said.

"Doesn't sound friendly."

I went to the door to ask for identification. A familiar voice barked back. "It's Cutter. You ain't stupid enough to not let us in."

The police had returned for another session. I was a question mark under a cloud of uncertainty surrounding Eddie Kelter's death.

"Surprise, surprise, it's the cops," Major Jack said.

I opened the door to face detectives Cutter and Pitman, both eager to make an arrest. They pushed their way inside.

"I don't know how I feel about all this attention. You guys were just here," I said in response to their aggressive moves.

"We checked on that guy, Damon Slade. He used to be a highway patrolman," said Cutter.

"You found Silver Kelter?"

"I'll tell you what you need to know. But him being a former cop don't make him a good guy. What can you tell me about Cecil Horry?"

"Who?" I asked.

"You know, the guy who runs the Pothole."

"What I've witnessed at the Pothole is he's mean, violent, an all-around asshole."

"Oh yeah? He said he was at the bar until two thirty last night. But of interest to us, he said Edward Kelter came by the bar earlier and told him you were looking to get him. Lugs said Kelter left around midnight. Why would you be coming after Kelter?"

"Lugs is lying. I've done nothing but help the guy. Remember: I bailed him out of jail."

"Maybe him owing you money, or something you haven't told us," said Pitman.

"Like I said, I came home early and never left last night. I have no idea what happened to him."

"Well, I'm gonna get to the truth. Tell me how we can find Damon Slade and that Kelter girl."

"Lugs will know."

"He said he doesn't know," said Pitman.

"That's another lie."

Cutter said, "Don't let me find out you're lying. Better not be lying to me."

Over Cutter's shoulder a black Mercedes sedan approached slow enough to read the house numbers. In our neighborhood, a late-model Mercedes was a visitor, not a resident. The car parked on the street behind the police sedan. Mr. Sedley got out in a dark suit, white shirt, and power-red tie. Cutter and Pitman turned around when they noticed my attention directed out the window. His approach confused the detectives.

"Who's that?" said Cutter.

"The attorney I worked for."

"Why's he here? How could we be any sweeter to you?"

"Let's see what he has to say," I said.

Mr. Sedley stepped up on our brick stoop, noticed the open door, and waited for permission to walk in.

"Come in, Mr. Sedley."

He cautiously came inside, halted, with a surprised look to find we had company.

"Good evening," he said.

"These are detectives, sir," I said.

"Oh. Okay. But their attorney should be present. Don't you agree,

Officers?" Mr. Sedley said.

Cutter said, "Just a friendly conversation, Counselor. Nice guys talking to nice guys."

"Gentlemen, I'll tell Mr. Zubell's attorney to call you tomorrow. Set up a meeting. That should work for you."

Mr. Sedley was impressive, in control. His polite firmness called for an end to the police inquiry.

But Cutter got in the last word. "Yeah, well, it ain't over yet. Stay available, Zubell."

The police strolled back to their sedan. Mr. Sedley took only a few steps into our living room. He appeared uneasy in the home of a person with furniture he couldn't imagine sitting on. He fought back the discomfort of an unpleasant setting with an insincere grin. I enjoyed seeing him feeling awkward.

"Sit, Mr. Sedley. You want a beer?"

"No. Thank you."

No way would he expose his expensive suit to cracked vinyl. He glanced around to nod hello to Major Jack, who stared back like a curious dog. The major's steely expression made him quite unsettled.

"Don't talk to the police without Lew present, okay?"

"Okay. But they weren't here for that. They're investigating Edward Kelter's death. He may have been murdered."

"What?" The disturbing news inundated him. "How does that involve you?"

"It doesn't. They just wanna find Damon Slade and Silver Kelter."

"Really?" More worrisome news, more concern for unwanted exposure. "How do you know where they are?"

"I don't. They're just inquiring."

"Tell 'em to make any inquiry with your attorney present. Understood?"

"Unless he moves in with me, I can't stop the police from coming here."

"You know exactly what I mean."

"No, I don't, sir. I don't know anything. You're using me, and I have no idea why. I've reconsidered. I'm not going to your meeting."

My intention was to rile, disrespect, and push him away as far as possible. And he knew it. His green eyes lit up for a moment, hot from my rebuff, but then doused the flame with surprising ease.

"It's in your best interest to go with me."

His accepting stare rejected my refusal to go with him. His involvement was too important to allow my disrespect to alter his plan.

"You're not wearing that tonight, right?" He pointed at my T-shirt and jeans.

He figured me out. He knew how to tap into my curious nature. "No. I guess not. I'll get dressed."

"Good."

I went to my bedroom for the every-occasion red jacket, khaki pants, short-sleeved white shirt, and army tie. While dressing, I listened to the silence coming from the living room. Left alone, Mr. Sedley and Major Jack could cool down a room five degrees in no time. I returned to the living room to find Mr. Sedley standing in the open front door.

"Why're you letting this guy bully you into going someplace you shouldn't?" said Major Jack.

No baiting Mr. Sedley into a setup argument with the major. He got what he wanted. He avoided eye contact with either of us.

"Be back after a while, Jack."

"It's a setup, Zin."

"Have a few beers."

"What else is there to do?"

This retired sergeant major, used to dirt and sweat, never experienced the comfort of fine Mercedes upholstery. I never expected the unattainable hope of earning such an automobile. I rubbed my rear across the seat to relish the feel of luxury.

"You kept our arrangement with the police confidential, right?"

"Your name never came up. Your staff has no idea what you're doing. It's the way you want it, right?"

"Don't say a word tonight. Let me do the talking."

There was no more conversation. *Why the urgency of a meeting with the church people to light me up? Or was Mr. Sedley just cleaning the mud off my troubles with them? Was it a mistake being available for this meeting?* No. Pro bono help was worth some humiliation, but it might be at a costly measure of my dignity.

Mr. Sedley parked his Mercedes in front of Endover Towers. My quick fuse might be in the offing without my truck to excuse myself. I envisioned ignoring his directive to stay quiet.

We walked down the long hall on the first floor to an open door with a nameplate marked "Conference Room." At the end of a conference table in the narrow room was a tall man in a black suit, with calming eyes, pronounced chin, oval glasses, and a trimmed salt-and-pepper beard—the look I associated with a college professor. We faced another challenge that neither of us expected. Damon Slade sat next to the tall man, staring at us like a cat ready to pounce. Dressed in a business suit with a Bible in his left hand, he soaked up the surprised look on our faces. His left eye socket was still black from my punch.

"Come in, please, Claude."

"Pastor Crigler. Nice to see you."

"Welcome to our church, as it were," the pastor said, rising from his chair to come forward and shake Mr. Sedley's hand. Holding on to the handshake, the pastor stepped closer to him, then said with a "saving your soul" intention, "Our church still grieves for your brother. He is missed, Claude."

"Yes, his death has been difficult for all of us."

"We're carrying on, as best we can, as I know he'd want us to," the pastor said. "Please sit."

Pastor Crigler ignored me, not offering his hand before returning to his chair.

"It was my understanding, Pastor, that this meeting would only be between us," said Mr. Sedley. No subtlety when it came to his obvious dislike for Damon Slade.

"It was, but you said you'd be bringing your associate. I thought it best to invite Damon Slade to clear the air. Get some things out in the open. Is that okay with you?"

"I have no choice now. I just want you to understand this is only about clearing up a misunderstanding."

Again, a misunderstanding? This could turn into an explosive meeting, with Slade displaying a contemptible smile as he watched us take our seats at the table. Mr. Sedley sat next to the pastor; I sat next to Mr. Sedley; Slade, on the other side of the table, next to the pastor. No one spoke up as everyone waited for someone else to speak first.

"It's always helpful to start a meeting with a prayer," Pastor Crigler said. "Guide us in your ways, our Lord and Savior, as we meet tonight. Open our hearts to your words. Your love is the guiding light that will keep us on the path to righteousness."

I didn't lower my head or close my eyes. Slade rested his chin on his chest, and his Bible-toting hand clutched the book tight enough to bend it slightly. *Was he hoping his piousness would distract God for a few minutes?*

Pastor Crigler concluded his prayer, and everyone, except me, said in unison, "Amen."

The pastor said, "Claude, again, thanks for coming here tonight—"

"Yes, thanks for coming, Claude," said Slade. "Let's get to the point. I'm not dropping charges against your boy Zubell. That's it. Shortest meeting ever."

"We talked about being respectful, Damon," the pastor said. He turned to Mr. Sedley. "We do have concerns about your interest in our church. We cooperated with your associates concerning the church finances regarding your brother."

"Yes, you did. And we're completely satisfied."

"Good. Okay, but why the troubling interest you still seem to have in some members of our congregation?"

"I want you to know I never instructed Mr. Zubell to do anything that would cause trouble at your church. I hired him to do an assignment that had nothing to do with the church. He is no longer associated with my firm. That's all I came here to say, Pastor."

I hated not having my truck. I would have made a quick exit.

"That's no apology, Sedley," said Slade.

"Damon, that's enough." The pastor looked at Mr. Sedley. "It has come to my attention that you're representing Bonnie Ridge."

Mr. Sedley squirmed in his chair and cleared his throat. The meeting veered off in an uncomfortable direction, to his displeasure.

"Pastor, I can't discuss anything about Bonnie Ridge."

"I understand, but I hear you haven't involved her husband in the counseling. He's upset about that. It's really upsetting to many people why you have any interest in Bonnie Ridge."

Me too.

"Pastor, with all due respect, I can't and won't discuss her."

"Claude Sedley won't tell you what's going on, but I will," said Slade. "He hired this goon, Zubell, to come to one of my shows and shove the police report on Bonnie's hit-and-run accident in my face. He's trying to pin her accident on me, of all people! I've worked with Bonnie for many years. You know, Pastor, Bonnie is the one who convinced me to join this church. I became a Christian. He's out of his mind 'cause his brother is dead, and he wants to blame someone for it. And he paid his goon to punch my lights out at Mosie's funeral. Who does something like that?"

"This just doesn't sound like something Claude would do, Damon. Billy spoke so highly of him." He turned to Mr. Sedley. "From what I know about you, none of this makes any sense, Claude."

"Pastor, I won't comment on the absurd fallacies this man is saying."

"Maybe, Pastor, you and me should remind Claude how close me and Billy were."

Ignoring Slade, the pastor said, "I heard rumors about Damon and Bonnie's relationship, Claude, but everyone denies it. And to clear up another thing, the elders hired an attorney to check with the police concerning any accusations about Bonnie's accident. It's unfounded, and there is no basis to any accusation."

Slade shook his head in agreement.

"So that makes it hard to understand why you're counseling Bonnie Ridge behind Blaine's back. You have such an upstanding reputation, Claude. Can you help me understand what all this is about?"

"I won't talk about Bonnie Ridge. You know it's privileged. You keep asking me over and over . . ." He paused, remaining even tempered in these choppy waters. But his expression read like he experienced a verbal punch to the gut.

Slade spoke up. "Ya know, Claude, your brother and Mosie were close. And Mosie and her daughter got into a bad place. I stepped in to help Silver out. But Mosie never approved of Silver traveling with me. And you'll never admit this. Billy and I were close friends. If you're trying to get even because you didn't like your brother and me associating, well, it won't work. I ain't gonna back down from fighting back against anybody, especially a lawyer who's nothing but a shyster. But I'm giving you a pass since I respected your brother so much. But that only goes so far. Got me?"

"I don't understand what's going on here. But know this: These accusations and threats are tearing apart the church's foundation. It has to stop. Hear me, Damon." Pastor Crigler displayed his conviction worthy of his position.

Surprisingly, Slade drooped his head as if cowering to the pastor's reprimand to be civil. "Ya know, I miss Billy as much as anyone. Claude Sedley don't like knowing his brother associated with the likes of me. But he did. And I still grieve." He oozed emotion like butter out of a hot biscuit.

Mr. Sedley seethed. More wood on his fire. He gripped the arm of the chair like he meant to break it.

Slade said, "Remember: I came over to you and your family at Billy's funeral to say my condolences, and you told me in an asshole way to stay away from your family."

"That's quite enough, Damon," said the pastor. "Claude, let me be direct: Have you spoken with any of the elders or any member of our church about anything to do with Damon?"

"Never. It's best that we leave now, Pastor Crigler. I wish your ministry the best going forward."

"One more question, Claude: Are you planning to counsel Bonnie Ridge again?"

"Her husband fired me."

Pointing at me, the pastor said, "And your man there?"

"He's done as well."

"Let's just leave it at that. Damon, I need to speak with you after they leave."

Mr. Sedley stood up and walked to the door, expecting me to exit the meeting with him. I had a different idea. It was time to cast doubt on Slade's posturing to his pastor.

"Pastor, Damon bragged about having sex with Silver Kelter and even showed me a nude photo of her."

Stunned silence filled the room. Pastor Crigler faced Slade with a disturbed expression. Mr. Sedley reacted with a furtive grin that only I noticed—a serious man was careful not to expose cracks on a steadfast face.

Slade couldn't maintain an unfazed look. "You son of a bitch."

"Is that true, Damon? She works for you. She's young and vulnerable, Damon," the pastor said with a disapproving, judgmental tone.

"You can't believe them, Pastor," Slade said. "They'll stoop to anything to destroy my reputation."

"Ask Silver Kelter. I also have a witness to verify Slade slugged her in Stuartville. Even manhandled her at her mom's funeral."

"You know, I did notice bruises on her face that she tried to cover up with too much makeup," the pastor said.

Slade stood up, fuming. "If you believe them, then I'm done here, Pastor."

"Damon, under the circumstances—"

He interrupted the pastor. "After all I contributed to this church and helped Billy Sedley . . ." He had more to say but held back his retort. He headed out of the room and slammed the edge of his shoulder into Mr. Sedley on his way out, moving him backward a foot or so. No chance Mr. Sedley would say anything or confront him in any way.

"And, Pastor," I continued, "one last thing: The police came to see me about Slade and Lugs's involvement with Eddie Kelter. You'll read about him in the newspaper soon enough. Now, Mr. Sedley, we can leave."

Pastor Crigler looked bewildered, struggling to find the right words to say. I had nothing more to add. Mr. Sedley was hesitant to leave the room, worried about Slade waiting to jump us. I walked ahead to see Slade leaving the building. Mr. Sedley hurried to walk by my side, without talking or making eye contact. He sighed—his dramatic gesture, which he used to emphasize his mood. We stopped walking when he reached out to grab my arm.

"What you said about Slade and that girl: Was it a grandstand play or the truth?"

"Are you still going after Slade for Bonnie's accident?"

"I deal only in facts."

"What I said was the truth."

"I told you not to speak, but you did anyway."

"And you weren't forthcoming about giving Slade the police report on Bonnie's accident. That's public information, not privileged."

"No reason to get into all that. But it looks like you poisoned Slade's well."

"Whatever that means, I—"

"Okay, Zinny. The pro bono offer still stands. But you stay clear of Damon Slade."

He reached out his hand to confirm his commitment. I would walk away from any involvement if I were in his position. My suspicions were digging roots.

"Why're you helping me?"

"I got you involved with him."

"But not to keep pursuing him."

Mr. Sedley said nothing on the drive back to my house. No pointless conversation about golf. He cleared his throat more times than usual. I intrigued him, no doubt, but it would be a challenge to understand one another.

"You're not curious about what I said about Eddie Kelter?" I said when Mr. Sedley stopped his car in front of my house.

"I don't know who that is." His quick response was a lie. He was quite attentive when I told him Eddie was the source of my knowledge about his brother at the Pothole.

"Well, he's dead. Murdered, so the cops say. What the hell have you gotten me involved in?"

He was speechless, which I expected. Entanglements were coming hard at him to retreat to a fallback position. My response to his nonresponse: slamming his expensive car door with the force of an ax to a tree.

CHAPTER 11

I sat up in bed, restless, awash in night sweats; awake most of the night with too many scenarios about Slade and Mr. Sedley tumbling in my head. The shadows from the living-room lamp, along with the major's pained moans, haunted our home like a bad horror movie. Major Jack insisted the lamp be on. He preferred to keep lights on at night while contending with vivid memories of the war, trusting his eyes more than his other senses.

The howling wind and the pounding rain heightened my senses as thunderstorms rumbled into the city. Nature's drumbeat recalled the nights I spent in 'Nam monsoons as a long-range scout trying to rest under jungle foliage, a respite from the war. When I dreamed of trudging through the jungle, I often woke up with a restless night ahead.

That night I heard movement on the mushy ground outside my bedroom. I rolled out of bed to peer out the bedroom window. I saw nothing to clear up what I heard, but my instincts told me someone or something was out there. I went to the living room and stared outside for a shadowy form or movement in the dark but saw no one. I heard only thunder in the distance.

Major Jack never stirred. I went back to bed. It took a while to relax enough to fall asleep. I had a short, terrifying dream about a presence stalking nearby. I wanted to face whatever it was and fight, which was unclear in the dense haze of my dream. Exposed. I knew that much.

I sat up when I heard movement again. Something outside made enough noise to trigger my vigilance. Thunder rolled. And there was a heavy thump against metal—two times. Lightning struck nearby; two neighborhood dogs barked. I listened in bed until, to my shock, there was a hard pounding on our front door. I reached for my pistol in the duffel bag on the floor, only to remember I stored it in my truck. I bent down for my jeans, grabbed a flashlight from the duffel, and went to the living room. The major was unfazed by the noise. I gazed through the window into the darkness at the hard rain. I fixed my stare on the yard and driveway. There were no streetlights on our narrow street. I saw no movement.

I opened the front door and stepped out onto the narrow, covered stoop. Was there someone by my truck? I left the stoop to jog across our lawn in the driving rain. There was no one at my truck. Examining it with the flashlight, I saw two deep dents on the driver-side panel. I ran to the edge of the driveway to gaze up and down the street for a person responsible for the damage but saw no one.

Who knew where I lived? The police knew. Mr. Sedley knew. I then remembered I wrote my address on the business cards I slid under the motel door for Eddie and Silver Kelter. Silver showed the card to Slade. That made sense.

"Zinny?" said Major Jack.

I jerked around to see Major Jack on the stoop with a confused expression about what I was doing in the rain. He placed his hand as a visor over his eyes. He grimaced, twisting his legs in a jerky motion to step through the puddles in the yard to join me.

"Someone sent me a message."

"What? What're you talking about?"

"Some asshole pounded big dents in my truck."

The dogs barked again. Other dogs on the next street over joined the alarming chorus. The neighborhood was on alert now. Not far away on the street perpendicular to our house, I heard tires screeching on the wet pavement. That was the culprit. It was pointless to pursue the fleeing vehicle.

"I didn't hear shit," said the major.

"You've slept through mortar rounds."

In the rain, Major Jack insisted on an examination of my truck. He grew up in a family of backyard mechanics. He got down in the muddy puddles to feel around the bashed side panels like a doctor examining wounds. After a few minutes of painful bending, plus the cold rain, Major Jack waddled back inside to dry off. He told me not to drive the truck until he checked it over after sunrise because the hood wasn't shut in place.

"Who'd do this?" he said.

"I know who and why. Slade or Lugs. A coward's way of sending a message."

"Are you listening?"

"Yes. And I'm also pissed."

I made us a pot of coffee. To pass the time until dawn, we reminisced about our struggles in the monsoon season in the Iron Triangle of 'Nam.

The rain ended at dawn. Major Jack took my flashlight outside to examine the engine. With the workman's tools I had collected over the years and stored in my truck cargo box, Major Jack went to work with the eagerness and care of someone tinkering with a classic car. He examined every connection in the engine well with the scrutiny of a dentist. No reason to ask him what he was doing, because he ignored everyone around him when in mechanic's heaven. I left him and went back in the house. An hour later he came inside to declare he had found something. From his expression, it was serious.

Major Jack had a fascination with booby traps. In 'Nam, he deactivated camouflaged mines and traps himself rather than leaving the tricky job to the bomb-disposal experts. He had the highest respect for the Vietcong and their creativeness to hide booby traps along trails that even seasoned soldiers would fall victim to.

"Somebody set up a booby for you."

"What'd you find?"

"They banged out a small hole in the fuel pump, just enough for gas to drip out on the intake manifold. What was clever was the fuse."

"Fuse?"

"Guy knew what he was doing. He smeared accelerant all over the manifold. My guess is it has a low flash point. When the car heats up on the road, boom. It's a bomb, Zin."

"Someone knows their way around cars."

"Your beautiful Cheyenne ten Super goes up in flames. Don't drive it until I replace the fuel pump and clean up the manifold."

"I should call the police."

"Cops don't like us already. Anyways, they won't bother until something happens. Someone's seriously messing with you."

"Cops are interested now. Eddie burned up in his car."

"Really? Jesus Christ! It's serious business now, Zin. Not the last play, whoever did it. I got reason to be alert. Hand me that .45."

"What? You're a sentry now?"

"I got no problem shooting bad guys." He smiled after saying that.

Major Jack used up what energy he had working on my truck. He had to block out the pain of being on his feet too long. He winced, collapsed into his chair, and rubbed his legs up and down.

"You know," I said, "Slade is too careful to do something this stupid. He'd announce his intentions to my face. This is Lugs's doing. Pounding on our door is his dumbass way to gloat about what he did."

"I thought I heard something."

"Yeah, right!"

"Let me guess. Gonna be some pushback at the Pothole."

"No. That's what Lugs wants. He expects me to come hard after him in front of witnesses. I'm not playing that hand."

"Then you're gonna be a pussy about what he did, huh?"

"Your opinion."

After Frosted Flakes for breakfast and a taxi ride to City Chevrolet for a fuel pump, Major Jack was at work installing the pump and cleaning up any remnants of the mysterious substance. Once again he fought through the pain in his legs. He even smiled. Remembering better days before his disability filled him with momentary happiness, drowning out the misery of what he couldn't do any longer. When he came into the house, exhausted from the repair work, the reality of doing nothing again clouded the satisfaction of a hard job accomplished.

"We should've reported it to the cops," I said.

"Report what? A lube job. I cleaned it up, and that's it."

———

By lunchtime we were in bad moods. We went to Anderson's restaurant to avoid an irritable afternoon. Begrudgingly, Major Jack agreed to use his cane.

After filling our stomachs and not talking for an hour, we walked out of the restaurant to find a disheveled man in layers of dirty clothes with a sign asking for money. What caught our attention was the phrase "Viet Nam Veteran" over "Hungry. Please Help." As expected, Major Jack stared at the sign, shaking his head in disgust. *Uh-oh.*

The unkempt man came over to him, grinning, thinking he would receive a handout.

"Hey, buddy, you served in 'Nam?"

"Huh?" The stunned man had no immediate answer; then he remembered the sign, "Yeah, right."

"What branch?"

"Huh? Don't matter."

"It does to us. We're vets. You in the army?" Major Jack stepped closer.

"Yeah, I was."

"What unit?"

"USA, man!"

"Twenty bucks if you tell me your unit."

More confused, frowning, the man backed up, then changed his mind and confronted the major. "Why you hasslin' me, man? I ain't done nothing wrong."

"You're lying about being a vet."

"Jack, drop it. He's right. It don't matter."

With anguish abounding, the man shouted, "Okay, man. Okay! Okay! Okay! I need my fix. It's for drugs and shit. Gimme anything you got, okay?"

The man shuffled to the major with an outstretched hand.

"Well, that's different. The truth just earned you a twenty spot. Here." Major Jack reached in his jeans pocket for a wad of folded money to hand the man a twenty-dollar bill.

"You're being an asshole, Major."

The man grabbed the bill and hotfooted away like we would change our minds and chase after him. He looked over his shoulder as he crossed the intersection in front of Presbyterian Hospital. When he was a block and a half away—a safe distance in his mind—he cursed at us, his arms waving like he was doing jumping jacks.

"So this is what it's come to? Confronting a junkie. We've got a well full of anger," I said.

We headed back home for a day with nothing to do and nowhere to go that mattered.

A day off from stress ended when the phone rang around dusk. I had a strong sense the call was trouble. But I picked up the phone after six rings.

"Is this Zinny?"

"Yes. Who's this?"

"It's Silver Kelter. See, I kept your card. I need a favor. I'm here at the Pothole paying the beer truck guy. Problem is, fuckin' Lugs won't let me leave and keeps pawing me. And won't stop. He wants me to strip for him. Listen, I need you to give me a ride to Goodman's Department Store. Damon's there buying clothes for our next sale. Okay? I'll pay you. I can't reach Eddie. Okay? Please do me this huge favor. Please, okay?"

Stunned. Silver didn't know her brother was dead. I couldn't utter her brother's fate.

"Why not call Damon? He can put a stop to it in a hurry. Anyway, you need to—"

I started to tell her to report Lugs's assault to the police, leading to the intended consequence of finding out about Eddie.

"No. Damon don't like to be bothered when he's buying. Please help me. Please."

Too much downside to get involved with Lugs at the Pothole. And how do I handle her emotions if, under the strong possibility of getting frustrated dealing with Lugs, I blurted out Eddie was murdered? No way could I be a white knight while facing the serious consequences of another assault charge.

"Silver, you know I got issues with your boyfriend. Can't you just walk away and call a cab with the money you said you'd pay me?"

"You know how big fuckin' Lugs is."

"He can't keep you from leaving."

"He has, and he will. Please, Zinny, I need help. Please, please."

"Tell Lugs what Slade will do to him when he sees him."

"Oh no. Damon will laugh and say Lugs was just kidding around. Please, Zinny. You're as big as he is. You ain't afraid of either of them. That's what you do, right? Help people. You said you'd help me and Eddie. Now I'm paying for your help."

"Get off the phone and get to it, Silver," Lugs said in the background.

Next I heard a dial tone.

Did Lugs intimidate Silver into getting me to come to their turf for a fight? It crossed my mind, although pawing his friend's girlfriend seemed like something Lugs would do. I was suspicious of everyone's motives. I believed everyone had an agenda. I wanted to believe she was in trouble. *Was going there the right thing to do*? I would find out soon.

Major Jack had a puzzled look on his face after I hung up. "What's up?"

I hesitated to tell him my plans, but I did. "Silver wants me to get her away from Lugs at the Pothole."

"Where's Slade?"

"At work."

"Is she worth more jail time?"

"Just walk her outta there. I won't do anything stupid."

"Yeah, you will. Pretty girls and stupid stuff go hand in hand. I know. I've done it enough times."

I shook my head. I left the house hearing Major Jack counting aloud the cash I would need to post bail.

———

Returning to the Pothole was risky. Major Jack was right. A high probability of arrest. And I was concerned this was a trap. Assess the situation with a cool head before escorting Silver away from Lugs. Likely Lugs had a different response in mind.

I walked into the Pothole not knowing what to expect. Patrons sat in groups in air fouled with cigarette smoke and popcorn and peanuts. In a corner booth, Lugs and Silver sat side by side, with his shoulder pressing her against the booth wall. Silver looked scared, on edge. They saw me standing in the doorway sizing up the situation. Lugs pointed a threatening fist in my direction.

"Hey, asshole, I know she called you. But you can't do shit since the cops got your number."

Lugs moved his right hand up Silver's print skirt. Silver struggled to force his hand off her. After peering about to see who was watching, his left hand swooped down her open-collar dress and grabbed her breast. Silver struck back, scratching Lugs's face with her nails. He grimaced and used his right hand to protect his face. He reacted with an enraged slap to her face. The force of the blow rammed her head against the wall; then she slumped in the booth.

Lugs ignored my approach to tend to his bleeding scratches. Silver rubbed the back of her head and protected her face with her left arm. Lugs raised his left fist to hit her again. I reached him in time to grab his arm and halt his swing, planting my right foot against the wooden bench seat, jerking him out of the booth. Even though he was massive, I had the leverage to haul him to the floor. I cocked the heel of my boot, aimed for Lugs's stomach, and stomped on the wide target. Lugs grunted, gasping as the blow collapsed his diaphragm.

Two patrons got off their stools to challenge me. I pointed my finger in their direction. "Don't concern you. Stay out of this." They backed down after hearing my threatening sergeant's tone.

Sammy, a regular every time I dropped by the Pothole, came over to aid Lugs. But he stayed on the floor trying to catch his breath and waved off Sammy's help.

Silver rubbed the back of her head, with tears streaming down her face.

"Get me outta here, Zinny."

I supported her with my arm around her waist to exit the bar. No one confronted us or followed us outside. If this were an army bar, a donnybrook would break out for the simple reason soldiers enjoyed a good fight. But these guys weren't soldiers.

"You able to drive?"

"Yes. I'm gonna tell Damon what he did. My head really hurts."

"Call the police."

"How much I owe you?"

"Nothing. But how about this? Get away from them both."

She stopped walking with an angry, wide-eyed expression. "I'm slashing his tires. He won't feel me up again. You got a knife?"

"Don't do that. Go call the police."

"Fuck both of 'em. I won't forget what you did."

No one came out of the Pothole to confront us. And no police siren in the distance. Silver unlocked a pristine white Cadillac, which, like Silver, was as out of place as a runway model in a biker bar. She sped away, sliding sideways in the gravel—much like her late brother would do.

———

"You stomped on his gut!" Major Jack said, after listening to the details of my encounter.

"Right in the diaphragm."

"You know, Zin, you're bringing the army way to civilians."

"He asked for it."

"You think Lugs will call the cops?"

"Think he's the kind of guy who handles things himself. He'll either come tonight or wait for the right time. Either way, he'll get his turn."

"And I'll be waiting."

"Meaning?"

"Shoot him and drag him inside and tell the cops he forced his way inside."

"Cops won't believe that."

"I'll wait for him to make the first fuckin' move."

"That's cowboy thinking, Jack."

"Suppose he goes to the cops?" he said.

"If he does, I can't do shit about it. Ya know, I'm not adapting too well to civilian life."

Being angry these days came easy. It replaced commitment. Our military service had ended abruptly, leaving us with an empty life. How were we doing? Major Jack threatened a homeless man; I stomped on a bartender. Both things beneath us.

At dusk I retrieved the .45 from my truck. I had every intention of carrying it as if I expected to use it when Lugs showed up at my house. Major Jack and I sat up for hours in a vigil watching out the living-room window. We rehashed stories of missions with Bike Crandell, our trusted helo pilot, each iteration with a slight embellishment, making the stories more interesting with every retelling. Near midnight our storytelling ended. That's when the major pushed himself to his feet to pick up the .45 on the sofa. He aimed the barrel at his temple.

"Ya know, I think about shooting myself. More than I ever thought I would. You believe that?"

"I believe that, but—"

"I could do it."

"That's not your way. Talk to someone."

"The VA? That's a joke."

"Someone around here?"

"I ain't gonna cry to some stranger."

I took the loaded pistol out of his hands. We had no more conversation.

I grew weary. After midnight I fell asleep on the sofa. Hours later I woke up with Major Jack vigilant in his chair, staring at the shades of gray illuminated by the harvest moon. While I was asleep, he put the .45 in his lap. I was too lethargic to take the weapon from him. I fell back asleep.

CHAPTER 12

The phone woke me early the next morning from a hard rest on the sofa. Major Jack was awake in his chair with the .45 in his lap. When he saw me yawning, he grumbled, "I wanted Lugs to show up."

Who's calling this hour of the morning? I thought about not answering, but after stretching, I picked up the receiver.

"Zinny, Claude Sedley. I apologize for calling so early. I've got some bad news. Bonnie shot Damon Slade yesterday." He sighed, allowing the shocking news to sink in before continuing. "She shot him at Goodman's Department Store warehouse late yesterday. I can't believe she did that."

"Is he dead?"

"I'm not sure. I called Lew and asked him to see what he could find out."

"You're in the middle of some dangerous stuff."

"I never imagined anything like this. How could I? How could I?"

He added kindling to a fire that was now scorching his world.

"I don't believe you, sir."

"Well, I, huh, I never heard her even hint about anything like this. If she ever mentioned anything like that, I would've—how could that vulnerable woman do such a horrific thing? She was afraid, but shoot him? Never."

"You've never had to-the-bone fear, have ya?"

Again, more sighs. Shame embedded in every sigh. And bewildered. There was no way to turn back the pages to see what he missed in his dealings with Bonnie Ridge.

"Why'd you feel like I needed to know this? I'm done with you and him and the rest of them."

"I thought you should know. That's all."

"I'll keep up with what's happening in the newspaper. Good luck dealing with your guilt." My statement, tone was intentionally meant to piss him off.

"Wait, Zinny. I need you."

I waited before responding to think over the possible reasons he said that. He was experiencing a real stunner—absolutely no control over something he set in motion.

"What?"

"I want you with me at Bonnie's preliminary hearing."

"Why? You've got a staff to escort you to and from court."

"No. You're familiar with the circumstances—"

"Yeah. You put me right in the middle of shit, right?"

My indignity was righteous. I wanted to be an investigator, not a bodyguard. My background and size had established the wrong reputation.

"Anyway, Lew is there for you," I said.

"No, he's not. I need you. No one knows what you know."

An honest admission from a cagey, manipulative man. I was naïve, but as I witnessed his maneuverings, he wasn't prone to work someone up to commit a violent crime. But trusting him to level with me? No. Not in his tightly wound world.

"I'll pay you very well, Zinny. And listen, everything I advised her to do was legal. I just . . . I just should do what I can to help her."

Mr. Sedley was out of his league navigating the dark streets of this side of his profession. Something he wanted to control but now ventured into deep waters. No other reason connected the dots to his involvement with these people. In time, that something would come out. One way or another.

"When is her hearing, sir?"

"Don't know. As soon as I know, I'll call you. Thank you."

"I'm not saying I'll go with you. But if I do, I want something in return."

"What's that?"

"Give me a reference. Tell any employer calling you I'm a good investigator."

"Yes."

"A good reference. A good one. And one more thing. I don't wanna be involved with anyone else you're involved with. Okay?"

"Sounds like you regret working for me."

"Ya know, Mr. Sedley, I wanted to know all you knew about Slade. Now I don't wanna know why you hassled a small-time hustler who was involved with a woman in a wheelchair. Seems beneath you, to be frank. And ya know, sir, when I talk to you, I get a bullshit headache."

"I suppose that's the way it is."

He was a careful man with an agenda he shared with no one. I gave him the benefit of the doubt that he had good intentions gone awry. Yet it was beyond my reasoning why he needed me at a public hearing.

"Can I count on you?"

"Maybe. For a good reference. And I'll hold you to your promise. I'll drive myself this time in case I need a quick out."

"I'll call you when I know the time for the hearing." Mr. Sedley hung up.

I sat down on the sofa, then told Major Jack about Slade. It took a lot to shock him. He shook his head from side to side with his mouth agape. His comment: "Boy, a few days in this town and you're right there in the headlines. How lucky can you get?"

"Gonna be interesting watching Sedley lie his way through all this shit. He's over his head. But I still got a bad feeling it's gonna come back on us."

"Yeah. Lugs will go apeshit with his buddy shot. And who'll be his target for payback?"

"Me."

"Good. Retaliation always makes me feel needed."

"If he comes around—"

"I'll shoot him and drag him inside. Say he broke in."

"No, you won't."

"I'm not worthless with a .45 in hand."

———

I waited all day for a phone call from Mr. Sedley about the hearing. When the phone did ring late in the afternoon, I anticipated Mr. Sedley's call.

"Zinny? It's Silver." With a shaky voice, Silver said, "Did you know Eddie's dead? He burned up in his Mustang. Oh my God, what's going on? I can't believe it! Damon's shot, and Eddie's dead. I'm scared to death, Zinny."

"Yeah. I understand. Is he dead?"

"No. But he'll probably wanna be. That woman shot him down there. Doc said the bullet tore his balls all up. He don't know how bad it is yet." She stopped to sigh in the shadow of a bad moon encircling her. I heard how difficult it was for her to breathe normally, as if her lungs were experiencing continuous malfunctions.

Revenge shooting? Sounds like it.

"Why us? Why all of us? Me and Eddie had our issues, but ya know, the last thing I said to him, I called him a fucking moron. I can't take it back. And last time I saw Mom, I told her that I hated her and never wanted to see her again. I can't say I'm sorry for being such a bitch." She made a gut-wrenching groan that came from deep in her emotional bank. "And I'm so terrified I can't even cry for them. I'm so scared I'm next, Zinny. All I can think about is . . . I screwed up everything. I'm so sorry for acting the way I did. But I gotta get outta here. You gotta help me. You gotta, please." She gasped, trying to breathe in a tunnel of panic.

"Where're you?" I asked.

"At the hospital. I can't deal with all this. I can't just hang around here. I gotta get my Corvette and be gone. I just got through burying Mom. I don't think I can handle another funeral. I just can't. How can I ask a man I hate for money to bury my brother? When he wakes up, he'll be crazy angry. Fuck! What kinda evil have I done to deserve this?"

"It's not you. It's who you're with."

"I had no choice. But now I do. I've earned my money and my car, and I'm gonna get it. I need your help. I gotta get my car, Zinny."

"You know I can't help, Silver."

"Drive me to Slade's place for the 'Vette."

"I saw you drive a white Caddy—"

"That's Damon's car. I'll pay you."

"Is Slade's place in town?"

"No. A couple of hours away in the backwoods."

"I don't know. The cops—"

"Please, Zinny. I got no one else to turn to. Please, please. I wouldn't ask you if I wasn't so fucking desperate!"

"I'll come there to talk about it."

"I'm really scared, Zinny."

"We'll see. We'll see." I served up a pile of uncertainty.

I thought my new career would be as an investigator. Not a courier, or a bodyguard, or a taxi driver. Like the major said, a pretty girl in serious need was difficult to turn down. Silver's nude photo drew me back in.

———

Charlotte Memorial was an eight-story hospital on the fringe of downtown.

A high-rise barracks was a better description of the building. I drove up the circular entrance to the hospital and followed the signs to an adjacent parking lot. Inside the entrance to the hospital, I walked up to the half-circle information desk to ask for Damon Slade's room.

"Are you family, sir?" the receptionist asked.

"Cousin."

"Room five twenty-one."

Getting off the elevator on the fifth floor, the medicinal smells reminded me of the time I spent sitting beside Major Jack's bed at the VA. The grim thought of being in a hospital for an extended period made me appreciate my robust health, even though my poor eating and drinking habits couldn't assure that would continue indefinitely.

Room 521 was midway down the long corridor. Before I faced Slade and Silver, I reminded myself to avoid any mentions of Bonnie Ridge. My tendency to distress people with my bluntness was a character flaw. My presence could turn into an ugly bedside manner, if Slade was cognizant.

I knocked twice. No response. I went inside the room, easing the door closed behind me. The single-occupancy room was dark; the blinds were closed. The position of Slade's bed shielded Silver's view of the door. She was asleep in a recliner by his bed. He was resting; his face, chalky; IVs in both hands and layers of bandages covering his lower stomach and groin.

"Silver?" I whispered.

She gasped, looked about with owl eyes, startled that someone was in the room. It took a few seconds of squinting to recognize me.

"Oh, Zinny. How long you been here? Thanks for coming."

I sat down in the hardback chair beside her. "Just now."

"Why would his Mustang catch on fire? It was his baby. A cop said it was on purpose. Who would do that? Eddie wouldn't hurt nobody."

"The cops will find out."

"A Mustang don't just catch on fire, right?"

"That's right. When did the cops come talk to you?"

"Last night. Briefly. Have the cops talked with you?" she said.

"Why me?"

"They asked about you and Eddie."

"And you said?"

"You had nothing to do with it. You tried to help us."

I withheld my opinion. I had no idea what the right words were to explain my hunch about Eddie's murder and her predicament without scaring her more than she already was.

"Thank you for coming, Zinny."

"Ya know, the cops warned me about getting involved again."

"But you'll help me, right?"

I could fault her for her choices, but at the same time, be sympathetic to the tragedies that went beyond the consequences of bad decisions. With Slade and Lugs in her life, she was in a cycle of fear and abuse. Why was an attractive, young woman with a man twice her age? Women and their choices was beyond my logical reasoning.

"Zinny, that woman, Bonnie, who shot Damon, seemed sweet when I met her at Goodman's. She was crippled in an auto accident, ya know, and Damon said it made her crazy." She frowned as if a troubling thought came to her. "I'm not stupid, Zinny. Something was going on. She shot him in the balls. Like she meant to do it there."

"Yeah."

"I know what Damon's like. I hate him most of the time, and when he hurts me, I wanna pick up a gun and do the same fucking thing. Wonder what he did to her."

"Makes you wonder, doesn't it? Where's your dad? Can he help you?"

"He left Mom after she threatened to file charges against him for beating her up. I haven't seen him since. I grew up without a father. Probably why I'm so screwed up."

"Silver, you're pretty and bright. That's two check marks for a better life."

"I dropped out of high school after Mom kicked me out of the house when I got busted for drunk driving. Damon paid for a lawyer to help me keep my driver's license. I told him about my dream to go to New York and be a model. He said I could model clothes for him at his sales. He said it would be good experience. Stupid to think I could be a model someday. For sure I'm worse off today than when I first started thinking about modeling. And I shouldn't have slept with Damon either."

"Silver, you've grown up too fast."

"You're a nice guy, Zinny. I hate that you know I'm this kinda person."

Slade stirred, moaned in obvious pain. He moved his torso until the pain stopped him. Licking his dry lips, his groggy voice pled to anyone present. "Who ya talking to? Is it the doc? I gotta have more pain meds, Doc."

"I'll tell the nurse, Damon."

"Fuck, fuck, fuck," he replied.

Silver pressed the call button beside his right hand. Slade swept his left hand across his bandaged groin. He gasped in pain. When he did catch his breath, he blinked rapidly in the dark room. His squinting eyes struggled to identify me. "Who's there?"

"A well-wisher for a speedy recovery," I said with abounding sarcasm.

"Who?"

A nurse opened the door to the room with medicine to insert into a tube in his wrist. She turned to issue instructions to us. "He'll be asleep for a while. The night nurse will check on him after my shift is over."

"Thanks, nurse. Let's go, Zinny."

The nurse left. Slade squirmed, squinted, lashed out in a weak voice. "Is that Zubell? Zubell? Why's that asshole here?"

"Go ahead, Zinny. I'll say goodbye and meet you in the hall."

"Get that asshole away from me, Silver."

Stepping out of Slade's room, I came face-to-face with detectives Cutter and Pitman. Bad timing on my part.

Cutter's reaction was to drop his head, massage his temple, and look agitated. "Well, well, well, lucky for us to find you here. And unlucky for you for being where you shouldn't. Why're you messing with this man in his condition? And don't give us a bullshit answer. You're not getting the benefit of the doubt. What're you up to, Zubell?"

"A favor for Silver Kelter."

"Really?"

"Yes, sir. We were just leaving."

"Not so fast. You're really pissing me off getting involved with these people again. Do I have to remind you again to stay away from the guy you assaulted? You can't be that stupid," said Cutter.

"Yes he is," said Pitman.

"I'm not here like you think."

"The man's been shot. Have some decency," said Detective Pitman.

"I know the circumstances look bad. But—"

"Ya see, I tried hard to like ya, but you end up coming here when you know there's trouble abound," said Cutter.

Silver came out of the room, quietly shut his door. She was surprised to see the police presence. "Oh, you're back."

Pitman said, "Did Zubell say anything to you or Mr. Slade that sounded like a threat of some sort?"

"Oh no, sir. I asked him to help me. Drive me to my car. And I was in the room the whole time. He didn't say anything to Damon."

"You asked this guy to help you?" said Pitman.

"I'm getting a headache, and that ain't good," said Cutter. "Anyway, young lady, you ain't leaving with Zubell. I got questions for ya."

"What? Why? I've told you everything I know, sir."

"We wanna clear up a few things with you and Mr. Slade," said Cutter.

"Okay. It won't take too long, right? Wait for me, Zinny."

"No. That's not gonna happen. I want Zubell outta here."

"That's not fair. He's driving me to get my car."

"What's right is what I say is right, Ms. Kelter. I'm asking you, please, to cooperate, okay? And for you, Zubell, get."

"I'm on my way."

Cutter grabbed my right arm before I took a step. "Why don't I ever want you to talk with Mr. Slade again?"

"Because it's an active police investigation."

"Now we're on the same page. Goodbye." Cutter released his grip, turned, and entered Slade's room. Pitman escorted Silver back into the room.

As ordered, I went to the elevator. But I didn't head home. I had to see Lugs's ugly face. And satisfy my curiosity about his reaction to Slade's shooting. When I arrived at the Pothole, there were no cars in the parking lot and a small white sign tacked on the front door. I parked my truck to check out the handwritten note. It read: "Closed. Go away."

CHAPTER 13

I didn't hear from Silver the rest of the day. Pleased about that. Done with them. And no phone call from Mr. Sedley. Did he change his mind about attending Bonnie's hearing? It was time to accept my life as a retired guy with no responsibilities.

Edna called the following morning at 0830 to tell me Bonnie Ridge's preliminary hearing was today. "Be at the Mecklenburg County Court at nine."

I stayed in bed fifteen more minutes, took a long shower, ate a bowl of cereal, and dressed. At 1030, I left the house in no hurry to arrive at the courthouse. With any luck, the hearing would be over by the time I arrived.

I stood at the back of the courtroom looking for familiar faces. On the back row of the packed, church-like benches was Mr. Sedley and Ableman. We acknowledged each other with nods. Unlucky to arrive before the hearing started. I looked for others I recognized as I sidestepped across the bench to sit with them. Bonnie's husband, Blaine, and Pastor Crigler sat behind the defense table. They seemed too preoccupied in prayer to notice anyone else in the courtroom. The pastor had his arm around Blaine Ridge, who was leaning forward with his head bowed as if in continual prayer. I recognized other church elders in attendance.

The district attorney was standing at a bench facing the judge loudly reciting the charges against a Black defendant. Mr. Sedley leaned across Lew to whisper, "Thought you weren't coming. Lew just arrived."

I responded with a faint smile and nod. Mr. Sedley whispered to Lew, "Tell us how Bonnie is holding up."

"Don't know," Lew whispered to both of us. "I went to see her at county. The arresting detectives said she hasn't said anything since being in custody. No one can get her to talk. And she hasn't eaten. It's not good, Claude."

"Are you representing her?"

"No. Another attorney I know was hired to represent her."

"That's all you could do, Lew. I appreciate it."

"I'll wait around to see if she answers the judge's questions," he said.

About forty-five minutes later, a deputy escorted Bonnie Ridge into the courtroom. She seemed comatose sitting in her wheelchair, oblivious to the legal setting, and didn't gaze about to see who was present. Not the panicky person I encountered outside Mr. Sedley's office building.

The clerk read aloud the docket number of the *State of North Carolina versus Bonnie Elaine Ridge*. The charge: attempted murder in the first degree and discharging a weapon in a public building.

"Mrs. Ridge, you are represented by counsel?"

A chubby attorney with bleached blond hair spoke up. "Yes, Your Honor. Wilson Simmons for Bonnie Ridge."

"Mr. Simmons, have you advised your client of the charges that were just read?"

"Yes, Your Honor."

"How do you plead, Mrs. Ridge?"

She did not answer.

"Mrs. Ridge, do you understand the charges that were read against you?" the judge asked again.

She still didn't answer.

"Mrs. Ridge, you must answer the court. This is a hearing to determine that you understand the charges against you and how you plead to these charges. Do you understand that?"

Still no response.

"Counsel, please tell your client that she must enter a plea, or I'm prepared to add contempt of court to the charges."

"Your Honor, I did advise her of the charges, but she hasn't spoken at all. In fact, she hasn't talked to anyone that I'm aware of and hasn't eaten in days. I would like to ask the court for a continuance to have Mrs. Ridge evaluated for competency. If that pleases the court, Your Honor."

The judge said, "One last time. How do you plead, Mrs. Ridge?"

She said nothing.

"I'm gonna grant the defense motion. Does the DA have any objections?"

"No, Your Honor."

"Mrs. Ridge, I'm ordering a psychiatric evaluation. You understand what I'm saying to you?" He paused for her response. "Mrs. Ridge, this order does not mean you will be held indefinitely. You have rights. Do you understand what I just said?"

Bonnie remained motionless, quiet.

"So ordered."

Blaine Ridge took the cue from his colleagues to head out of the courtroom. Blaine didn't try to get his wife's attention as a show of support. He appeared sleep deprived, angry. The church group noticed us staring as they exited. Blaine stepped toward us with his index finger pointed at Mr. Sedley with a brawler's glare in his eyes. "This is all on you, Sedley," he said. "You see the harm you caused."

"Order in the court," the judge said. "Bailiff, clear these people from the courtroom. Any more outbursts, I'm ordering arrests for contempt of court."

Three bailiffs approached us. Ableman stood up in front of Mr. Sedley while the church group surrounded Blaine to escort him out. Pastor Crigler whispered in Blaine's ear as they left the courtroom. My attention was on Bonnie's reaction to the outburst. She appeared encased in a soundproof bubble with no reaction to the disruption her husband caused. A bailiff wheeled her out of the courtroom.

We halted in the corridor right outside the courtroom, where Lew said, "Don't be concerned, Claude. Wait for them to get a good piece away."

"I'm concerned about Bonnie. She will be sent to Broughton now," Mr. Sedley said.

"What's Broughton?" I asked.

"State mental hospital."

The three of us watched the church group walk away with the pastor and the two elders bookending Blaine, who turned around to scowl at us.

"Thanks for coming, Zinny. I won't forget my commitment to you."

"I'll be in touch, Zinny," Lew said.

That was the end of our conversation. We parted ways.

On my way back to the house, I thought, *Her reason for shooting Slade would remain a mystery if found incompetent to stand trial. He paid a life-changing price for an affair.*

———

Later that day, I went on a two-mile run around our neighborhood. Feeling light-headed, panting, my side aching, I returned home to see Major Jack rising from his chair for the first time that afternoon. As I stood in the living room to cool off, the major stretched, with his arms reaching for the ceiling before sitting back down.

"Who're you trying to impress shuffling down the street?" he said.

"I'm paying for it."

"I need to exercise my arm. Bring me a beer."

I went to the refrigerator for two beers. Major Jack, oddly enough, didn't ask about the court hearing. I asked him why.

"Don't give a shit. Why should I?"

"I'll tell you anyway. She won't talk to anyone. Not even the judge."

"What're you doing, Zinny?"

"I told ya."

"What do you want from all this?"

"Legal help to get us out of the shit we're in. I told you that."

"And now you want a chance at Silver. A long shot for an ugly guy like you."

"When did I ever say I wanted that?"

"Why else would you do whatever she asks? At least you've got one thing in your favor: your nut sack is intact. She'll get tired of a guy who can't satisfy her."

I gulped the rest of my beer without responding. Time for a shower and nap.

———

That afternoon we were surprised by a knock on the door. I walked to the living-room window to see a black sedan and a squad car in our driveway. Two police vehicles there meant serious business. Detectives Cutter and Pitman stood at our front door motioning me to let them in. One uniformed policeman approached our house to join up with the detectives.

"Who's there?" Major Jack said.

"Cops. Can't be good."

"Well, here we go again."

"Remember, Jack: don't be a smart-ass."

There was a harder knock on the door. I watched the other uniformed officer stroll around behind the house. I unlocked the dead bolt. The cops pushed me aside without asking permission. Cutter and his men had hard questions on their minds.

"Zubell, you're gonna let us go fishing around here, right? I got a permit just in case you think this ain't legal. But, of course, it's okay, boys. We're all on the same side, right?" Sarcasm was his stock in trade.

"You're welcome anytime."

"Be gentle, Wilson." Cutter motioned the uniformed officer to do a physical of our home.

"What're we supposed to think about all this, Detective Cutter? You're searching for what, may I ask?"

"I'm beginning to wonder if you're running a back-door investigation. I don't know why you'd do that. Is that lawyer paying you to do something like that? The truth, Zubell. I'll find out eventually."

"Detective, like I told you, I don't work for him any longer, and Silver Kelter asked me to come to the hospital because she wanted me to drive her to Slade's place."

"For what?"

"Pick up her car."

"Why you?"

"She said she has no one else to turn to. With her brother murdered."

"Listen, Private Dick, you're getting under my ornery skin. Are you running your own investigation for some goddamn reason?"

"I don't have the authority to run an investigation. Just doing the girl a favor. But not anymore."

"You got no shot with her, ya know?" said Cutter.

Starting to develop a complex about my looks.

"I see even you found a wife," said Major Jack to Cutter, pointing at his wedding band.

"Oh, it speaks," said Cutter.

Major Jack was ready to mouth off again, but I shook my head. He followed my cue. Silence was the best response.

Cutter walked around supervising the search as Pitman and the uniformed policeman turned our house upside down, checking every drawer and closet. Cutter never wandered from our living room, keeping a curious eye on us.

About ten minutes later, Pitman returned to the living room to sit with Cutter on our sofa. Cutter propped his feet up on the crate we used for a coffee table. They were in no hurry to pry information out of us. As any experienced investigator knew, the tried-and-true method of circling around the hard questions boxed a person into admission.

The patrolman returned to the living room with my hunting knife and .45 in hand, having removed it from a duffel bag. He handed it to Cutter for examination. The patrolman searching the outside of our house joined up with the posse carrying a rusty gallon gas can. He handed the can to Cutter, saying, "Gasoline."

Cutter checked for our reactions. "So, Zubell, you told us earlier you had no weapons in the house. You lied to the police. That's not good."

"I told the truth, Detective. When you asked, I had the pistol in my truck."

Cutter smirked with the grunt of pig eating slop. "Tell me, Zubell. We're on the same side, right? Why the gas can?"

Major Jack answered before I could respond. "Comes in handy to burn up things."

"We can all go downtown to the station. You want that?"

I shook my head. The mean-spirited stares on Cutter's and Pitman's faces gave away their dislike for smart-mouthed answers. Cutter, the quarterback in charge of the police team, motioned for his men to huddle up at our front door. He handed the gas can to the patrolman with stripes and told them to return to the station. Cutter and Pitman returned to sit on the sofa. I stood by the major.

"Boys, we're gonna have a frank conversation, right?"

"All right, Detectives," I said. "Once again, I was hired to deliver a document to Damon Slade out of town—"

"What document?" asked Pitman.

"Never saw it. For Slade's eyes only. And hired again to watch for Slade at the Pothole. Just watch for him. Then he fired me. That's the extent of it."

"And you met Eddie Kelter there?" said Pitman.

"Yes. And I see where this is heading. Eddie told me about his missing mom and the violent relationship his sister, Silver, had with Slade."

"Cecil Horry told us you were the last person to see him alive. Is that true?" said Pitman.

"The last time I saw him, he left his home, drunk, and drove off without noticing me. Slade and Lugs weren't there. So how would they know I was the last one to see Eddie alive?"

"We're looking at everyone involved with him. I'm looking hard—believe me," said Cutter.

"Seriously? Seriously, you think we had something to do with Eddie's murder? Keep this in mind, gentlemen. Major Jack is a twenty-two-year army veteran with the Silver Star and three Purple Hearts. And me, a twenty-year veteran. So, seriously, think about it."

"You're not going near Slade again, right?" said Cutter.

"Right."

Pitman said, "Why would Horry lie to us about you being the last person to see Eddie alive?"

"Because he's a liar."

"After we spoke with him, he disappeared. And he closed the Pothole. So you wanna be an investigator? Where's Cecil Horry?"

"No idea."

Pitman said, "You guys came back from Viet Nam and got no respect. Hippies turned you guys into the enemy. And the commies in the press wrote about you guys killing women and babies. You got a raw deal. It pisses me off you guys didn't get to win the war. That's gotta burn a hole in your gut, right?"

"You served, Detective Pitman?" I asked.

"Well, no. I wanted to."

"Fraternity parties kept you tied up, huh?" said Major Jack.

I took offense at Pitman's clumsy maneuvering to tap into our emotions about serving our country. "You got your opinion, Detective, but you got no idea what pisses us off. Don't tell us you have any clue about how we feel about 'Nam, because you don't."

Pitman stood up to confront us. Cutter shot up to halt his aggressive move.

"We're done here, Pit. Go out to radio in we're on our way back to the station. Go on," said Cutter.

"He's not gonna talk to me in that tone again. I promise you that," said Pitman.

"Go on, Pit. Go on."

Pitman left our house stomping on our hardwood floors. Cutter waited until he was out the door to say, "You guys were soldiers, and I respect that. I served with Patton's Third Army in the Second World War. But making waves when you should be getting respectable work won't cut it." Cutter stepped over to us. "Silver Kelter backed up your story. She said you had nothing against her brother. Guys, I don't wanna develop a much closer relationship with you."

"We don't want that either, Detective."

"I'm leaving your toys," Cutter said, pointing to the hunting knife and pistol on our sofa. "Heed my warning, Zubell." He closed our door hard behind him.

Major Jack had a wide grin.

"What?"

"Proud of you, man. The way you put that frat boy in his place showed me the real Zin."

"Asshole pissed me off."

"But ya know, Cutter has a point. What good are we these days? We're no longer soldiers, and that's all we've ever been. You're no investigator. But at least you're trying. You're not a worthless slug who sits on his ass all day like me."

"Point taken."

The cops were right. All we did was talk about the past more than we should, embellishing experiences for no one's benefit. We had too much time on our hands.

For about ten minutes, I watched Major Jack staring out the window. His day consisted of watching leaves fall, eyeing scampering squirrels, studying cars driving in and out of the neighborhood. That was his life. He never talked about doing anything more meaningful. I had no idea what to say to get him to change.

"Jack, stop smarting off to the cops. Ableman doesn't need an attitude to hamper his negotiations on our behalf."

"I'll be gone before they get around to sending me away."

That statement shut down the conversation. After he gulped three beers in less than thirty minutes, he was asleep. He was snoring within a few minutes. I tiptoed over to whisper in his ear, "Get right, Jack."

The phone rang shortly after six. Sometimes I tried to guess who was calling before I picked up the receiver. I thought this call might be from Silver. No more favors with Slade in her life, I would say. I was surprised to hear an unfamiliar voice.

"This is Chip Sedley. Remember me? I'm the guy who tore up your business card when you came to our office looking for work."

"I remember you, sir."

"I hear you went with Dad to Bonnie Ridge's prelim this morning. I'm wondering why you did that."

No small talk from him—a direct question straight to the reason for his call. "He asked me to join him. I'm surprised you don't know about that."

"Edna has been very curious about you. She thought I might know something. But I don't. Our business office doesn't have a 1099 on you."

"A 1099?"

"Contract employee."

"No. I was paid in cash."

"Interesting. Dad doesn't do things like that. Hire freelance people without an explanation. It's for Damon Slade, right?"

"He told me not to discuss him with anyone."

Surprising, but not shocking, I thought, *that Chip wasn't in the loop about my brief work for his father.*

"I respect that. Edna said you go by Zinny. Do you mind if I call you Zinny?"

"Sure."

"Edna was stunned that Dad hired you. You left his office after the first meeting with an envelope. But she hasn't seen a file on Damon Slade."

"Don't know anything about that."

"Do you know what was in the envelope?"

"Again, he said not to discuss anything. Can I call you Chip?"

"Yes."

"Well, Chip, ask your dad about Slade."

"Edna said you were paid to watch for him at a bar called the Pothole. Is that right?"

"You already know the answer to that. Not to be rude, sir, but why all the questions? I don't work for your dad any longer."

"Bonnie Ridge met with Dad. I have no idea how often. I never met her, but I recognized her name in the newspaper. Her shooting Damon Slade raises a lot of serious questions. And my dad's dealings with him troubled me, so I asked a law school friend who works in the state attorney general's office to check him out. Seems he has a checkered past as a highway patrolman. He wrecked two cruisers after high-speed pursuits. Two speeders died at one accident. And accused of taking bribes to tear up tickets. He waived a hearing and resigned. My friend is checking into Slade's business dealings. The Pothole, in particular."

"Seems you're as curious as I was about him and your dad. He's tight-lipped about something. Have you told him that you're asking questions about Slade?"

"No. Not yet."

"Be careful. I wasn't, and he fired me. He doesn't want you or Edna to know something."

"He honors client-attorney confidentiality, but still—"

"Let me ask you this: Did your dad have reasons to go after your uncle's church?"

"Why would he go after Uncle Billy's church?"

"There has to be people in the church wondering about Billy Sedley's suicide."

Chip Sedley took a couple of deep breaths. His voice was introspective when he said, "There are a lotta questions that can't be answered. No one says it was suicide. I believe he had too much to live for to do that. His new church kept him really pumped up."

"Ask yourself this question: Why would your dad, in his prominent position, have anything to do with Damon Slade and Bonnie Ridge? Something doesn't add up, Chip."

"Again, I apologize for tearing up your business card. Have a good day."

Bringing up Billy Sedley's suicide unearthed raw emotions with the

Sedley family. I got the same reaction when I mentioned suicide to the pastor. Too fresh in their memories, I supposed. But there were serious connections between Slade and Billy Sedley. Had to be. Slade said as much to us and Pastor Crigler at the meeting. Now I learned Chip Sedley was digging into Slade's past, going behind his dad's back.

There was smoke surrounding Billy Sedley's death. Doubtful I would ever find out what it was.

CHAPTER 14

No one wanted me in the middle of the night. The phone kept ringing as I struggled to free myself from the clinging sheets. I tripped over the duffel bag Major Jack left in the hall and almost fell to the floor. Annoyed, I trudged to the phone on top of the television in the living room, only a few feet from where Major Jack was snoring. I cursed aloud.

"Hello?" I said.

"Hello?" said a raspy woman with a pumped-up tone. "Who was I calling again?" the woman said to someone within earshot.

"Who's this?" I demanded.

"Tell him to come get me," said a frantic female in the distance.

"I don't wanna get involved," said the raspy woman.

"I'm hanging up." And I did.

Within seconds, while standing by the phone, it rang again. "What do you want?"

"You gotta help her, okay? I can't get involved." The woman sounded as distraught as a mother whose child was in danger.

"You must have the wrong number, lady." I hung up again. Hopefully this madwoman wouldn't call back.

She did call right back. She spoke before I could hang up. "Silver, Silver.

You know her? She says you know her."

"Yes. I know her. Please stop screaming."

"A son of a bitch beat her up. She says you can help her. I can't get involved."

"How bad is she hurt?"

"Blood all over her face and clothes ripped up. That bad enough for ya?" The woman had the temperament of Major Jack's late mother.

"Are the cops on their way?"

"No. She don't want the cops. You her boyfriend?"

"No. But I know him," I said without thinking beforehand.

"A friend of yours? Men are animals. My late husband beat me till I creamed him with a skillet. And that was that."

She wanted no part of the fraternity of men. The woman took the phone away from her mouth to shout at Silver to call the cops. I heard Silver yell back, "Tell Zinny to come get me."

"Zinny, come get her. I ain't gonna get involved."

A hairy situation. Helping Slade's girlfriend could draw me back on Detective Cutter's radar. But thinking it through, what choice did I have? She knew I would come to help her.

"Tell me where you live, ma'am."

"Listen, if ya come here to hurt us, ya better know I got dogs and a shotgun, and I ain't afraid to use 'em, ya hear me?"

"No reason to threaten me, ma'am. I'm a good guy."

"Why don't her boyfriend help her?"

"He was shot and in the hospital." Again, speaking before thinking.

"My God, what kind of people are ya?"

Great question. I asked her again for her address. I waited at least a ten count before she had the courage to tell me her name: Winetta. My revelation about Slade with a gunshot wound made her hesitant to give me directions to her home. Dangerous circumstances had come to her door. I told her that I was retired from the army and respected her concern. Before she gave me her address, she warned me about her prowess with a loaded shotgun. I thanked her for the alert.

Major Jack moaned during the phone call, never roused even when I cursed aloud before answering the third time. I dressed and stuffed my .45 and hunting knife in a small duffel bag. Major Jack was snoring again when I returned to the living room.

Having a premonition about something bad brewing for unmindful people was one of my strong suits. On certain occasions, for certain people, I enjoyed their bad consequences. Not this time.

⎯⎯⎯

Strip clubs, abandoned buildings, cheap diners, a fleabag motel took root where Winetta lived in the western side of the city. Years ago her house might have been a desirable outlying Charlotte location. These days overgrown vacant lots and uncaring neighbors damaged her neighborhood like a bad bruise that wouldn't heal.

My headlights flooded her small brick house built deep into a dense plot of pines, poplars, and oaks. She tended a row of roses and an impressive flower bed beside her driveway. Despite an established mental picture of Winetta, I would be concerned about a woman living in this neighborhood.

I parked my truck beside the narrow sidewalk to her small front porch. I opened my car door, then heard deep, menacing barks coming from inside the house. I stayed in my truck. She opened the front door for two Dobermans to dash to my truck. Racing with the intent to dismember me, they stood on my truck door and barked with their fangs inches from the driver-side window. Often when I had nightmares, vicious dogs were the predators lurking in my subconscious.

A woman in a light-colored bathrobe strolled out on her porch with a shotgun in hand. She looked like I imagined: wrinkled face, silver hair, an unkempt appearance. She called her dogs to heel, gesturing them with her shotgun to approach the house. They obeyed her command. I stood outside the safety of the cab, shouted, "No need to sic those dogs on me, ma'am!"

"You Zinny?" she said.

"Yes, ma'am. I haven't done a thing to warrant that."

"Neighborhood's gone to hell. I'm an old woman. I need protection."

A drunken fool might challenge her, but not me. I left the truck door open and took my time stepping to the front of my truck, but no farther. I watched Winetta put her right hand on the trigger housing of her shotgun. The Dobermans snarled at my every step, sitting like gargoyles next to Winetta's bathrobe. How Silver got past these beasts was due to the grace of a dominating master. One of the dogs exposed his fangs and growled at his prey: me. Winetta stopped the dog with a stern command. "Stay."

"Winetta, don't point that shotgun at me. Did Silver call the cops?"

"No. Why she trusts the lot of ya is beyond me."

"Tell Silver to come here. I don't trust you and those dogs."

"Some soldier you are. Don't make a sudden move."

No way was I going near her. The Dobermans kept up the vicious barking, sending chills through me. Winetta spun around with the dogs beside her like henchmen and walked through the open door. She glanced over her shoulder to see if I had approached her porch. I backed up to my truck cab.

In no time, Winetta and her dogs returned, followed by Silver, who wore an old print dress that had wrinkles and stains of gardening garb. From a distance, her hair looked wet, her legs shaky, her head down.

"Child's gotta have more trust in men than I do," Winetta said.

"Thank you for helping me, ma'am," Silver said.

"Come help her," said Winetta. Her dogs joined in a barking chorus. "You forgot your clothes, young lady."

"Throw 'em away."

I walked a measured ten paces toward the porch. Silver walked at an exhausted, deliberate gait. I wrapped my left arm around Silver's waist, guiding her to my truck, consistently glancing over my shoulder. The alert Dobermans growled for my flesh. I stared at the blood around Silver's nose and mouth longer than I should have. Silver wrapped her arms around her ribs and winced as she stepped up into my truck. I hustled around behind my truck to the driver's side as Winetta's dogs barked, and she shouted, "Treat that baby right!"

Her dogs chased me out of the driveway. Winetta was safe from danger with those beasts hunting for an invaders' flesh.

Back on Wilkinson Boulevard, Silver said, "Thanks, Zinny."

"You need a doctor?"

"No."

"Was it Lugs who attacked you?"

She nodded with quick, short motions. I saw how fearful it was to confirm the identity of her attacker.

"Don't let him get away with this."

"I gotta get my car. Please, I gotta."

"You can put Lugs away for this."

Silver was less interested in pursuing the assault charge than getting the car. Her escape, I assumed. My pushing her to report the crime was my desire, not hers.

I headed back toward downtown, not knowing where I was going and on edge. I convinced myself, difficult as it was, to do exactly what she wanted. At what cost?

She struggled to catch her breath. "I gotta do something." She rolled down the window, stuck her head out, then threw up. When she stopped heaving, she screamed as if attacked again. She screamed twice more, startling me each time. I drove on at a slower speed, expecting more understandable emotions. Fortunately, no cars were near us. She then vented her anger on my dashboard with raging slaps of both hands.

She faced me with eyes prepped for more outbursts. "Zinny, I'm not a stupid fuckin' bimbo. I know what fuckin' Lugs was capable of. Don't you dare think I deserved what Lugs did because I went with him."

"No, I don't. He belongs in prison."

"The cops told me to stay away from you. Fuckin' Lugs showed up at the hospital all sweet and apologized for the way he treated me. He told Damon what he did just to be an asshole. Damon was crazy mad but couldn't do anything in his condition."

"You have to get your car that bad?"

"Yes. I gotta get out of this fuckin' mess." She took a moment to rub her mouth with the sleeve of her dress. "When Damon fell asleep, Lugs said he'd drive me for the 'Vette. Crazy to trust him—I get that. He drove right to a strip club. I said no way. He tried to pull me out of his truck. I fought him until he slapped me real hard and made my mouth bleed and hit me again. He said he'd keep hitting me unless I gave him a blow job. That's when he pulled out his junk and started ripping off my clothes. I said okay, okay, okay. He relaxed and thought I'd get down to business. But I remembered what Eddie taught me. Duck you head and wrench the guy's balls hard till he screams for mercy, then run like hell." She blew her nose on the sleeve of her dress. "He hurt too bad to chase me down."

"That was brave. How'd you get past those hounds?"

"That lady heard me screaming and held them back. I'm done bein' treated like trash. Ya know, sometimes it's real shitty to be pretty. That's all you guys care about. And I never had a daddy to protect me from assholes. Sure, I made some bad choices, but not bad enough to deserve this. What chance did I have with a mom who threw herself at any guy with money? Some role model. Well, from now on, I'm doing what I want with the 'Vette and the money Damon promised me."

"You know, Silver, he'll come after you."

"Let him. I'll be okay when I get Damon's gun."

Silver leaned against the truck window for support. I glanced at her repeatedly. The courage she displayed in the face of brutal violence was akin to the grit I implanted in raw recruits. I stood with them then, and I would stand with her tonight.

"I'm heading the right way, right?"

She nodded.

Wilkinson Boulevard became Independence Boulevard, then NC Highway 74, heading east out of the city. Leaving the Charlotte city limits, traveling east toward Monroe, I was understandably uncomfortable about what we might be facing at Slade's place—a troubling sense Lugs would be waiting there, since he already knew her intentions. But that wouldn't waylay her frantic decision to remove herself from Slade's death grip. Even given time to reconsider the possible danger, I doubted she would change her mind.

"How long to Slade's place?"

"About an hour more. That won't make any difference, will it?"

"No. You think Lugs is there?"

"Maybe. I don't know. I know one thing: he's hurtin'."

"I'd prefer the cops to pick him up before we get your car—"

"I'll fuckin' lose it if I don't get my car. I won't be able to control what I'll do."

Before proceeding, I must believe in a workable plan—careful, thought-out steps—requiring no confrontation with a hostile man. I imagined the stealth movements to assess the situation with a level head. And with it came a knotty feeling about how to keep Silver under control.

"Are there guns at his place?"

"Everyone's got guns. You got plenty, being an army guy, right?"

A gunfight would double down on Cutter's threat to jail me. I doubted self-defense would stand up in his investigation. Movie PIs could shoot, kill, then walk away with the distressed woman. But not in real life. Investigators warned to stay on their side of the street must stay there.

We drove through Monroe heading east on Highway 74. Neither of us spoke for a while. Glancing at her, she was becoming more anxious, nervously squirming and twisting her hair around her fingers. I asked her if I was heading in the right direction again. She nodded. She started breathing heavy as we left city lights and headed into the black countryside.

"You don't expect nothing, right?"

"No."

"Guys are usually nice to you 'cause they want something."

"All I want is not to get shot at."

"You're an army guy. You can handle stuff like that."

Her experiences with men left doubts about trusting the lot of us. I got that. She hardly knew me but was desperate enough to trust me to help her. The car was more important than the possible danger awaiting us.

"You won't leave me alone with him, right?"

"I said I won't. And I won't. You gotta keep telling me that I'm heading in the right direction."

"Yeah. Look for Highway 109. I don't wanna stay at Damon's tonight, even if Lugs isn't there."

"If you need a place to stay—"

She reacted fast to my untimely offer. "You just said you weren't that kinda guy."

"No, I didn't mean that. Nothing like that. Forget what I said." Considering what had happened, Silver had reason to suspect I had a motive for offering a bed.

After more miles down the highway, she leaned out the truck window and screamed as loud as she could to let the quiet world know she was upset, hurting. Driving through a dark world with limited traffic was eerie enough; her scream put me on edge like an amusement park's haunted house did to a kid. She leaned across the seat to massage her face in the rearview mirror. I heard her moan. She mumbled something.

After more tears, she calmed down enough to say, "I'm not getting the rest of my stuff. Just the 'Vette."

"How much farther is it?"

"A ways still."

"Tell me where to turn again?"

"Highway 109. You didn't answer me about a gun."

"I have a .45. But I don't wanna need it."

We rode in silence, until she shouted unexpectedly, "I can't get outta my head what Eddie kept telling me that Damon had something to do with Mom's disappearance. And how did she end up in a lake? How does that happen, Zinny? I'm so angry and scared. I don't understand why all this is happening to my family."

Even my disruptive nature wouldn't burden her with theories without any proof. Too much trauma tonight.

"Who do I believe, Zinny?" She insisted on an answer.

"The only proof is the coroner's report. Accidental drowning."

"Yeah," she said, then paused to reflect. "But Eddie's dead, and Damon shot by a crazy woman. How do I deal with that?"

"You can't. I can't."

"Lugs kept saying I don't really know the truth about Damon."

"Yeah, well, I don't know."

"I don't believe what anyone says anymore."

"Agreed." That conclusion was a good start.

I had no map in my truck to locate Highway 109. Before sunrise, miles on a two-lane highway were as isolated as a night voyage at sea. Silver leaned over to smooth out the tussled knots in her hair. She asked me to turn on the heat.

I was weary. My heavy head nodded often. The drive seemed endless, until Silver cleared her throat and pointed ahead to let me know Highway 109 was coming up.

"Thataway, ya know. It's bad when a girl gives a guy directions."

"Which way?" I asked, with the NC Highway 109 intersection in sight. "Right."

"How far on 109?"

"Don't know. But I know it when I see it."

I checked the odometer reading to mark the starting point for my mileage calculation. Silver tensed up the closer we got to Slade's place. She gasped often, as if her mouth was in a paper bag. She banged her head softly against the car window with the anticipation of facing her tormentor. I felt for her. I reached across to comfort her with a gentle pat on her arm, but she recoiled when I touched her, like anyone would after an assault. I said, "Sorry."

Up ahead, I saw an emergency turnoff alongside the highway. I pulled my truck off the road as far as I could and stopped.

"You gotta do this. You gotta. You promised, Zinny," she said as if I had changed my mind.

"I know. I need your word you'll listen to me and do exactly what I say. Agreed?"

"Of course. You're the one with the gun."

No turning back now. I checked the odometer to mark the miles again. We drove past a dozen isolated family homes. Not Slade's style. I had a hunch he lived in an isolated home with no likelihood of drop-in neighbors.

"Turn right around the curve up there."

About a quarter of a mile ahead, we came to an unmarked, unpaved, single-lane road cut through a field. "Here," said Silver. I slammed on the brakes, throwing us forward, then turned onto the dirt road. My head-lights sliced through the dark. I motored forward at ten miles per hour to anticipate any turns. I saw no power line, no telephone line, no home in view. But I did see tire tracks.

"Stop," Silver said, anxiously.

"What?" I said, braking to a stop.

"There's a gate up ahead. If it's open, Lugs is there."

She was scared. With good reason. And seeing me with Silver would set him off. Gunfire was a huge problem. I proceeded at five miles per hour, prepared to back out at twenty miles per hour if the gate was open.

The dirt road had to be a dead end. We could end up in peril in these backwoods. Out here Lugs had isolation and knowledge of the terrain on his side, which was a huge advantage in a place where no one could help us.

I drove about five football fields out of sight of 109 before coming to a right bend in the road. Silver gasped when I stopped my truck. Up ahead, the gate was wide open. I was about to face a crazed civilian who had already committed a felony tonight.

"Silver, anyone else live down here?"

"No." Silver put her face in her hands.

I cut off my headlights and kept the truck running. "Here's the plan: Lugs is sleeping. Doubt he'd think you'd show up tonight. That's our only advantage. No way will I drive my noisy truck right up to the door. We're going on foot. How far?"

"I don't know." She quivered from the chill or fright. "Not that far."

"Okay. I'm turning my truck around, in case we gotta get away in a hurry. I've got a flashlight in my duffel. And my .45. You stay right beside me. When we're close enough, I'll stop to plan our next move. Understood?"

She nodded in agreement.

"No normal talking. We talk in each other's ear. I mean, my mouth touches your ear. Got it?"

She nodded.

"If Lugs sees our approach and comes after us, we'll see what to do next."

"You'll shoot him, right?"

"I don't wanna think about that. That's a problem."

"Oh, I forgot my shoes at that lady's house. Stupid, stupid, stupid."

"Got some old boots and socks in the storage bin back there. After I turn the truck around, I'll get 'em."

It took seven maneuvers on the narrow road to turn my truck heading toward the highway. I left the truck running. I went into the storage bin for the army boots, socks, flashlight, and my loaded .45. Bringing my pistol could jump-start trouble to a tense situation. But still, I had to even the odds.

Silver stuffed the stiff green socks into the boots, then laced them up tight. She reached for my arm. Pointing the flashlight on the ground in front of us, with the .45 in my right hand, we walked at a lazy cat's gait in the middle of the road. I worried that my running truck engine signaled our approach.

Not far, like she said, I saw the shadowy outline of a mobile home among a grove of pine trees. No lights were on. I heard the motor hum of what I thought was a generator. I turned to press my mouth to Silver's ear. "Generator?"

She nodded.

"Good. May cover our approach."

She squeezed my arm when we were about thirty yards from the front door. I pulled her down to where we were kneeling in the road. I whispered, "Is that Lugs's truck over there?"

She nodded yes.

I pointed the flashlight at a third car parked beside the Corvette— Chevrolet Impala in bad shape. The front bumper was gone, and the car hood crushed in.

"There's a third car, Silver. Is that a problem?"

"No. It's Damon's. He won't fix it. He gets mad every time I mention it."

"Why?"

"Who knows? He gets crazy all the time. Let's get the 'Vette and get outta here."

"Where's the key?"

Spoken with heightened concern, she said, "I couldn't tell you this before. It's in the bedroom."

"We're done here. Not going in there. We'll get shot."

She twisted around to talk loudly in my ear. "Give me your gun. I'm getting my 'Vette."

I leaned too far toward her, and we banged heads. Neither of us yelled out.

"It's your car, right? The law can take it from Lugs." I caught myself talking too loudly.

"Well, Damon said it was mine to keep."

"My God, Silver."

"Lugs said he'd never let me have it."

I motioned her to lower her voice.

"Lugs went to prison for running a chop shop. At the strip club, he said he'd rip the 'Vette to shreds 'fore he'd let me get it. Give me your gun."

"The place is probably locked up."

"It's never locked. No one comes down here."

"You know exactly where the car key is?"

"In a jar on top of the chest. Okay, don't give me your gun if you're that scared. There's a baseball bat by the door. I'll use it on Lugs and get the key."

Silver stood up and walked toward the front door of the mobile home. I hesitated a moment, then went after her. I guided her back to our former position, where I whispered, "What're you doing? It's too dangerous."

"I'm not leaving without my car. I'll scream if you try to take me away."

When would I learn? A bad decision usually led to a bad outcome. But I was committed now. I couldn't walk away, leaving Silver with Lugs, especially with her threat to beat him with a baseball bat. She would beat him to death. With good reason. And I'm with her. An accomplice.

Silver again made a move to walk to the mobile home. I reached out to stop her.

"Okay, okay. No lights inside. Assume Lugs is asleep. Stop right inside the door, and I'll assess the situation. Follow my lead. Got it? Don't do anything until I'm okay with it."

"You'd better not leave me alone with him."

"I'm here." I was worried about what Silver might do.

Leading the way, I painstakingly opened the front door to the mobile home, cringing with each squeak that seemed as loud as worn-out brakes. I stepped up into the dark living room with my .45 aimed ahead. I heard loud snoring. Silver reached down to pick up a baseball bat behind the door. She tugged on my arm to keep us heading to the bedroom. We stepped carefully like we were walking on ice. In the bedroom, Lugs's snoring was a tugboat horn as I raised the flashlight up to the bed, across it quickly to see Lugs lying naked on top of the covers. I moved the flashlight to my side and pointed the .45 at Lugs, in case he woke up. Silver tiptoed toward the chest of drawers by the bed. I stepped toward her and raised my flashlight to see her holding the baseball bat over her head, cocking it for a downward swing at Lugs, letting her justified anger rule over rational thought. I blocked her with my forearm before she could slam the ball of the bat into Lugs's midsection. She resisted, but I held on and pulled her tight against me. I shook my head.

Lugs stopped snoring, turned on his side away from us, and grumbled. I squeezed Silver tighter. I kept my eyes on Lugs for any sign he was waking up. We stood together for a minute or longer; he didn't move. I shined the flashlight at the chest of drawers as a reminder to get the Corvette key. I then took the bat out of her hands.

Silver felt inside a mason jar to locate the Corvette key. She lifted the key out of the jar; dropped it to the top of the chest of drawers, making

184

a tinny sound; then fumbled the key again for more unwelcomed noise. Lugs groaned and turned on his side toward us. I cut off the flashlight and quickly grasped her arm to lead her out of the bedroom.

We halted our careful exit when Lugs grunted like a pig, rolled out of bed, and lumbered out of the bedroom in our direction. The front door was about five steps away. Silver buried her face in my chest. I aimed my revolver in anticipation of Lugs discovering us. But Lugs stopped in the hall to open a door. Silver tried to pull away, but I held on to her. The next sound was Lugs peeing, sighing in relief. He farted while heading back to bed. I held her tight to keep her still. We stood near the front door, waiting for Lugs to fall back asleep. I had no idea if he was asleep when I nudged her toward the door. She kicked the leg of a chair we avoided with the flashlight on, which made an alarming noise. Wasting no time to find out if the noise alerted him, I gently pushed her out the door.

Outside I joined Silver in the Corvette. There we got a huge surprise—a key in the ignition. The key in the mason jar was the spare.

"Pretty dumb, huh," Silver said.

We shared embarrassed smiles in the starlight. Short-lived. Lugs screamed from the cabin door. "Who's there?"

"Go, Silver. Don't turn on the headlights. Go."

She backed the Corvette away from Lugs's truck. She released the clutch too fast, and the car stalled.

"Can you drive a straight drive?" I asked.

"Yeah!"

She started the car again and drove ahead, using the silvery moonlight to guide her. I twisted around to see Lugs step outside, aiming with his right arm.

"Back and forth, Silver! Weave!"

The first round from Lugs's pistol glanced off the car bumper. On my command, Silver veered hard to the right, then swerved to the left, then back straight ahead. The next round ricocheted off a nearby tree. Silver made the serpentine maneuver again as Lugs fired two more rounds. One round hit the trunk of the Corvette, causing me to duck.

I heard Lugs cursing. More rounds hit nearby trees. Silver slammed on the brakes when we reached my truck, almost rear-ending it.

"Follow me. No headlights."

I hurried to the driver's seat, spinning my tires in first gear as I sped up the road. Lugs stopped firing. We were out of sight. Silver followed my lead, never turning on her headlights until we arrived at NC 109. I relaxed a bit without Lugs in hot pursuit.

We traveled at fifteen miles per hour over the speed limit to reach NC 74, the road back to Charlotte. Silver tailed my truck close enough to where her headlights blinded me in my rearview mirror.

———

The living-room light backlit the major rising from his chair as we turned into our driveway. Leaning forward, he strained to see Silver's Corvette in the faint light from the distant streetlight. He raised his arms to greet my return, which he had never done before, after seeing Silver get out of her car, thinking I was successful convincing a woman to come here. His excitement didn't ebb as he squinted for a good look at the woman. While walking up, I looked over my shoulder to notice Silver lifting a suitcase out of the trunk of her car.

I stepped inside the house. "Jack—"

"Way to go, man. She looks a bit rough, but we like it that way." He remained standing to greet my guest.

Silver, toting her bulky suitcase, stopped after one step into our living room. "Hi."

"You remember Silver Kelter?"

"Wait a minute. She's, uh—"

"Yes. Slade's girlfriend."

"You hooked up with Slade's girlfriend?"

"Hook up?" Silver stared at me.

"No hookup. Didn't you hear the phone ring?"

"Yes. I pretended to be asleep."

"You were snoring."

"Okay. But I woke up when I heard you drive off. What's going on?"

The bruises around her right eye and her swollen lip were more obvious in the living-room light. She turned her head away from our stares and appeared embarrassed by her unkempt look in a frumpy dress and weatherworn army boots.

"I don't want any trouble, Zinny. Just let me change into something decent, and I'll leave."

"It's safe here. Relax a minute."

"No time, Zinny. Can I change in your bathroom?"

"Sure. What about the cops?"

"No. I want Damon to see what Lugs did."

"Bathroom is down the hall."

She was timid leaving the living room.

"What's going on, Zin? You're bringing trouble to our door?"

"Lugs attacked her. She asked for my help."

"So you brought her back here. Well, okay. We could use some excitement."

I remained standing. The major sat down. In less than five minutes, she returned wearing a bright blue dress and black loafers, her hair pulled back in a ponytail. She cleaned the dried blood off her face. As far as I could tell, she wore no makeup.

"You always keep a packed suitcase in your car?" I asked.

"You never know when you gotta leave in a hurry."

"She's like us, Zin."

Silver was nervous standing with us, swaying back and forth with her suitcase in hand. "I won't forget what you did, Zinny."

"Be careful out there."

"You got a gun I can borrow?"

"No. The cops are the help you need."

"They won't do nothing. I went with him . . . anyway."

"Get away before Lugs finds you."

"Don't worry. I'm gettin' Damon's gun at the motel. I gotta go."

We watched her struggle with her decision to leave a safe place. She moved backward toward the front door. Her body language had enough anxiety to keep me concerned. Heading off by herself was a bad decision.

She took short, slow steps out our door. I noticed the major moving his head up and down, smiling.

"What?"

"She's a turn-on in combat boots."

I filled him in on the rest of the details of my long night's journey to Slade's place. He grimaced as he twitched his body to a more comfortable position during my detailed narrative.

"You coulda used me."

"You'd have returned fire."

"Fuckin' A. What have I got to lose?"

"Everything."

"You see me as a useless cripple."

"No. That's not it."

"Yes, it is. Well, you're back in the crosshairs again, helping out a pretty face just 'cause she's a pretty face. The cops will be pissed all over again."

"Yeah. But I don't know what other choice I had."

"You don't have a chance in hell with her, ya know. Even with a wad of RIF dough."

"Don't want one."

"Bullshit. Maybe I'll give it a shot."

"Good luck. You've been a fool for good-looking women before."

"Roger that."

I was weary lying about my reasons for helping Silver. She was a beauty. Why I helped her when she asked. A pretty, gutsy woman was the starting point of a turn-on.

"Ya know, Zin, you see me as a useless cripple. You do. And I do too. But know this: I'm just as capable of screwing things up."

"I can't make your life better, Major."

"Don't want you to."

"How about trying harder. Get off your goddamn ass sometime."

Harsh truths spoken without thinking of the consequences strain relationships. But in our case, brutal words never etched in out psyche. I raised my eyebrows and shrugged. The major smiled. I said what I thought. He accepted it as a truthful aggravation. Conversation was over.

I headed for the bedroom as the major said, "Silver would shoot Lugs. I like that about her."

I read his mind. I went back to the sofa to hand him my duffel bag.

"If Lugs shows up, shoot him."

"Love to."

I continued to the bedroom, laid down with my clothes on, and was asleep in minutes.

CHAPTER 15

I jerked awake. The shadows of the trees confused me about what time it was. I never napped longer than an hour. I sat up on the side of my bed, then felt how stiff my back was. I stood up, stretched, yawned, yelled, "Jack? Jack?"

No response. I stretched as far backward as I could. I reached over to the nightstand for my watch to see the time—1545. I stared at the time for at least five seconds. I lost seven hours of daylight.

"Why didn't you wake me up, Jack?" I shouted.

Again, no answer. I walked out of my bedroom and called out to him once more. In the living room, I saw his chair was empty. I checked the second bedroom and shower—no Jack. I went back to the living-room window to see my truck in the driveway. He never went anywhere, never talked about going anywhere, never asked to go anywhere. I thought over the situation. I remember the phone ringing. Did it happen, or did I dream it? Where did the major go? No way he went for a walk. He never exercised since the surgeries. He'd take a cab for a full day of binge drinking. I reached underneath the cushion of his chair for his black sock stuffed with five hundred dollars. It was gone. My money? I went to the refrigerator freezer to find my five hundred dollars in a tinfoil wrap. I had a disturbing thought about his disappearance. I returned to the living room to see the unzipped duffel bag on the floor by his chair and clutched my concern— my .45 was still there.

The major sat around, comatose, never voicing any plans to go anywhere, which was why his sudden departure confused me. Why today? Leaving without notice made no sense, when he had a roof over his head and ample beer in the refrigerator.

I was hungry. He left because there were no frozen TV dinners available. I picked up my truck keys and wallet for an early dinner at Anderson's. Something wasn't right about him leaving now. *What happened while I was asleep? Who called?*

———

An hour later, a hamburger and french fries filling my stomach, I turned the corner onto my street and heard the neighbor's German shepherd barking, an uneasy distress signal for a quiet neighborhood. The agitated yelping spooked me. I parked in my driveway and peered over the fence into my neighbor's yard, but I saw no dog.

I stepped inside my house, closed the door, without seeing or hearing anything, but felt a presence, someone in my house. I trusted those instincts. Saved me more times in combat than I could remember. I froze. I heard a foreboding crack on the wooden floor. Someone moved closer. I saw the shadow of a big man in the kitchen doorway outlined in the light coming through my kitchen window. I had nothing in hand or close by to use as a weapon. I squatted in front of the major's chair, lurched sideways, and used the leopard crawl toward the front door.

"Don't move, motherfucker! I'll gun you down right where you are, soldier boy!" yelled Lugs.

He turned on the kitchen light with a malicious grin, aiming a pistol.

His stare screamed out crazed, full of intent to shoot me.

"We got no beef, Lugs. Let's just leave it at that. Okay?"

Think! What're my options? How could I get out alive?

"Oh yeah? Let's see, fucker. I got no fuckin' money now that my business is closed. Slade's gonna get even for what I did to his bitch. And she's gonna file charges against me. So I'm fucked. Now you're gonna be fucked."

Panic overtook me. *Reach for the front door, a sudden move, catch him off guard. But shit, fuck, I can't get out of here without taking a bullet. Reason with him. Reason!*

"C'mon, Lugs, you don't wanna do this. Ya know, I stopped Silver from splitting your head open with a baseball bat."

"I'm eatin' it up seeing you beg."

I stood up. No way to show weakness now. Images of those I cared about flashed in my head. *Frighten him. Rush him, screaming as loud as I can. That's the only hope I got.*

He motioned with his pistol to follow him out the back door. "Okay. Let's go, Zubell. Time to die."

"Five hundred dollars. Cash. In the freezer. It's yours. I can get more."

"Five hundred bucks for fuckin' up my life? Really? That's all you think I'm worth? Only pleasure I got left is watching you dig your grave. Let's go."

"Lugs, c'mon. C'mon, c'mon, man."

"You're on your way to hell, asshole. I can't wait to watch you die. Just like I did to that moron Kelter."

I walked slowly toward him with my hands in the air, making him smile like he was in control. *Distract him long enough and rush him—count down five, four . . .*

There was a crash at the rear of my house. The back door exploded from its hinges. Armed men dressed in combat fatigues with flak jackets rushed inside. Three excited voices with assault rifles aimed at Lugs ordered him to drop his weapon. Lugs turned around to face them. He dropped his pistol and raised his arms in surrender. The assault team rushed forward.

More cops stormed through the front door. A strong arm pushed me forward. Stern voices ordered me to get down. I threw myself to the floor and remained motionless. Cops shouted at Lugs to put his arms behind his back, which he did while yelling at them not to shoot. I heard a familiar voice order his team to secure the premises. Heavy footsteps rushed through my house. I was relieved to be alive. I rested my head on my hands. Lugs was in custody, with prison growling for his bones.

"Don't move," a husky voice said over my head. "Stay down."

The magnitude of what could have happened overcame me. I was sweating, about to chuck dinner. The thought of facing my execution made my head spin.

"Nice. Real nice," said Detective Cutter.

I saw him out of the corner of my right eye bend down over me when the heaving stopped. Still sweaty and spitting out vomit, I pushed up to my knees with my head down. Cutter leaned on my shoulder to stop me from getting to my feet.

"Stay down."

"No, I'm okay."

"No. Stay down there, Zubell. You'll listen better on your gut."

I extended forward to lie prone on the floor, sliding my hands as far as they could reach. I rested my head on the gritty hardwood floor. Lying in a humbling position was far better than lying face down in a pool of my blood. I braced for a tongue-lashing.

"You keep showing up on my case, Zubell."

"Lugs was waiting here. How could I know that?"

"Maybe you'll think it over and realize we saved your life. Just in time, Zubell."

More dry heaves. I did glance off to my left to watch Cutter walk over to where Detective Pitman was reading Lugs his rights. My stomach was calming down, and my head was clearing. I started questioning how the police timed their arrival with weapons drawn at the exact moment to intercept my execution. This was a scene out of a movie.

"It's not your style to show gratitude, huh?"

"I owe you my life," I said.

"Now that's what I wanna hear."

"How'd you know Lugs would be here, Detective?"

"There you go, questioning me. And doing things you shouldn't and going places that ain't your business. And here you are in an active police investigation again." He paused to collect his thoughts. "You weren't minding your own business yesterday when you drove that Kelter girl to Slade's place, were you?"

Detective Cutter was good.

"Just doing a girl a favor after Lugs attacked her."

"Told you to stay away, didn't I? Huh? Didn't I? Yes, I did. What were you thinking going with that Kelter girl? Not thinking is my guess. Really stupid going after this guy. Kelter girl said you never fired back. Is that right?"

"Yeah."

"So you wanna know how we happened to be here in the nick of time?"

"If you—"

"Well, Horry—or Lugs, whoever the fuck he is—called up Slade at the hospital while we were bugging his line. And Slade got him to admit to killing Eddie and doing you in before leaving town. So here we are to save the day. Like Joe Friday."

"Thank you, sir."

"You're in way over your head, Zubell."

"I tried to stay away."

"Try harder. A lot harder."

From the prone position, I had an angled view of three uniforms escorting Lugs out the front door of my house. He said nothing to anyone.

"Can I get up now?"

Cutter was thinking, breathing heavily. His eyes told me that he was searching for the right threatening words to keep me away from the case.

"Where's your boyfriend, Zubell?"

"Don't know."

"Think about staying out of my hair forever, Zubell. Maybe getting the shit scared out of you by a lowlife like Horry will do it."

I waited on my knees as the police filed out of my house. I experienced degrees of fear during my military service, but this incident felt like one of the worst. Memories of near-death experiences in war flashed in my head at a rate that made me flinch. I did my best to unplug those images when they played in my head.

My self-esteem spiraled out of control. Since I chose a PI career, I was trending backward, helping no one. It was time to cut the line with that disappointing assessment. To the Charlotte police, I was a buffoon. I worked hard to prove they were right. As bad as that reality was, I needed no more reminders my short career as a PI was over.

CHAPTER 16

I walked a circular path around the living room, down the hall, and back for an hour after the police left, but I couldn't burn up all my adrenaline. I had to get out of the house. I drove to an A&P grocery for two six-packs of beer, still wired into the terror of facing my execution. Returning home, I plopped in Major Jack's chair. Three beers dulled the image of digging my grave; two more beers faded Lugs's vicious grin. I hadn't been this revved up since the fury of war.

Sleep was out of the question. I sat up hour after hour, with no radio or television blaring and no book of interest to pass the time. Every passing vehicle, I thought, was a taxi bringing the major home. His prolonged disappearing act had to be a drinking marathon. My concern for his well-being waned with each elapsed hour.

The night passed like a slow train through a city. I was bored sitting in the major's chair for just one night. It was unimaginable how he sat here day after day enduring pain without end.

At six in the morning, I drifted off. It took sunrise to relax me enough to fall asleep. My internal cycle was off.

Around noon I woke up and realized Major Jack hadn't come home. No idea where he could be. Anything was possible. I imagined the worst, with him on a drinking binge, and hoped for anything right above bad.

At 1330, I decided to visit Mr. Sedley's office one last time to inform him about Lugs's attempt to kill me. He wouldn't see me. If he did allow me into his sanctum, I should expect the news of an attempt on my life warranting a stern lecture, then a quick exit.

Mary Lou, the receptionist, waved me into the firm without a break in my stride. Stares peppered me as I walked to Mr. Sedley's office in jeans and a T-shirt, a casual invasion of their buttoned-down world. I was an unwelcomed person who would be the subject of continual gossip. Edna gave me the approving wave to proceed into Mr. Sedley's office. I hesitated before entering his office, thinking something was awry with unquestioned access. I opened Mr. Sedley's door. He looked up and walked across his office to shake my hand with a salesman's smile.

"What a coincidence. Pastor Crigler and I have been talking about you. You must have a sixth sense when to show up. The pastor asked to meet me but just stepped out for a minute." He paused while frowning at my casual togs. "You know what? I miss the red jacket." He laughed at his joke.

"Yeah, well, okay, sir."

"Come to think of it, I don't remember if I instructed Edna to pay you for Bonnie's hearing. Is that why you're here? Have you found work yet?" He smiled, pleased with his stab at a friendly banter. He returned to his desk chair.

I had no time to bring up the reason for my visit. Pastor Crigler entered the office in a black suit, white shirt, navy-blue tie, and sleep-deprived eyes. He glanced at me like an uneasy pitchman in the presence of an angry client. The pastor continued to stare, unsettling me to a point I almost left. Mr. Sedley motioned both of us to sit. I obliged.

"Pastor Crigler came here out of concern for Blaine and Bonnie Ridge,"

Mr. Sedley said, with a paternal tone.

"Seeing you both in court upset Blaine and the other elders, and me in particular," said the pastor. He was downbeat, like he aced morose at seminary.

"Let me be clear. We have no intention of counseling the Ridges for any reason," said Mr. Sedley in his definitive voice.

The pastor choked up a bit. "Some good Christians won't be coming to our services any longer. I can understand that. First Billy's untimely death. And now Bonnie, Damon . . . the only way I can keep going is to put my faith in our Lord Jesus Christ."

"No words can appreciate how difficult it's been for you," Mr. Sedley said. "We'll be praying for all of you."

How politically insincere could he be?

"It's shaken our faith. But we must go on. God's plan for us must continue. We've made mistakes—placed faith in converts without really getting to know them. We'll make changes in the ways we disciple to bring good folks to Jesus. We won't make the same mistakes as Damon and Cecil."

"Both Zinny and I thank you for coming here today. We'll support you and your congregation in any way we can."

The pastor swiveled his head and focused on me with an uncomfortable silent plea. He leaned sideways to lay his hand on my shoulder. I slid my chair out of his reach.

"I owe Mr. Zubell a thank-you for speaking out about Damon Slade's lascivious behavior."

So that was the reason for his surprising acknowledgment of my involvement with his ministry.

"Pastor Crigler, thanks again for coming." Mr. Sedley stopped short of making further comments, even though he quietly mouthed a few more words. He stood up. If he had an unspoken way to beckon his associates to enter and escort us out of his office, he would do it. Pastor Crigler strained to rise like his arthritic knees struggled to support his weight. It was time for my news.

"Gentlemen, I've got more bad news."

Pastor Crigler dropped his head in anticipation of more unwanted anguish. Mr. Sedley wasn't pleased.

"Is it really necessary, Zinny?"

I ignored him. "Lugs came to my house last night to kill me. The police showed up in time to arrest him."

My statement was jarring. All shocked stares in the room. Mr. Sedley seemed to hyperventilate as I watched stress build on his face. He sat down. More emotional agony welled up in the pastor's eyes. The consequences of the incidents involving his congregants were crushing what remained of his calling. His head became too heavy for his neck.

The pastor dealt with his distress with a soft-spoken prayer. "Guide us in your ways, dear Lord, and bring the love of Jesus to everyone's heart. Each day tests our will to go on. Good people are looking for answers. Please help me lead them. Amen."

I'd done enough damage to the spirits of both men. I stood up to leave the office, but Mr. Sedley beckoned me with a stern tone. "Zinny, we need to talk this through. I apologize for my rudeness, Pastor, but I need to talk with him in private. Please excuse us."

"My heart is broken," Pastor Crigler said. "Damon and Cecil professed to Billy and me that they had changed their ways and had accepted Jesus Christ as their Lord and Savior and would follow the path Jesus set out for us." He gazed out Mr. Sedley's window. "It was Damon who brought Cecil to us. How were we to know what was in their hearts? Now we find out who they really are." He paused for a momentary reflection. "I never knew anyone who worked harder for Jesus than Billy. He loved Jesus and was fearless and would go anywhere to spread His message. He didn't want a church to be just a social gathering of similar folks. He went places I would never go. I'm not naive about who Billy brought to our congregation. He believed in folks I never felt comfortable with, but that was his way."

Mr. Sedley hung his head down to rub his forehead. He showed a level of emotion about his brother that was honest, pained.

The pastor continued. "Billy challenged everyone to bring new members to our congregation each month. Some voices disagreed with the direction we were heading. Each Sunday they grew louder and louder." The pastor's emotions swirled around his face.

"Pastor, please," said Mr. Sedley.

Pastor Crigler reached into his coat pocket for a small notebook, then said, "I'm thinking about Romans 8:28: 'We know that in all things God works for the good of those who love him, who have been called according to His purpose.' We'll never understand why these horrible things have happened, but there must be a purpose in God's plan for us. We can fill our hearts with Paul's words and work hard to bring Christ to many and be 'servants of God's mysteries.' But you know, Claude, there was something troubling Billy. He didn't share his worry with me or anyone. Is that why you got involved with Bonnie, Claude? Did Billy share his troubles with you? It may help us rebuild our church."

Mentioning his brother evoked the effect of a scalpel to Mr. Sedley's throat. But he remained steadfast, even with his emotions close to the surface. "I can't talk about Bonnie. As much as I want . . . you know my position, Pastor."

"Claude, I beseech you." Emotions overcame him.

"My only advice to you, Pastor, is to help Bonnie. She needs all of you now."

Pastor Crigler left the office without shaking hands with either of us. Mr. Sedley leaned forward with his hands intertwined on his desk mat. He started to say something but changed his mind.

Time to leave. "I won't show up here again."

"What you told us about that guy threatening to shoot you sounds unbelievable."

"You think I'm lying?" I was loud, indignant. "I know I crossed the get-back line. But you, you set me up and pointed me in their direction. You knew all along how dangerous these guys were, didn't you?"

"How would I know that?"

"Call Detective Cutter."

"I don't have to do that."

"Yes, you do, sir. You know you do."

He paged Edna to call Detective Cutter, then swiveled his chair at an angle to gaze out his window. I sat facing him with my arms folded at my chest. His impatience growing, he tapped his fingers on his desk, from pinky to index finger, over and over. After a few minutes, without facing me, his phone rang.

"Hello? Detective Cutter? This is Claude Sedley, an attorney working with Zinny Zubell. I have a few questions about an incident I heard about."

He listened to Detective Cutter's loud iteration of the Lugs incident. "Yes, I agree."

I heard Cutter's warnings about my involvement in his investigation.

"I'll go over that with him. Good day, sir."

His disappointed frown confirmed what happened was the truth. He withdrew deeper into his thoughts. I had no patience with another lecture. I stood up to leave his office for the last time.

"Sir, with all due respect, I won't be lectured. If you want me to pay the legal fees from here on, I'm okay with that."

"Please, stay"

I obeyed orders from superiors most of my life. The chain of command trained me well. I did as he said.

"You didn't deserve that ordeal." Under his breath, he said, "Never knew anything like that would happen."

"Sir, you're not a careless person. Did you really think those guys would run scared?"

No response. He stared with a standoffish expression—not an admission of personal accountability. Never support a person who went beyond his permission.

"I'll never understand why you wasted precious daylight on something that didn't line your pocket."

He had more going on than he could handle. My sense was he was shutting down.

"You're a smart man. No one will ever know what you're covering up."

I stood up again, walked toward his office door, but stopped when he erupted with uncharacteristic anger.

"I told you to stay away from all of 'em."

"You did. And I didn't. But you're still lying about something."

"Lying! Lying!" The entire office should be on alert now. "I never met that Lugs guy. For that matter, I've never met anyone named Kelter."

We glared at one another like a quarreling couple who had nothing more to say. I saw the energy he applied to his braking system to keep his anger in check. He was bound for a heart attack. What confused me was why he kept me in his office this long? I said things I would never have said to a superior. I was a subordinate who wouldn't succumb to an angry dressing-down. In the end, he never wanted me on his team anyway. Weeks from now, I would be a forgotten man.

"Don't leave. Okay, okay, okay. You're right. It's time. I'm gonna show you something."

"No."

"You wanted an explanation. You pushed for an explanation. I don't owe you an explanation, but you deserve to know the truth."

"Why now? Ease your conscience?"

"You wanted to know why I had to do what I did. You're goddamn good at making someone own up to the truth. I was dead wrong hiring a guy like you."

His penchant for evasiveness made me wonder if he would come down off his high-handed pedestal. Or was he teasing me with another duplicitous statement? If he started another lecture, I would walk out. But I gave him the benefit of the doubt. I sat down.

He leaned back in his chair to ease up on the drama of the moment. "I've been asked to run for the Senate by three influential people who have the resources and connections to make it happen. It's been a dream of mine since I met Barry Goldwater." A faraway gaze took his thoughts away. He grinned as if he experienced the euphoria of power.

"You'd be a good politician, sir."

His demeanor told me that he accepted my comment as a compliment. I meant it otherwise.

"To be honest, you have legitimate concerns about my involvement with Bonnie and Damon Slade. But I wasn't forthcoming. I had to protect my family, my firm."

"Obviously." I squirmed, trying to hold back my rage.

I witnessed his doubts about troubling revelations to a subordinate. "All I wanted you to do was a simple job. But now you're in too deep to not know why I did what I did. I'm not pleased. But at the time I felt— too late for regrets."

"Okay. Noted. You used me."

He thought about my statement. "I accept that. It's true."

Mr. Sedley was a performer at heart. After what seemed like a minute of awkward silence, he spun around to the credenza behind him. He unlocked the long middle drawer, reached for something on his mind, and revealed a yellow manila folder and a white envelope. He handed me the white envelope.

"Open it."

Inside I found a firm check with my name on the pay line for two hundred dollars.

"You're working for the firm. Official. No more cash transactions."

"Why?"

"The check is dated a week ago. I had it available if I needed to take you in my confidence. What I'm about to show you is privileged. Work product. I'll deny everything you read if you report it. And I'll use all my resources to discredit you."

"And if I just walk away?"

"You won't. You're too curious not to want answers."

Damn him! He was right. He clutched the manila envelope like it bore his fate. He wrestled with his decision to hand me the envelope but relented. He glanced away after I accepted it.

"My brother sent me this letter before he died."

The handwritten letter read:

Claude,

I love you, brother. I never told you that often enough. I regret many things, and that is at the top of the list. All I wanted to do was be a good husband and father and disciple for our Lord Jesus Christ. I wanted to build a new church to lead sinners from all walks of life to Jesus. I failed all around. I tried to build a congregation too fast. It is now time to face my infidelity and admit my sins. I gave in to my lust for the flesh. I wasn't strong enough to weed out any thoughts of those sins before they took hold. I sought out a woman in our congregation who worked for the church and trusted me. Her name is Mosie Kelter. I used her devotion and led her into adultery. My sins brought about an unwanted pregnancy. The sin of adultery will never justify the loss of an unborn child of God. My sanity has been tested. I didn't seek your advice. I'm ashamed to tell you that I sought the confidence of a member of my congregation, Damon Slade. He told me that he loved our church and wanted no one to destroy what we were building. Damon told me that he would give her five thousand dollars to leave Charlotte for a new life. I could repay him over time. He said he could convince Mosie to give up the baby for adoption. I was desperate. I believed him. I went along with his plan and told no one else about it. I never talked to Mosie or saw her again. I asked Damon where she went. He told me not to worry. She's doing well in another city. I wanted to believe him. Eddie Kelter, her son, has called me many times about his mother's disappearance. He said she left at night without taking her possessions. Eddie believes something bad has happened to her. He reported her missing to the police. They haven't located her or her car. Mosie wouldn't just disappear like that. She said she loved me. I asked Damon about Eddie's concerns for his mother. He got angry. He said she was fine. He told me to stop worrying about the situation. I'm convinced Damon is lying about Mosie because he came and asked me for help with his problem—Bonnie Ridge, another member of our church. She told me in confidence that Damon was the driver of the hit-and-run accident that crippled her. But she must have told someone else. Damon heard the rumor and told me to cast doubt about her mental stability. He was the driver who crippled Bonnie. He could have done the same to Mosie. The truth will come out. Damon is threatening to tell the congregation about Mosie and me if I don't help him with Bonnie Ridge. He said he will tell everyone I was behind Mosie's disappearance if I don't help him with his problem. Something bad has happened to her and the child. I know it. I feel it. It's driving me insane. How could I be that blind to trust him? He lied to all of us about loving and living for Jesus. Claude, I can't go on knowing what I have done. I can't face the truth. I can't sleep. I can't eat. Something will turn up, sooner or later. And you and my family will face the consequences of my horrible judgment. I can't bear to think about what I have done to Mosie, the child, my family, the church, and you. I've confessed my sins to our Lord Jesus Christ and put my life in His hands. If Jesus wants me to come to Him, His will be done. My faith is in the Lord Jesus Christ. Please keep my *confession a secret. I don't want my family hurt by my immoral failings. If I do go to our Lord Jesus Christ, I want my family and the congregation to believe it was God's will. I want them to be strong in their faith. I love you, Claude. You are a rock. Please be there for Rachel, Will, Beth, and Debbie. I love my family more than anything. I can't live with what I've done. Claude, keep a close watch on Damon Slade. Keep him away from my family. In my heart, he is an evil man. Please pray for my soul. God be with you.*

Forever in Christ,

Billy

An outburst of expletives filled my head. But I remained outwardly calm. His brother's suicide letter intensified the indignation I felt for Mr. Sedley's deception. He cleverly evaded entanglements as a man who released the hounds but couldn't stomach the blood of the kill. His intent to hide his brother's involvement with Mosie Kelter's death would be hard to establish. He wouldn't need his legal clout to cement doubt to stop any investigation after Mosie's body was ruled an accidental drowning.

But why let me read his brother's confession now?

"Go ahead. Say it," he said.

"Who else has read your brother's confession?"

"No one."

"No one else?"

"No one."

"Does anyone know a confession letter exists? Your son? A trusted colleague?"

"Asked and answered."

"Hard to accept, sir."

I got exactly what I expected: a cold stare. A thought occurred that made me wonder—would I have covered up my brother's bad decisions in similar circumstances?

"All for your brother, huh?"

It took more than a few seconds for him to say, "I had no knowledge of that woman's drowning."

"You can't even say her name," I said, louder than I should have.

"Mosie Kelter . . . Mosie Kelter . . . I did what I had to do. Okay, you've handled the situation differently, but . . ." Another dramatic moment to reflect. "I expected you to react differently after reading the letter. Shouting or something. You're a hard guy to figure out, Zinny."

An invisible knot wrapped around his throat and squeezed his guilt-ridden face. He strained to breathe normally, locking his hands. In a low voice, he said, "I honored my brother's wishes. My duty to my family. I was put in a bad situation that wasn't my doing."

"You know Mosie Kelter's drowning wasn't an accident, sir."

"I don't know that."

"Damon Slade was a former highway patrolman. Driving hard and fast and chasing people was his training. You know he caused Bonnie's accident to end their affair. And he rammed Mosie off the bridge to solve Billy's problem. But there is no way to prove he did either of those things."

I witnessed the considerable internal struggle he went through to keep his guilt in check—a countercurrent for a man positioned for unquestioned authority and unnoticeable remorse. He twisted in his chair to hold back his emotions. His deeds, cloaked and planted in a sense of familial duty, were in his subconscious for a lifetime.

Mr. Sedley rose from his chair, came around his desk, grabbed the letter, tore it into pieces, then walked back to his desk to funnel the paper into his trash. Billy Sedley's confession was gone.

"You can't say anything to anyone, Zinny. You're smart enough to know my word counts far more than yours."

"Yeah, you're right. But ya know, we could've saved the life of an innocent man, Eddie Kelter." I dropped the envelope with the firm's check on his desk. I left his office at a slow walk.

———

In the parking lot, my truck steering wheel suffered the brunt of my anger with an open-handed slap. I calmed down when the pain of an untreated wrist injury reminded me of the stupidity of that response.

Personal and political motives. That was driving Mr. Sedley's cover-up, which was a dangerous brew when difficult challenges led to bad decisions. It was flashes of insanity. Under different circumstances, Mr. Sedley wouldn't withhold information about a crime from the authorities. Would I do the same if faced with similar circumstances? I didn't know.

———

I was suspicious why Mr. Sedley hired me for what I thought was a simple yet baffling delivery. I tried to well up a level of empathy for Mr. Sedley and his circumstances, but that feeling bounced hard against my disgust for his manipulation. Nothing confusing about his intentions now. I played a role in the orchestrated cover-up of his brother's misdeeds, a pawn in his stratagem.

Many conversations, many interactions with all parties involved came cascading back as I flipped the pieces to sequence the events. No way to parse the depth of the bad blood between Slade and Mr. Sedley. I wanted to play it smart, trying not to miss any obvious clues. My instincts were on target. That was all I had. But I failed to follow up on an important clue.

I missed one huge clue: Staring at my business card, a churchman in the parking lot of the Pothole said, "Another one." It was obvious. I failed to follow up. Mr. Sedley had hired another investigator to dig around in the church's business, with Billy's confession letter in hand. The investigator had heard about Bonnie's accusation of Slade being the hit-and-run driver. Armed with his brother's complicity, Mr. Sedley had the ideal threat to keep Slade quiet about Billy's involvement with Mosie's accident. He hid the truth about Mosie's murder.

———

Major Jack wasn't there when I returned home. I burned up more of my anger doing push-ups and jumping jacks. Being alone gave me more time to rant without having to explain my actions to the major. He was on a bender with plenty of money to find trouble. It was his doings, his responsibility, to get himself out of whatever situation he might be in.

I laid down on the sofa to clear my head of any thoughts, assumptions, ponderings about anyone or anything. I got up and walked around the house for what seemed like an hour. Nothing relaxed me. At least I had no more impulses to slam my fists into anything immobile.

The phone rang an hour later. The call I was anxiously awaiting.

"Hi, Zinny. You okay?" Not the call I expected.

"Yeah. I'm okay, Silver."

"Listen . . ." Her tone intensified. "Listen, Zinny. Please, listen—"

"Silver, it only gets better when you leave Slade."

"Don't keep saying it. I know. I know. I know, but there's something you gotta do."

"I can't. I can't."

"Damon won't let me leave."

"I can't help you. Not anymore."

"I can't handle Damon's shit anymore. I can't. So angry I can't breathe normal. You have to do something—"

"Silver, please. I can't get involved."

Her tone was now right below a scream. "Damon convinced me to take him outta the hospital. So I came by your place to get you to drive his Caddy to his place. But you were snoring. So, so . . . Jack said he'd drive him."

"Wait a minute. Wait a minute. Slow down. What? What? Jack did what?"

"Jack drove up here with Damon. He did okay. I drove the 'Vette."

I was suspicious. Doubtful any physician would approve Slade leaving the hospital in his condition. And Jack driving him to his mobile home? That made no sense. How could she expect me to believe that? "Is this some kinda joke, Silver?"

"It's true. I'm not lying. Is Jack there with you?"

No. The major was known for some wild stunts. Driving Slade away from the hospital was too crazy, even for him.

"You gotta come get Jack, Zinny. He and Damon been drinking since we got here. They're jawing at each other. Damon said he's gonna shoot Jack if he keeps calling him a killer. If that's true . . ." Her voice, worry, reached another level. "Maybe y'all are right about Damon."

"You swear you're telling me the truth?"

"Fuck yes. Why would I lie to you now?"

I wanted to believe her. "Tell me again how to get to the mobile home."

"No. His other place. In the mountains. I'm getting my stuff together, and I'm done. Do you have any idea what it's like to hate someone so much but be totally dependent on 'em? It's fuckin' awful!"

"Where are you?"

"Bridle Path."

"C'mon, Silver. What street?"

"I don't know. It's a gravel road."

"Goddamn it, Silver. Give me something. Describe something."

"I don't know. There're lotta mountains. They're all the same. I gotta get back. Damon gets real angry if I'm gone too long."

"Wait." My plea was of no use. She hung up.

She was desperate. And not specific about her whereabouts, which made sense since she couldn't be calm about her circumstances. I never caught her in lie before, as far as I could tell, so I believed her.

The major with Slade. At times he did crazy things, especially when drinking. In my wildest scenarios, the major driving Slade anywhere was unthinkable. How could he act on a stupid voice in his head telling him to do something that irrational? But there was no waiting for the situation to play out. I was headed to Bridle Path.

CHAPTER 17

Studying the map, I estimated the drive would take about three and half hours to Bridle Path in the Appalachian Mountains. "Hang on, Jack, and don't do anything stupid," I said aloud to any higher power listening.

Slade made his traveling clothing show known in out-of-the-way towns. Like Stuartville, his presence caused a stir of a big fish in a small lake, which might make locating him as easy as asking a local for his address. If that failed, spotting a white Cadillac and a red Corvette parked together in a small burg like Bridle Path wouldn't be that difficult, unless he took refuge in a tucked-away home for privacy.

He was cooperating with the police. So why flee suddenly to the mountains instead of convalescing in the hospital? My reasoning was to avoid further suspicion regarding Eddie's murder. He feared Lugs might implicate him to plea for a lesser sentence. Nothing else made sense.

I put on a flannel shirt, jeans, heavy-duty wool socks, and hiking boots; then I packed my regulation army fatigues and army field jacket in a duffel bag. My search might take me places where an army uniform would garner respect. I went to the storage locker in my truck bed to inventory my gear—fifty feet of rope, machete, hunting knife, sleeping bag, canvas tarp, and a various assortment of camping and maintenance tools. Returning to the house, I packed my .45-caliber pistol and two boxes of ammo in a small duffel bag. I searched through my filing system in the far corner of my bedroom—a paper bag stuffed with unsorted papers and letters—for a photo of the major, the one Sally took of us leaving for 'Nam on our third tour. I folded the picture to fit in my wallet. On my final check around the house, I took the five one-hundred-dollar bills wrapped in tinfoil in the freezer.

On Interstate 85, I drove over the speed limit to arrive in Bridle Path before dark. The sunny day become a rainy afternoon as I approached the Appalachian Mountains after turning on US Highway 321, then 221. It was hard to appreciate how the major could drive this distance without his legs cramping up. The more pain he felt, the more his personality would clash with Slade's mood. With their physical challenges altering their civility, violence was in play.

The mountain roads in the Appalachians were a winding splendor. The two-lane highway was busy with gazers taking in the beauty of the red, gold, and green foliage forming a quilt over the mountain ranges. Shame I was in no mood to enjoy the autumn beauty.

———

At the town limits of Bridle Path, my heart raced, and my stomach knotted up. Drawn into Slade's world, close to the serrated edge of police threats. An unanticipated confrontation was at hand.

I parked my truck in a small lot off a narrow side street in town. I walked in the steady rain with my eyes gawking at the tourist shops. It was dinnertime, and all the shops were open. The fall colors lured crowds as they milled about.

I stepped into trinket shops and asked the owners if they knew Damon Slade. No, no one knew him. Across the street from a row of shops, I saw an Exxon station about a block and a half away. I asked the attendant at the cash register if he knew Damon Slade.

"Nope. Does he live around here?" he said.

"Yep."

"Probably know his face."

The rain began coming down harder. I jogged back to the center of Bridle Path to the Mountain Morning Café. The diner had an elderly cashier at the entrance and a young girl to show me to a table, a two-seater on a row between the larger booths sandwiched along both walls. My seat bordered tables where diners smoked. As a former smoker, I enjoyed the aroma. At six thirty in the evening, the café was lively. The regulars enjoyed cross-aisle chats with friends seated in nearby booths. An overweight waitress with an updo coifed about a foot over her head asked for my order. I said a chop sirloin with mashed potatoes, green beans, and coffee. Before she left, I inquired if she knew Damon Slade.

"Nope," she said.

"Would the restaurant manager be in tonight?"

"Yep."

"Where is he?"

"That's him over there. Joe's always here," she said, pointing at the short, husky man standing by the cashier in a green polyester sport coat. His round red face had a big smile while talking to a patron.

I strolled over to ask, "Hey, is your name Joe?"

"Yes, sir," Joe said, extending a welcoming grin, a thick hand bearing many rings.

"Hi, I'm Zinny Zubell. I'm looking for Damon Slade. Seen him lately?"

"Damon Slade? Damon Slade? Damon . . . Slade? Nope, don't think I know him. Live around here?"

"Yep," I said.

"Well, I know everyone around here, but never heard his name. I can't imagine him not coming in here on occasion."

"Is there a mobile home park in the area?"

"Yes, sir. Down along the highway right outside town."

"Thanks."

"Enjoy your dinner. Thanks for coming in."

After dinner I walked up and down both sides of the main street, moseyed through open shops, and went down the side streets checking out the cars parked there. I saw no white Cadillac parked with a red Corvette in town.

———

The Green Mountain Inn was a roadside motel built on a graded overhang along Highway 221, about a half of mile out of town. It was a single-story green plank building with about thirty rooms facing the highway and narrow balconies with panoramic views of the valley below.

The motel manager told me that he had just received a cancellation. I paid for three nights to secure a room. It was in the center of the motel. The room had a standard-size bed, a small desk, and an even smaller bathroom. I opened the curtain on a sliding glass door and stepped out on the balcony. The rain and darkness teased me about the view below.

After storing the duffel in the closet, I continued my search for Slade's place. I spent an hour driving through the neighborhoods. Outside town, cloud cover and no streetlights made the car search more challenging. The isolated homes on land stripped of trees and level with the highway were no problem seeing the parked vehicles, even on the winding road. But it was difficult to spot the cars at homes tucked away on ridges like tree houses or homes built down in gorges. Three miles outside Bridle Path, I checked out a small mobile home community with no resident owning a luxury car. I returned to the motel.

I found no visual leads on where Slade was located. I returned to town to call information at a public telephone booth. No local listing. I could ask the local PD for any information on Damon Slade. No. Too risky to inquire about a man who could be a local hero and raise questions about the reason for my search.

I returned to the motel. Frustration made for a restless night.

———

Early the next morning, fog shrouded the mountains, with visibility down to fifteen yards at best. The gray light coming over the mountains and the rolling fog isolated the inn. I stepped outside my room to enjoy the damp morning air in the packed parking lot. I returned to my room for my fatigue jacket and hiking boots for a morning stroll.

I walked across the parking lot to the highway. I continued along the grassy overhang of the serpentine road and peered down the slope into the misty abyss. Along the edge of the overhang, the highway department had rooted a series of posts positioned at even intervals to stop a car from careening into the ravine. I stayed on the asphalt to avoid the wet grass.

A tractor trailer emerged from the fog. I was right in its path. The driver turned to avoid me and laid on his air horn as I jumped off the road. I lost my balance on the wet grass, fell hard on my butt, then slid downward. In a desperate maneuver, I outstretched my arms toward a nearby guard post. I wrapped my left arm around the damp wood and swung my right hand around the post to grasp my left wrist, forming a loop. My legs slid down in the direction of the ravine.

I hung there as I dug my feet into the ground for a base. I released my right hand on my left wrist to grab the post. It was damp, slippery, but I had a firm grip. I slid my left arm across the post for another hand grip. I attempted to get a foothold, but the wet weeds offered no resistance. My boots slid free. Panicking, I had to pull myself up. My first effort would be my best attempt. I grunted, lifted my body up to where I could use my elbows as a bipod, but I still couldn't get a foothold. I inhaled deeply to fuel determination through my body. With my torso touching my elbows, I swung my left leg up to get more weight over the edge. I wrenched my left leg forward to form a twisted tripod. Using that leverage, I wiggled my chest and left leg to where my right knee came to the edge of the overhang.

"Mister? Mister?" A desperate voice yelled for my response.

"Over here."

The truck driver rushed to grab my left arm and leg to pull me up to the overhang. He pulled me across the grass to the highway edge.

"You okay? You okay?" he said.

"Yeah," I said, panting.

"Really sorry, mister. I'm so sorry. Didn't see you." He helped me to stand up.

"It's not your fault. I'm okay."

"Praise Jesus, you're not hurt." He placed his right hand on my shoulder to comfort me.

"Better get back to your truck before something else happens. Thanks for your help," I said, offering my hand.

He asked again and again if he could do anything to make things right. No, I replied, over and over. He stopped apologizing to thank God for saving my life. He was back in his truck as I walked in the road to the motel. The semi moved forward on the next leg of its climb up the highway. I was exhausted. I wouldn't be a bowling ball down the ravine.

My muscles quivering, my heart racing, I took deep breaths to regain my composure. The visibility beyond twenty feet was all gray. A car heading up the highway with headlights on honked to warn me of its approach. Still on edge, I responded with extended arms and an annoyed shout.

In the room, my arms shook while removing wet clothes. I examined the red marks and scraps on my arms and hands. I took a shower, put on my fatigues, and flopped on the bed for a short rest.

———

After breakfast and a lot of coffee at the Mountain Morning Café, followed by another slow sweep of the roads in and around Bridle Path, I parked in a public lot in sight of the main street in town. Two hours passed as I waited for any sign of Silver driving either car.

Knowing Slade had a mobile home in the backcountry, it was logical to assume his second residence was in a remote area of the mountains—difficult to find in a hurry. I had an idea how to speed up the search, but improbable to pull off. It called for friends to take risks—an eagle in the sky, a helo pilot who worked a search like an aerial scout—that they wouldn't even consider.

Back at the motel, I called General Haywood's office. A recorded voice reprimanded me for attempting a long-distance call from the motel. I called back through an operator to make a collect call to Sally Aberdeen at the Pentagon. The phone rang once. She accepted the charges. "How am I gonna explain a collect call to finance, Zinny?"

"Sweet talk 'em."

"Zin, call me tonight. I've got a lot to do."

"I need your help. Actually, Major Jack needs our help."

"Not now, Zin. Call me tonight."

"This guy, Slade, I told you all about."

"What guy?"

"The guy I was hired to tail. Jack went off with him."

"What's that got to do with you calling collect to the Pentagon?"

"The major might be in trouble."

"Don't be dramatic, Zin. I've got work to do. Call me tonight. I'm serious."

"No, I'm serious. Slade's girlfriend called me at home to tell me Jack and Slade got into it. It could get bad, Sal. That's why I'm asking for your help."

"Goddamn it, Sergeant Major, what can I possibly do?"

"I'm up in this mountain town to find him, but it's an impossible search from the ground, Sal. I need Bike to search the area for a red Corvette and a white Caddy. I know it's a lot to ask. I need the best asset I know."

"What? You're out of your mind. He's regular army at Bragg. Bike can't fly a helo for a civilian."

"He's a couple of hours in range. Sal, get him TDY for a day, and he can rent a civilian helo for a search. No rules against him flying a civilian bird off duty, right?"

"That won't work, Zin. Where's he gonna find a helo on short notice?"

"Just ask him to check around the area for a private helo or something."

"You're out of your mind."

"We look out for each other, Sal. I'd move heaven and earth for you or Bike. You know that."

"The army can't get involved in any civilian activity. C'mon, Zinny, you know that."

"Yeah, but you and the general can get Bike relieved for a day. A search, nothing else, Sal."

"Zin, I won't ask the general this. He won't agree to what you're asking. It sounds like John Wayne shit."

"A day search, Sal."

"Zin, it's a long shot Bike can even find a helo. And what if Jack is fine, and you look like a crazy fool pulling a stupid stunt."

"I gotta try—"

"Three problems, Zin: I won't ask the general. Bike can't afford to rent a helo. And Bike can't get relieved for the day."

"Ya know, Sal, I'm not turning my back on the major."

A long silence. She was either considering my idea or mulling over the right words to tell me no way. Either way, my best move was to be patient and wait for her to speak.

"So that's what this is about. It's about them, isn't it?" Sal said. "You can't let it go. Mickey, Bingo, and the rest of the special ops team knew the risk. You and Jack did too. All of you knew."

"And what did the general risk?"

"Zin, I care about Jack. But how do I ask General Haywood for something like this?"

"In plain English!" I shouted at her.

She gasped. She knew how demanding I could be when I pursued a course of action. "You're asking for more than we can do, Sergeant Major."

"Work your magic."

"No matter the circumstances, huh? And the consequences? What about the consequences?"

My determination swelled to push for what I wanted until I heeded the voice in my head to back off. What I asked for was improbable at best. I came to terms with the obvious: my demand was way beyond her boundaries.

"You're right, Sal. It's too much to ask. Too many eyes and hands in the way. It's just . . . I don't know. What else can I do? The major is in serious trouble."

"Sometimes you want too much too soon." She waited a bit longer before continuing. "No matter what. You can be a real asshole sometimes, Zubell."

Don't say a word, I told myself. I was bullheaded. At times unreasonable. And Sal was right. I deserved to hear the truth, like a cymbal, to get my attention. I only considered unreasonable demands of my friends, which was unfair.

"We're out of control. I'll deal with it. Forget I ever called."

"Zin, don't even think about trying to convince Bike to do anything.

Got me?"

"I won't."

"I don't know where you are."

"It don't matter, Sal. Like I said, I'm sorry I even asked."

"Give me your phone number, asshole."

I repeated my phone number twice. Sal hung up without saying goodbye. Not a good sign of consideration for a time-tested friendship.

My only plan for finding Major Jack was to go business to business in and around Bridle Path, asking if anyone knew Damon Slade. Hardly enjoyable talking with strangers, but necessary.

CHAPTER 18

The following morning I canvased more businesses in Bridle Path. I got strange frowns from the store managers wondering why a uniformed soldier was looking for a man no one knew. Another strategic mistake thinking a military uniform would assist my search. I decided to return to the motel to change into civilian clothes before continuing the search.

I unlocked the motel door in time to hear the phone ringing.

"Zin, where ya been? This was gonna be the last time I called you."

"Hi, Sal."

"Well, Bike had an idea. I don't know about this, but I issued an op order from General Haywood's office for a test flight of a decommissioned Huey that the army is selling to a big honcho contractor. It's at the NC National Guard armory in Charlotte."

"Are you kidding?"

"Do I sound like I'm kidding? I can't believe I'm getting involved, but Bike convinced me this will all be above board."

"You guys really came through. It wouldn't take a lotta convincing to get the general to sign off on an order to help an army contractor."

"I got a bad feeling about this."

"It'll be okay, Sal. Bike can spot a white Caddy and a red Corvette up top. Bike won't be involved in anything else."

"He can't, Zin. My ass is on the line. Get that through your thick head. Anyway, it's in the works. Do you know an LZ near where you are?"

"Yesterday I saw a field about three klicks south of Bridle Path on two twenty-one. Bike can spot it from up top."

"You sure?"

"Bike is the best."

"He knows you're looking for Major Jack. And he knows how sensitive this flight is. Just get Bike out of there pronto. He's already on his way to Charlotte. I'm guessing three hours to rendezvous. Give me your word Bike doesn't get involved."

"I promise. Search only and return to the armory."

"Zin, this could end up bad. What's your plan to get the major out of there?"

"Through the front door. I'm walking the major out. Nothing else."

"You have to be the one with the cool head."

"I promise. I won't let you down."

"I mean it, Sergeant Major." Using my rank was her shutdown statement. "I saw your ex-wife last week. We talked."

Ex-girlfriend talking to ex-wife. No man would want to eavesdrop on that conversation. Too much comparing notes for any man to hear unedited.

"She said you weren't worth it."

"You agree with her?"

"No."

Sal hung up before I said thank you. Issuing official paperwork for the search exposed her to untenable questions. She might not be able to cover her tracks. We must avoid any footprints to her.

Going through the sliding glass door to the small deck, I gazed at the expansive green valley below, with visibility for miles. Clear skies to search the area. The plan had a chance of succeeding.

———

Master Warrant Officer Bike Crandell was the best helo pilot I ever flew with in 'Nam, bar none. His technical skill and courage notwithstanding, he flew with an uncanny sense of control, anticipating each maneuver like a bird flying between the trees. He walked away from a helo crash in 'Nam, then went back flying with the same cool hand. But his career stalled because he was cut from the same mold as Major Jack: never by the book. Deviating from orders—when they believed it to be the right call—was their SOP. Yet they had a powerful ally in General Haywood, a man willing to clean their slate because he needed their daring for covert operations. Major Jack and Bike were the general's men.

I transferred gear from the storage box in my truck to a duffel bag: rope, hunting knife, .45-caliber pistol, and a box of ammo. I was on edge waiting to hear from Bike to go over the faux military operation and the rendezvous point. I was about to lie down, when the phone rang.

"Hello?"

"Hello, bubba. What the fuck is this all about?"

"Bike, how ya been?"

"Great, son, but what's this I'm hearing about the major? Sal says he's in Dutch with some asshole, and you've gotta snatch him outta there. You've grown a bigger set of balls, bubba."

"You know it, Bike."

"A huge fuckin' risk, man. Not like you. But I love it. Way off SOP, but cool as shit. You think this asshole will make trouble for us?"

"No. He's hurting too bad. We just gotta locate the major in a tight area search. The guy has a red Corvette and a white Cadillac. All you gotta do is show me the way in and outta there."

"Let's find him. You know a rendezvous?"

"There's a level clearing for landing."

"Approximate distance and location away from town?"

"My guess about three klicks south of Bridle Path on two twenty-one."

"Okay."

"You'll have no trouble spotting it on approach."

"No worries."

"I got the same truck. I'll be there."

"Gimme two hours, tops, bubba."

"Gotta make sure nothing gets back to Sal and the general."

"You worry too much. You're a good guy, Zin. The army fucked up when they RIF'd you. Gotta get airborne."

"Roger that."

———

I drove into Bridle Path, which was alive with tourists. I went to the Mountain Morning Café for a meat loaf, mashed potatoes, salad, and sweet tea lunch. Joe, the manager, remembered me. He complimented my uniform, and we chitchatted about his stint in the navy. I listened, nodded, adding nothing to the conversation.

An hour later I arrived at a glade on Highway 221, a strip of land on hiatus from farming or development. The field was near a sharp bend in the highway, and no curious neighbors in sight. A brief helo landing would attract little attention. I parked my truck about fifty yards off the highway near the center of the field to wait for Bike.

Sitting in my truck, I nodded off, with the sun warming up my full belly and the quiet smoothing my restless nerves. The distant cars passing on the highway didn't disturb my sleepy state.

A disturbing knock on my truck window startled me. I had no idea how long I napped. Never heard an approaching car. I jerked up to see a highway patrolman motioning me to roll down the glass. He was suspicious of a truck parked in the middle of a barren field.

"Good afternoon," he said.

"Good afternoon."

"Some identification, please, sir. I bet you got a good explanation why an army sergeant is sleeping in the middle of a field."

"Yes, sir, I do. I'm waiting for my army team to arrive." I balanced my butt on my left hip to reach for my wallet. My pulse raced. I never had reason to worry about a police inquiry until only weeks ago. I was concerned about the trooper checking me out in the state police network with the assault charges pending, further delaying my search for Major Jack. I could miss the rendezvous.

"I'm retired from the army. I've been contracted to scout out locations for special forces maneuvers in these mountains." I handed him my driver's license and military ID. "Officer, the army uses these mountains for training. Special forces training."

I had said enough. Nervous babble might prompt suspicion. The trooper stared at my IDs longer than I expected. *How far I could go with believable lies?*

"Sergeant Major Zubell. You served in 'Nam?"

"Yes, sir, three times."

"I'm taking my sergeant's exam next week."

"Good luck. How long you been a state trooper?"

"Ten years."

"You're due," I said, grinning, sucking up.

"You say you're waiting for your army buddies out here. Why in the middle of a field on private property?"

"Got really sleepy, sir, so I got off the highway. Not to be a traffic hazard. I should have thought it through."

"Why aren't you with them?"

"Pentagon hired me for contract work. Retired now. The rest are active duty at Bragg."

"Where're you living now?"

"Charlotte."

"I'm gonna check something out."

The trooper headed back to his cruiser parked behind my truck with his blue light flashing and my identifications in hand. I watched him sit in his car too long. I waited for his inquiry to turn up my name in the system. He walked back to my truck with a serious look.

"Sergeant Major, step out, please."

Fear realized. He found my name in the police network to warrant further questioning. I did what he said. He stepped closer and reached out to shake my hand.

"I never served. I respect your service, Sergeant, but you must move on. Good luck to you," he said, nodding, handing back my license and ID.

"Good luck to you as well." My relief showed in a wide grin.

I made a wide U-turn back to the highway. The trooper followed me off the property. He tailed me as we headed back to Bridle Path. In the city limits, the trooper drove south on Highway 221. I waited until he was out of sight before I backtracked to the rendezvous point. I parked right off the highway near a grove of trees, trusting I was still visible to Bike.

No more than thirty minutes passed before Bike flew over the nearby mountains in the Huey—the Bell UH-1 series Iroquois, the workhorse helo for the army. The Huey hovered over the field, then set down within a safe distance from my truck. My eye in the sky had arrived. The plan was on.

I grabbed the duffel, locked both doors, and jogged over to the copilot's door of the Huey. Inside the familiar helo, I sensed soldier's sweat and spent M60 rounds, bringing back memories of 'Nam. Seeing Bike in the pilot's seat dressed in fatigues lifted my edgy state. He bent sideways to extend his hand. The last time I saw him, he was hardened for combat. He was now slightly overweight, mustached, and for a soldier, a full head of curly blond hair stuffed under his fatigue cap.

He said over the roar, "Zin, you're a fat ass now."

"You too." I got comfortable, buckled the seat belt, then noticed he had a .45 clipped to his belt.

"Why the issue, man?" I asked.

"Habit. Remember: Jonesy said always be prepared."

"Search only, Bike."

"I know. I know. Sal's ass if we screw this up. Nothing's gonna happen, 'cause, ya know, bubba, a helo up this guy's ass will make him shit his pants before doing anything stupid."

"Searching for a red Corvette and a white Cadillac parked together. Anything else you need to know?"

"Yeah," Bike said, checking the maps of the area. "What the fuck is Major Jack doing with this guy?"

"I was paid to tail him. It got ugly, and without my knowing Major Jack left Charlotte with him."

"Why?"

"I don't know. He hasn't been right since the injury. He's trying a grand-stand play. I don't know what that means, and I just said it."

"Kinda fucked up, ain't it? This guy capable of killing Jack?"

"I'm worried."

"How'd you get the heads-up?"

"Slade's girlfriend called me. She's with 'em."

"All right. Got it."

Bike seemed anticipatory, shaking his right leg rapidly, unlike the cool pilot who flew us in and out of firefights. *Is he nervous about the ramifications of his idea to misrepresent the flight plan?* I doubted it. He loved—lived—for the edge of danger, just like Major Jack.

"Ya know?" he said with serious thoughts in mind.

"Know what?" Now I was concerned.

"I know these mountains, bubba. Raised in Murphy. We gotta consider the slope."

"What?"

"The northern and eastern mountain slopes get less sun, making for wetter ground cover. My guess is this guy's place is on the western or southern slope. Easier to cut a road through there."

Bike, as usual, had prepped for the search with clear thinking. I grabbed the maps lying on the floor of the Huey. Bike had topographic maps of the Blue Ridge Mountains to assist us in the search. He lifted the helo at a gradual angle up and away. A blustery cold front moving in bounced the chopper around. My stomach got a bit edgy during the ascent despite many years of riding in assault helicopters. Keeping the helo steady calmed him down.

"Bubba, ya know how hard this is gonna be in the short window I got, right?"

"You're my best shot, man."

"The guy have money to build up high?"

"Don't know. But he's got expensive rides. Down east he lives in a mobile home."

"In a clearing down in a valley. We need a lotta luck. You sure he ain't in town?"

"Yeah. I checked. Don't go there. Too many curious eyes on us."

"I got about an hour for a hard search. Can't come back either." Bike appeared troubled, embarrassed having to put a time limit on helping a friend. "Start with a sweep—figure eight and head to the New River near town. Okay?"

"You're the eagle."

"Get it done."

Bike banked hard to make a figure-eight search of the mountain ridges surrounding Bridle Path, one thousand feet above the red-and-gold leaves camouflaging the roads and homes. Viewing the ocean of trees—a high tide covering the life below—could be a challenge spotting two cars in the vast panorama.

Bike located Highway 221 and swept down to follow the road to view small clusters of homes outside the city limits. We spotted no red Corvette or white Cadillac. Without expressing any frustration, he realized locating cars in this setting might be futile. Without discussing a change in course, he slowed to check the map, then dropped down at a gradual angle toward the New River. There he decelerated to wind up the New River, reminiscent of our excursions in 'Nam to challenge Charlie to show us his hardware. Bike swung back and forth like a pinball to give us different angles to view the homes on the shoreline. Fishermen, boaters, and vacationers waved as we swooped by their position.

"Zin, if this guy don't have a place on the river, we'll, uh . . . we'll keep looking. We'll keep looking. You think this guy's looking for us to show up, bubba?"

"Who knows?"

"Folks get real curious about a military helo flying around."

After searching each bank of the New River, luck smiled on us. I spotted a red Corvette and a white Cadillac in a small clearing ahead. "Got it," I said. "Two o'clock."

Bike hovered over the river as I studied the tight group of three cabins forming an arc with a common front yard lined along a mountain base. A Corvette and a Cadillac in front of the middle cabin—Slade's cabin.

I scanned the surrounding area for an approach to the cabins. There was nothing in sight but thick woods. Bike made a banking turn toward the cabins, circling them once at an angle to get a view of any activity below. I anticipated Silver appearing from a cabin to wonder what was going on.

"You see what I see, Bike?"

"Not sure."

"No other cars."

"Yeah."

On a second pass, I saw the two cabins sandwiching the middle one had closed wooden shutters; the front and rear shutters of the middle cabin were open. Bike pointed out a narrow gravel road cut through the woods leading to the cabins. That was my approach to rescue Major Jack.

"Isolated cabin," Bike said. "Hard to drive up without him noticing."

"Yeah, but I'm going anyway."

We hovered right over the cabin. Now Slade had to know something bold, and alarming was reconnoitering in his vicinity. Bike flew to a nearby ridge above the cabins. He maneuvered the Huey to hover about a hundred feet above the trees, waiting for orders, like we did so often in 'Nam.

"What's the plan, Zin?"

"Could you follow the road out to an entry point? The highway?"

"Roger that. No way to land down there and extricate the major."

"Landing down there never was the plan."

From a bird's viewpoint of the rolling mountains, Bike studied the valley surrounding our hovering location with a thought in mind, an appreciative grin.

"Remember, bubba, when we snatched that NVA honcho before dawn when nobody thought we could get a helo in there? We grabbed the guy before Charlie knew what hit 'em."

If he is thinking about landing the helo on the small tract of land in front of the cabins, he is crazy. No reasonable pilot would consider landing on that real estate.

"Not a chance, Bike. Just follow the entry road. I'll drive to the cabin. You can't engage."

"I know, but fuck!"

"What?" I was concerned something was wrong.

"We got each other's back. It pisses me off I can't do more."

"Bike, you found him. That's everything."

Bike was a gifted aviator with an innate sense to find his way in and out of places, no matter if he strayed off course. Bike flew the helo to the gravel road leading away from Slade's cabin to follow the serpentine path despite the winds pushing us toward the mountainside. Even when trees covered our view from up top, he stayed on course until the road was visible again. He was a bloodhound in the air.

We weaved along the mountain ridges as he charted a course to backtrack to Highway 221. Arriving at the highway intersection, he veered toward my truck. He said, "I'll guide you back. But I ain't leaving until I get a thumbs-up about Major Jack's condition."

Bike guided the helo to the narrow glade to touch down near my truck. He assured me the flight back to the cabins was clear to him, as if he had done it multiple times. I unbuckled the seat harness to shake his hand.

"Owe you."

"What friends do," said Bike.

Still holding on to Bike's handshake, I said, "You're okay about all this?"

"I got enough years in. I'll make a safe landing, bubba. Maybe real soon I'll make some serious money for a change."

"Wish us luck, Bike."

"Get the major."

"See you on the other side."

"Follow me back to the cabin," he said.

"Not necessary. I got the route."

"No choice, bubba. I'm the lead dog. If you give me the thumbs-down,

I'll engage in a bad mood. Anyway, stay out of the headlines for a while. If anyone questions you about the Huey, I got the paperwork and general's orders to cover the contract work. Don't think you're alone on this. Call Sal if any shit comes up."

Bike saluted. I sprinted to my truck. I made a U-turn to drive south on Highway 221. Bike flew above me like a guardian angel. I traveled about five miles to the gravel road leading to the cabins. Up above, Bike was hovering at the intersection of the highway and the road. After making the turn, he flew off to the cabin. I had no time to consider a plan for what to do when I reached Slade's cabin. I had to play out the hand that I set up.

Chilling concerns got a brief audience as I sped down the road and slid in the tight turns. My status with law enforcement might rest on the events about to unfold at Slade's cabin. There were three turnoffs on the way, but I guessed the right route each time. Bike returned to circle above me to insure I followed the course.

When the road reached the clearing for the cabins, I slowed down with my foot pressing on the brake. I let the slope of the road guide my truck past the outside cabin. Bike hovered the Huey at the shoreline. I turned into the clearing and came to an immediate stop when I made a surprising discovery.

The Corvette was gone.

CHAPTER 19

I parked beside Slade's Cadillac, facing away from the cabin. I removed my .45 pistol from the holster, clicked off the safety, and ran low, straight for the door. All doubts pushed aside. The front door to the middle cabin was open. I offered no white flag to signal a peaceful approach or any diversions to mask my entry.

I was no longer nimble and made too much grunting noise running across the yard. I rushed inside and crouched behind a cushioned chair near the front door to limit my exposure as a target. I panned the room to assess the situation. Slade was lying on a sofa in the far corner; Major Jack was lying on his side facing the wall near my position, a blanket up to his neck, his head on a pillow. I looked back at Slade, who had a .38 pistol in his right hand resting on his chest. I aimed and squeezed the trigger to the tension point. I had enough anger to follow through with my threat aiming at Slade's chest. I felt the cold-blooded impulse to shoot the man.

"Slade! Slade! Don't do anything stupid. I'm here for Jack."

No response. No movement. My eyes hadn't adjusted to the dim natural light in the cabin. I was on alert for a response, expecting Slade to shoot out of fear.

"Slade, I'm taking Jack with me."

Again, no response. There were Jack Daniel's bottles on the floor near him. Had he passed out from drinking? That was my guess.

"Slade!" I screamed as loud as I could. Again, no movement from him, but the major moaned. That was a relief.

Focus, Sergeant. Signal Bike, who was hovering over the river, anxious about the situation in the cabin. I hurried outside to give him a thumbs-up. I shook my head up and down, waved him off as a signal of no engagement necessary. He hesitated to fly away until he was certain my fingers pointing skyward were confirmations everything was okay. He returned my salute, then piloted the helo over the mountain ridge.

I rushed back inside. I slowly walked to the sofa without relaxing my aim, still in his line of fire. Beer cans and Coke bottles and half-eaten food littered the coffee table and the floor by the sofa—sandwiches, pizza boxes, chips, and popcorn bags scattered about like this was a typical bachelor party.

I stopped close enough to smell the stench of his body excrement. I relaxed my aim. Was he still breathing? The light from the window was enough to see a black stain on his khaki pants from his waist to below his knees. A significant blood loss. No one could survive such trauma. He had the look of death. Silver left him in a bad state.

Hurrying to the major, I knelt to check on his condition. "Jack? Jack? It's Zin." No response. He reeked of alcohol; a broken whiskey bottle lay near his head. His eyes closed, the left side of his face swollen and stained with blood, his color chalky. I put two fingers on the artery in his neck. His heartbeat was strong.

"We're on our way to the hospital, Jack. Hang in there."

I stared again at Slade. The right thing to do would be to carry them both to the emergency room. I played out a difficult conversation with the emergency room staff about my involvement with Slade's condition. That conversation would be troubling to the staff and would be passed on to the local police. I wasn't that good a person. Leave Slade where he was for others to seek answers.

I bent over the major. I placed my hand on his shoulders to arouse him. He moved his head slightly and opened his right eye. His left eye was swollen shut. He tried to tell me something, but his voice was too weak and garbled to make any sense. I leaned down with my right ear almost touching his mouth to listen to whatever he wanted to tell me. "Say again, Jack. It's Zin."

But he drifted off.

Before lifting Major Jack, I noticed a pile of woman's clothes lying in and around an open suitcase at the door leading to the bedroom. Beside the suitcase was a single stack of strapped twenty-dollar bills. Clothes and money weren't important to Silver—leaving in a rush was. To avoid explaining what had happened here, and out of fear of the helo circling the cabin, she fled in the Corvette.

I lifted Major Jack's arm across my shoulder and wrapped my other arm around his waist. He was in apparent shock, but his right eyelid blinked. He again mumbled. I made out he was complaining about the pain. I reassured him that we were on the way to a hospital. I lifted him into my truck with one hand under his armpit and the other one in his belt at his spine. I ran around to the driver's side as the major slid down the bench seat to where his head flopped in my lap. I left him there.

He tried to speak once more. I said, "It's Zin. You're with me now."

There was no easy way to sidestep the truth when asked what had happened to the major. I rehearsed the story I would tell the medical staff: Scouting locations for an exercise to train special forces units in mountain terrain. Major Jack lost his footing and fell off a narrow footpath to a rocky gully. I told the story aloud to Major Jack in hopes he would recall a few details when he regained consciousness. Eventually, he had to tell the medical staff what had happened to him. But not to the police. His appreciation of our cover story was critical.

After repeating the story aloud, I realized how unrealistic it was to think the major could deliver a precise lie in his condition.

I had a dilemma. Without Silver's explanation, my presence at the cabin had poor optics. It could end up badly.

CHAPTER 20

Heading up the gravel road to the highway, my emotions ranged from concern for the major to anger at his insane decision to come up here. He put himself in position with a violent man. Like he wanted it to happen. *Did he have a death wish?* He almost succeeded. His wiring was so damaged.

Now I faced a dilemma: I had no experience lying at this level to explain the major's injuries. Without consistent practice, I had doubts about my ability to convince anyone our cover story was the truth. I mulled over a cocktail of blending truths and lies for a difficult sell to justify the major's injuries. But I must be unwavering to protect our friends.

An obvious explanation came to mind that might work. The major reeked of whiskey. Was it sellable the medical staff would buy he was drunk when he fell off a footpath? I had to sell it. With strong conviction.

Another fact would add credence to our story. A military helo flying low around a small town had to draw attention from the local authorities. Eyes watching were the truth. That was our red herring. If someone in authority was curious about our presence in the area, there was an op order from the Pentagon authorizing the flight. The red flag had an explanation.

Focus on being a Good Samaritan, I thought. That was my pitch.

The community hospital outside Bridle Path on Highway 221 was a one-story concrete building located in a narrow valley. I carried Major Jack into the emergency entrance and asked the nurse on duty for help. She called for an orderly to assist Major Jack onto a gurney. She informed me how fortunate I was an experienced physician was in this afternoon.

"What happened?" asked the attending nurse.

I recited the story like lines in a play. The nurse and two emergency room aides began taking Major Jack's vitals. A bearded man in a long white lab coat, with a full head of gray hair and a bounce in his step, walked to the well-lit examination room. He introduced himself as the doctor on call and asked if I was family.

"Army colleagues."

The nurse said, "Sir, please go down the hall to the admittance office. We'll let you know about his condition soon. He's in good hands."

The admittance clerk questioned me about Major Jack's insurance coverage. "The VA has been covering his war wounds since returning stateside," I replied. To collect payment from the VA, I told her the hospital must be persistent feeding paperwork into the VA pipeline. I attempted to empathize with her job, relating my duties over the past year at the Pentagon, processing form after form, over and over, day after day, using the overused cliché "brain-dead work" when I described the monotonous job she had. She glared like a teacher with a migraine.

I waited an hour and a half in the small hospital waiting room for any information on Major Jack's condition. Hours of waiting and watching in the army taught me controlled patience. When determined, I could outwait a glacier to move. But not today. At the beginning of the second hour, I walked to the nurse's station, extended both arms out to form a cross, and stood with an impatient stare to get the nurse's attention. The redheaded nurse responded with a visit to the major's room for an update on his condition. A few minutes later, the doctor walked up with a clipboard in hand.

"Sir, you brought him in, right? Your name?"

"Yes. Sergeant Major Zinny Zubell."

"What happened to him?"

Here we go. I told him the major and I were retired army, consulting with special forces at Bragg. Major Jack lost his balance and fell into a rocky gully while scouting suitable locations for mountain maneuvers with the Green Berets. *I'm slowly starting to believe my lies.*

"The injuries look like a beating, not a fall."

"I can't answer why that is, sir." He knew from experience the difference between injuries from a beating and a fall. He stared, sighed with disbelief. The doc wasn't buying my free-flowing lies. He studied the medical charts like the information there would reveal the truth.

Time to sprinkle in a truth to head off more doubts.

"Major Klinkscales has a drinking problem, Doc. Hard to miss that smell."

"He has extensive scars on his legs. Surgical scars. I'm quite certain he couldn't climb in that condition."

"I have a number you can call at the Pentagon."

"I believe what I see."

"I get that. But booze was his painkiller, Doc. Nothing for him to do but get drunk since his war wounds. I sought out this assignment in hopes it would center him. We all told the major he couldn't climb with us, but he's quite stubborn and one tough guy. Doc, he lost his balance and fell."

He hesitated longer than I expected. "I'm concerned about the swelling in his brain. He may need surgery in Asheville. We'll see in twenty-four hours. How do we contact you?"

"Staying at the Green Mountain Inn."

He had more questions in mind with a perplexed scowl on his

marshmallow face. He wrote at length in the medical chart.

"Can I see him?"

"No. He's sedated now." He started to walk away, then changed his mind. "I'm obligated to report a criminal act if in my judgment anything like that occurred."

"I understand." No need to add anything to that concern.

The doctor would eventually question Major Jack about his injuries. Without an opportunity to prompt the major on how to answer his questions, he would spill the truth to implicate Slade for the assault. The dilemma I was concerned about was brewing.

I sat in the waiting room for a report on Major Jack's condition. Another hour passed. I walked down the hall to ask the attending nurse about his condition. "No change," she said. When the nurse left her station to check on other patients, I went into the major's room to see his head bandaged, an IV in his right hand, and his face still stained with dried blood. Like the doc said, he was resting.

Around midnight I left for the motel to shower and get some sleep.

———

Under the constant wail of the hard-driven water, a disconcerting knock alerted me. I stood outside the tub, dripping water all over the floor, and listened for another knock. I sensed the person hadn't gone away. I was right. No casual taps on my door, but pounding, attention-grabbing knocks. I dried off quickly, then tromped across the room for a peek, assuming someone not friendly was at the door. I separated a small opening in the drawn curtain to see a wonderful sight: Sally, in jeans, a sweatshirt, and her hair pulled back in a tight ponytail. That beautiful woman had come all this way to see me. I was excited she was here, ignoring how upset, weary she appeared and forgetting I had only a small white motel towel wrapped around my waist.

She stepped inside, stunned to see me in a towel. I had movement below while thinking how happy I was to see her. Her face crumpled into a frown as she stood before me, shocked at my appearance. I made a slight move to hug her; she halted me with an upturned hand.

"You open the door to anyone practically naked?"

"Saw it was you. Well, I'm now a little embarrassed."

"You should be." Sal looked away. "Put some clothes on. Certainly not here for anything like that."

My excitement over a reunion with Sally lasted less than a minute. How I imagined she would rush to give me a long romantic embrace was proof of my delusional expectations. I backed up so as not to expose my butt in a towel that was more like a washcloth.

"I'll—I'll get dressed."

"Where's the major?"

I paused before answering out of imagined fear of her anger. "He's in the hospital."

"Hospital! Bike said everything was okay!"

"Yeah, I know. I promised Bike wouldn't be involved. I—I didn't know how bad it was till I got inside the cabin."

"How bad is he?"

"He took a beating."

"A beating?" She paced around the room, frantic, edgy, quick gasps between steps, an inescapable shroud enveloping her. "How could you get him involved with a guy like that, Zubell? All of us."

"I didn't want him involved. He did it on his own for reasons I can't understand. But I had to do something, Sal. I thought maybe—"

"Maybe what? You could pull this off without a hitch? Now I delivered you and Bike to a crime scene. This is fucking bad, Zubell. Fucking bad!"

"I didn't know, Sal. I thought maybe it wouldn't be so bad."

"Oh my God. It's Leavenworth," she said. The potential reality slapped her hard.

"Sal, you authorized a legit flight. No engagement, no cowboy stunts."

"Legit, my ass! I signed for the general. He trusted me to sign for him. How do I explain what happened when the general finds out Bike picked up a civilian for the test flight?"

"Me, Sal. Bike picked up me, a lifer."

"And how does Bike explain the full-day test flight to the command staff at Bragg?"

"He runs with army bullshit in his veins. Just like us."

"Oh, you got all the answers. It ain't fuckin' funny, Zubell. You of all people know the consequences. There will be a court-martial. Both Bike and me. Heads will roll."

"The general won't allow implications to get out," I said, hoping to ease her apprehension. "He'll keep the questions buried deep. 'Cause it's you. And Bike."

I was developing a throbbing headache. I gestured with both hands, a plea to make her feel better. I forgot about the small towel loosely covering my midsection, allowing it to fall to the floor, exposing my partially excited privates.

Sal gasped and spun around, shaking her head. "My God, Zubell. Put some clothes on."

Leaning over for the duffel bag on the floor by the dresser, I grabbed boxers, jeans, and a flannel shirt. I made sure my front was away from her. Almost fell over putting my jeans on in a hurry.

"We won't get past this, Zin. Can't believe I went along with you. I can't handle a court-martial. I just can't."

"The general won't allow that."

"You seriously think the general will fall on his sword for this? He will deny all knowledge. And who will they believe? A major general or a first sergeant? Huh?"

"Bike knows how to cover for us."

"This time your shit is on me."

"I won't ever understand why Jack went off with this guy. But I promise I'll do whatever it takes to protect you."

She sighed over and over, forcing herself to calm down. "Nothing seems like the right thing to do anymore. I don't know how to get far away from this, Sergeant Major." We stared at each other with eyes needing a hug, but neither of us made a move. "You think Jack's gonna pull through?"

"Think so. But I don't know. Some days I wonder if he's done living."

"I should be with him. I passed a hospital on the way here. Is he there?"

"Yeah. I'll go with you."

"No. I can't stand to look at you right now. What makes me crazy is, I can't hate you. Don't come. I mean it."

The possibility of collateral damage to my friends' careers was devastating. She would never forgive me. Any chance of her getting past this was hard to think about—the end of a valued friendship.

I was worried about her anxiety. She fled Washington posthaste. *Had something already happened or been reported that scared her to come here?* I thought.

"Has someone already approached you about this?"

She turned away, then left the room, slamming the door. Her nonanswer troubled me.

My anger at the major for getting involved with Slade surged again. I dropped to the floor to do push-ups until I collapsed. I laid there on the shag carpet as I imagined all the serious consequences that could happen. Good intentions be damned. Jeopardizing the careers, lives, of your best friends was as bad as it could get.

I laid down with my clothes on and the bathroom light on. It took an hour to fall asleep.

———

Someone sat down on the bed beside me. I jerked up to stare at an unwelcome face: Detective Cutter sitting at my feet like a friend comforting a friend. Detective Pitman stood over me. The stir I brought to Bridle Path attracted the Charlotte police. Cutter was out of his beat after his punch-clock shift. He hadn't shaved, a lit cigarette hanging down—his scowl, mean. To come this far at night wasn't routine.

"Detective Cutter, long way from home." I sat up on the edge of the bed and leaned forward to rub my eyes awake. "Never heard you guys knock." I checked my watch—five in the morning.

"No sleep makes me an unhappy guy. So your boyfriend fell off a cliff, huh?" Cutter said. "Yeah, and a pig gets an erection when you say *barbecue*."

He perfected his one-liners over the years in interrogations. His humor worked. His quip would get a laugh if dread didn't trump his sarcasm.

"Yeah. Major Jack is in bad shape."

"What're you doing up here, Zubell?" Cutter asked, still sitting on the bed.

I was in the center of an investigative circle. Hard questions would follow. I wanted to assume his visit was more inquisitorial than accusatorial. I would find out soon enough.

"What am I doing here? Contract army work. Suppose I could ask you the same question."

Pitman revved up his tone. "Shut up, Zubell. Park the attitude."

After an extended yawn, Cutter said, "You can't expect us to believe your boyfriend fell off some footpath. A crippled guy ain't going hiking."

"He's a stubborn guy."

"Trying out your lies now, huh? Okay. Let's hear 'em."

"I'm here on army business." I blended truth with fiction to concoct a story easy to swallow for doubting detectives. The alibi I was selling was trickier to traverse than a mountain trail. They heard my story out before making comments.

"Bullshit," Cutter said.

"You're lying," Pitman said.

Mixing in plausible deeds within the framework of a lie could be sellable if told in a confident narrative, but I wasn't that good of a salesman—why attorneys commanded high fees for their services. It was difficult for me to cobble together a convincing lie without a doubt in my voice.

"You still working for that lawyer?" Cutter said.

"No. He fired me."

"Makes sense."

"We know Slade lives around here, asshole," Pitman said.

I shrugged while frowning like I had no idea about what he was saying. I was in trouble.

"We know you know where Damon Slade lives, Zubell," Cutter said.

"How would I know that?"

"You remember Cecil Horry? Or Lugs, as you call him," Cutter said. "Remember: We saved your ass in the nick of time. You owe us. You can repay the debt with the truth about why you're up here. Let your conscience be your guide."

The force of the law landed right on my head. And the weight was getting quite heavy. "Sir, I told you why I'm here."

"Okay. Let's start at the beginning," Cutter said, displaying his wicked grin. "Lugs gives up Damon Slade for a deal. He tells us Slade was responsible for Bonnie Ridge's hit-and-run and Mosie Kelter's drowning in her car. But why should we believe scum like him? A guy trying to save his hide from the death penalty will lie about anything. But we're curious. We go the hospital to talk with Slade. And do you know what we found? He's gone. A staffer saw him leave in the middle of the night with a young girl and a crippled guy. A crippled guy? And who would that be? The description we got sounds like your boyfriend, Jack Klinkscales. So we go back to Lugs for Slade's whereabouts. We're told about his cabin up here. We check in with the local PD and hear an interesting story. An army helicopter was flying back and forth around here yesterday afternoon, looking for something. Huh? What's that about? The local PD gives us a report from a doctor at the hospital about a head-trauma patient that he believes was due to a severe beating. That patient just happens to be your buddy, Jack Klinkscales. And who brings him to the hospital? Z. Zubell. Anything you wanna add?"

Admit nothing, I reminded myself over and over. I had to stay in the crosshairs of Cutter's investigation to protect my friends, no matter what legal trap I faced. *Stay true to the story*, I thought.

"Contract work for the army, like I said. Got a .45 and a hunting knife and climbing gear in my duffel bag. Check it out."

I volunteered information to appear cooperative, although evasive about knowing where Slade's cabin was located. Any reference acknowledging Slade's whereabouts, I was in jail as fast as Cutter's fat fingers could hunt-and-peck the paperwork.

"We got grounds—we got grounds to haul your ass back to Charlotte for a more personal chat. Got me?" Cutter warned with his index finger poking my chest.

"You've been stepping in our path too many times," Pitman said.

Pitman reached down for the duffel bag beside the nightstand to rummage for my .45 and hunting knife. He sniffed the barrel and examined the blade. He shook his head at Cutter.

Cutter leaned over to whisper in my ear. "It's not good to be disliked, Zubell."

I nodded in agreement.

"Wonder what Klinkscales will tell us about what happened. The same bullshit you just did?" Cutter said.

He gave me no time to answer the incriminating question. He slapped a firm hand on my shoulder. "Like I said. It gets harder now."

"Stand up," Pitman said.

Pitman gathered my duffel bags. They escorted me out of the motel room to the brisk predawn air. Outside the door to my room was the night manager of the motel. His gaze, a brew of disdain and fear, watched our slow path across the parking lot as he backed up to give us plenty of space. At a comfortable distance to speak without concern, he yelled, "Your kind ain't welcome here."

The detectives walked me to the motel entrance sign beside their squad car. Detective Pitman opened the trunk of the police sedan and tossed my duffel bags in without regard for any damage to the contents. Pitman ordered me to hand over my truck keys, wallet, everything in my pockets.

"Am I under arrest? For what? What about my truck?" Nervous questions asked at an untimely moment.

"Your goddamn truck is the least of your problems, son," said Cutter. I anticipated being handcuffed and shoved into the back seat of the police sedan for a long ride to jail in Charlotte.

Cutter surprised me when he grabbed my shirt. He shoved me hard against the post holding the motel sign. Even though the temperature was chilly, my sweat glands worked at capacity. Cutter took his time to light a cigarette. He blew the smoke in my face. I inhaled the fumes to calm my nerves.

"You're a clever fella, Zubell. You found Slade faster than we did," Cutter said. "And that really pisses me off."

Cutter moved closer, dropping his cigarette to the pavement. My reaction to his approach was to brace for more accusations. It was hard to maintain a poker face. Cutter forced a half grin across his lined face, then clutched my shoulder.

"I told you to stay away from Slade and our investigation. But you're one stubborn son of a bitch. Now you've done some serious shit."

He squeezed my shoulder with his powerful left hand, jabbed his right fist into my gut, then blocked me from collapsing or moving away with his right forearm. He caught me off guard. I gasped for breath as he held me against the post. Ten years ago, at a strip club near Fort Benning, a drunk sergeant surprised me with a hard punch to the stomach. I knocked him out with a right cross to his chin. But retaliating against a cop was different. I took it.

Cutter released his forearm on my chest. "Tell me something I don't already know."

His punch caught me in the diaphragm. I opened my mouth wide in a desperate effort to breathe again. His experienced jab landed in the right spot to overpower me.

"You're gonna pay if I gotta work this hard for the truth. I'm never wrong about my hunches. And don't say I'm wrong. I'll slam you in the hole."

I refused to break eye contact but couldn't respond to his demand, even if I wanted to. He knew it.

"Any help from my ass is only good for the next few seconds."

Even with extensive prisoner-of-war training, I fell back to a state of dread when cornered by stern interrogation. I showed a please-don't-hit-me-again expression.

"All right. All right. Last chance is over. I'll find out what went down with Slade. You'll be dancing to my beat now. Put him in the car."

"Cuff him?" said Pitman.

"No. Not yet."

Pitman guided me to the back seat of their black sedan. The consequences of my do-anything attitude to rescue Major Jack were real and harsh.

We drove away from the motel at a deliberate speed. I was on edge, my heart racing, sandwiched in with no place to release my nervous energy. My mind sprinted to line up plausible denials for each step I took to retrieve the major. The lies were there, as plain as midday. The holes in my cover story would entrap me, and Cutter knew it.

At the intersection to Highway 221, we headed away from Bridle Path to worm along the winding highway in the Appalachians at twenty miles per hour. A chilled fog rolling across the highway with the morning wind diffused our headlights. No hurry ruled the early morning. The narrow highway was as remote as a vein far from the heart.

I had a good idea what was in store. More interrogation until I asked for my lawyer.

Pitman reported on the radio, "We're on our way." We slowed to ten miles per hour as Cutter strained to see the road ahead. At the end of a sharp turn on Highway 221, Cutter made an immediate left turn onto an unmarked dirt road. Images of a beating to get a confession came to mind.

We drove down the steep road with Cutter pumping the brakes. Down we went for what seemed like miles. Ahead bright lights came through the thickening fog, the focal point of our downward drive. At another sharp curve, the lights became brighter and more directed, illuminating the surrounding trees like huge actors in a massive Halloween drama. The road straightened out. The light source were headlights. We stopped in the middle of the narrow road. Straining to see through the windshield, I made out police cruisers in a line facing a row of cabins.

Cutter pulled me out of the sedan. Without a word spoken, Cutter and Pitman walked me downhill toward the lights. Ahead the sound of rushing water in the distance grabbed my attention. The headlights were focused on a center cabin between two other cabins on a small piece of land—Slade's place.

Bringing me to his cabin was the last thing I expected. Three cruisers with headlights on faced the cabin. Policemen were inside with flashlights. Cutter halted our approach when we were only a few steps from Slade's front door. Pitman walked ahead. With a quick move, Cutter grabbed my shirt to pull me close. He was hoarse, clearing his throat in my face. "We're here. And you know where here is, don't ya?"

I shrugged. A bad situation. The words—*I want a lawyer*—were right on my tongue.

Cutter frowned, grabbed my left arm, and pulled me with him into the cabin. The other cops in the cabin had the "what" expression. Cutter stepped behind me and shoved me across the room to the sofa where Slade lay in the same position as I found him.

"Damon Slade. Dead a day. We're gonna find out what killed him when the coroner gets here. Looks obvious he bled out. Here's the way we see it went down: You found Slade's cabin faster than we did. I'm gonna find out how you did that. Maybe hitched a ride on an army helicopter. How? I don't know. Anyway, you find your buddy Klinkscales, who we know came up here with Slade, near beaten to death, and you lose it. You stomp on Slade where it would do the most damage. And you leave him to die and take Klinkscales to the hospital. Sound about right, Zubell?"

His scenario made sense. He'd never believe my denial about assaulting Slade. I wouldn't either. His experienced questionings might even trick me into admitting I was here and did something. My fate was an accusation of assaulting and killing Damon Slade.

"Maybe Lugs is telling the truth. Slade is a bad guy. Shit, if I saw what some asshole did to my buddy, I'd do exactly what you did," said Cutter. "Maybe the DA will take that into consideration. Just tell your side of the story. It was anger that drove you to lose it in the heat of the moment. I'm gonna get a pad and pencil so you can write down your side of the story. Join me, will ya? Unless you wanna say a few last words to Slade."

"It's time to talk with my attorney."

Cutter stepped closer. "You see a goddamn phone around here?"

"I won't admit to something I didn't do, Detective."

My refusal to cooperate fueled Cutter's spitfire anger. He pushed me toward the door. Pitman grabbed my arm to escort me outside. We quick-stepped across the yard. There was no doubt in their minds as to my guilt. At their sedan, Cutter slapped me on the back of my head. I started to get into the back seat, but Cutter stopped me.

Pitman said, "Zubell, you have the right to remain silent—"

"No. Not yet. I want Zubell to think long and hard about his only option. Just admit what you did."

"Am I under arrest, Detective?"

"Are you gonna write down what happened?"

"No."

"So get the fuck outta here."

"What?" I asked.

Pitman was as confused as I was.

"Start walking. Clear your head about doing the right thing. You did the right thing for your country. Go, Sergeant. Move it."

In disbelief, I said, "Walk where?"

"Get outta here. Get outta here."

Cutter grabbed me and pushed me hard enough to where I fell to the ground. I looked up at a raging man believing he would hit me again. I stood up to leave the area. No reason to stand here to question an impassioned detective. I walked up the road at a climbing pace that was difficult. I never looked back.

CHAPTER 21

My lungs labored from the slow, steady climb up the gravel road into the gray morning light. I walked away with no cruiser following me. I never turned around until I was out of sight of the police headlights. The trek burned up little of my adrenaline; the distance from the scene in a dense forest only intensified my anxiety.

I had a full-body shiver wearing only a flannel shirt. I was weary but kept pressing on. I passed the time watching the fog float across the narrow road. When a misty, ghostlike patch floated in my path, I swung my fists through it to ward off the numbing chill.

Unexpectedly, Mr. Sedley came to mind. I imagined the satisfaction he would feel when he heard of Slade's death. His duty to cloak his brother's involvement with Slade was successful. Through his skillful maneuverings, his family was sheltered from Billy's complicity in Mosie Kelter's death. I shook off more spiteful thoughts about the man while ramping up the self-reproach for unwittingly diving headfirst into his cover-up and staying there. A costly leap of faith on my part.

Morning broke over the far slope. I stared up at the foggy mountains, tracing an outline of the treetops. I lingered for a long ten count listening to the forest sounds of the early mountain morning. I thought about trekking off into the wilderness, using my wilderness survival training to avoid jail, but it would only be a matter of time before I got lost or fell to my death or got picked up by the police. After another full-body shiver, I hiked straight up the road.

A noise startled me out of a stressful trance. Heavy, deliberate movement cracked dead tree limbs, and something tromped through thick, fallen leaves in the woods to my left. Not far away. I whipped off the road to my right in expectation of something, someone moving again. But the noise stopped. I waited motionless, crouching on the edge of the dense woods. All I heard was birds awakening for their food hunt. My eyes darted back and forth in the direction of the noise while trudging backward a few steps, difficult high steps through underbrush. In 'Nam, curiosity and the mission would urge me to check out what was out there. But not this morning. I incubated a new level of fear in a place where danger was unexpected. I crouched in a full squat and waited for any movement again. Seconds later a dead tree limb cracked under heavy weight, and in the silvery backlight a black mass moved among the trees across the road. The mass was large—a buck or a bear.

A distant siren then disturbed the quiet. There was panic movement. Crushing leaves and cracking fallen tree limbs, it fled without regard for the noise it made. Its flight was back up the slope and into the safety of the dense woods. I heard the nonstop fleeing until the blares from the siren drowned out the noisy runaway. The reach of the approaching headlights sent a cold shiver through me, and I ducked behind a rhododendron to hide from view. Recent run-ins with law enforcement made me hide from sirens.

After the ambulance passed me on its way to Slade's cabin, I listened for any fleeing noises. Nothing. I stepped out of the woods, down across the narrow ditch, and up the damp grade. Seeing and hearing nothing, I resumed my isolated walk up the road toward the highway.

I heard rocks pressed against the road with the approach of a vehicle in no hurry. Headlights jumped on my back, surrounding me with more dread. Cutter arrived to pick me up. He ordered me to get in. I did what he said, sliding into the back seat, where the warmth of his sedan was of little comfort. There was no bridge to strike up a conversation with a weary cop. He was alone. I was confused as to why he was without his partner.

"Zubell, I'm the only person who's willing to give you another chance to come clean."

Detective Cutter was convinced he alone could get my confession. He could be right.

"So you know the situation. Slade's dead. So now we can't run his stories up against his buddy Lugs to get to the truth. That leaves only you and me to find out what happened to Slade."

I was on my way to a human pound.

"Okay, suppose you tell me something I don't understand. Why was your friend Klinkscales with Damon Slade? I told you to stay away from him, but I never figured your boyfriend would go there. Was he doing your bidding, huh?"

The words—*I don't know why*—were right on my tongue, until I realized that answering his question would place me at Slade's cabin. Cutter's seasoned interrogation was clever. I kept quiet.

"You're a smart guy. My partner wanted to cuff you and take ya to jail. But I'm still not sure what you did outright. You don't wanna be a bad guy, so at least admit you were at the cabin and hauled Klinkscales to the hospital. Okay?"

His homespun good-cop manner could trap even a careful perpetrator. I didn't fall for his second trap question. I slumped in the back seat. After more sighs, Cutter headed up the road at a turtle's pace, slow enough I could almost count the rocks we ran over.

"If asked, will my superior hear about me tryin' to beat a confession outta you?"

"I didn't confess to anything."

"Smart boy."

"Am I under arrest?"

"In due time. Ya know, some things still don't make sense. Why get involved with these people and their nasty business in the first place? I don't get it. I know there's something that ties all this shit together. My old bones tell me it's bad. That sounds about right, don't it? I really believe you know what all this shit is about, but you won't tell me. And you won't tell me until we put you in a bind where you have to come clean." Cutter cleared his throat, coughing hard, almost gagging. "Gotta stop smoking. Okay, Zubell, at least tell me this: Where can we find that young girl who hung out with Slade? What's her name?"

"Silver Kelter." I had to answer a question.

"Yeah, her."

"Don't know. Maybe at the apartment above the car repair shop."

I regretted giving him an opening to question me further as soon as the words bounced off his windshield.

"Zubell, you've been one step ahead of us dumb cops. Are you protecting your boyfriend? I can appreciate that. Really can. Looks like he and Slade did a lotta drinking, and things got outta control."

"I should talk with my lawyer."

"Ya know, the coroner will check out the blood found in Slade's cabin. If it turns out to belong to your major friend, he could be in deep shit. You wanna help me out with what we'll find there? Could be to your benefit. What about it?"

His experienced hunches were right at the truth. We exchanged glances in his rearview mirror. He stopped the sedan at the intersection of the gravel road and Highway 221 to light up a cigarette. He twisted around, with his right arm on the back of the seat. With a controlled tone, he said, "You asked about charges against you. At a minimum, I can make a case for obstruction of justice to the DA right now. More coming. Count on it."

No weaving denial would work on this detective. I couldn't deny being in the area, since I had already lied about scouting for the army. The trap would be set when the coroner confirmed Major Jack's blood in the cabin.

He took two drags on his cigarette. He squirmed and cursed his involvement with this case. He shifted his body to make the turn onto the highway.

"This gets worse for you. Why a soldier goes messing around in trash cans for cheap bucks is beyond me. But you're involved."

Cutter was as relentless as I was. It would be easy to say more than I should, then nibble at his bait. Charlotte was a safer place with him in the watchtower.

He accelerated up the road toward Bridle Path. No further interrogation for a few more miles. Why stop now? He was at the truth to the troublesome case. He glanced over his shoulder and spoke like a guy at a bar at the end of a hard workweek.

"Ya know, you're a smart, determined fella. It's a real shame you ain't on our side."

CHAPTER 22

Cutter drove to the parking lot of the Bridle Path Hospital. He parked at the front entrance, turned off the engine, lit another cigarette, and took a few moments to collect his thoughts. As was his typical gesture, he sighed loudly and got out while jiggling the loose change in his pocket. Before closing the squad-car door, he leaned down to glare with eyes that would burn my skin. "I wanted to like you. No more."

He slammed the sedan door with much force to release his pent-up anger, then turned to stare at me. He surprised me with an expression that read as regret for what he was about to learn about my involvement with Slade's death.

Gut-troubling circumstances gripped me. Cutter sniffing around for damning confirmations of my presence at Slade's cabin would find two willing corroborators: The major, loopy from the meds, had no reason to lie about what had happened. And Sally, on edge about abetting the rescue, would fall for Cutter's clever questioning about the major's extraction. Cutter was close to unraveling my lies. Grilling Major Jack and Sally was a simple one-plus-one equaled me at Slade's cabin.

Jail time banged in my head as the truth. Cutter had boxed me in to where I couldn't answer his questions without incriminating myself. It was time to call Ableman.

I checked my watch every few minutes. A couple dressed like they were going to church headed into the hospital. The husband stooped to glimpse a local disreputable in the squad car. I slumped in the back seat, closing my eyes to avoid eye contact with him and anyone else. I needed a strategy. I pushed down on the door handle. Locked. Quick, another plan. I came out on top of perilous situations. But nothing came to mind. I was in police custody. All I could do was admit to nothing and call my attorney when charged today.

———

About twenty minutes later, Cutter opened the car door on my side. "Stand up." With downcast eyes and a surrendering nod, he stepped away, relaxed his shoulders, and paced slowly in a small circle. He came close again, reached into his jacket for a pack of Camels, and offered me one. I took it. He lit our cigarettes with a silver lighter etched with engravings.

We took more drags in silence. *What is he doing*? Was this plan B to introduce a cooling breeze before returning to the stagnant heat of an interrogation? *Don't fall for his friendly gesture. Admit nothing.*

"Bonnie Ridge talked to us a few days ago. Finally. Seems she and Slade had an affair. And it came to a head at the Pothole the night she had her accident. She and Slade left the bar arguing. He followed her. Said she couldn't lose him, and with no other car around he rammed her until she lost control and hit a tree at a high speed. She told everyone she didn't know the driver of the hit-and-run. Why? Because she never could admit to having an affair. She consulted with your lawyer, Sedley, on how to get Slade to confess without admitting to the affair. He told her that he was working on a strategy and to be patient. Then her husband found out about Sedley and fired him and forbid her to see him again. She lost all hope and saw an opportunity—shot him right in the balls."

"Was she willing to testify against Slade?"

"Maybe. But too late now."

"Now you'll charge her with murder, right?"

"Likely. But Slade leaving the hospital before he healed kinda clouds things up."

"Slade was a bad guy. I had a feeling—"

"Got no patience for your feelings, Zubell. You been talking about that Mosie Kelter woman in the lake. Maybe Lugs is right about that. Just maybe Slade had something to do with her being the lake. Why would he do that? Who knows now, 'cause all parties are dead."

He tossed his cigarette to the sidewalk and stepped on it. "Now to you. What to do with you? Can I establish you and Klinkscales were at Slade's cabin? You bet, in time."

"Detective—"

"Don't talk. For once, shut the fuck up. Been around too many bad guys in my time. Doubt you're one of 'em. And I got my doubts you did something to Slade. Maybe hard to prove anyway. Your army friend Sally backed up your story. Showed me the flight order with your name on it. You're too clever for your britches."

"Sir, like I said—"

"Anyway, your buddy is still doped up. And I don't much give a shit what he says anymore. So I don't clog up the system with what I think happened. You're in my fuck-it file now."

One of my worst tendencies was to ask questions at the worst possible time. I kept quiet. Dared not to look happy. I looked away when I noticed Cutter expecting me to say something. I took the last drag on my cigarette. I dropped it to the sidewalk, then sighed like Cutter.

"Nothing to say now, huh?" he said.

"No, sir."

"Okay, okay. But get this: if I see either you or your boyfriend's names on anything coming across my desk, I'm coming after you both. Count on that."

His last in-my-face threat was easier to take knowing I wasn't under arrest. I worked not to smile or acknowledge any relief.

Cutter reached into his pants pocket to hand me the truck keys, my wallet, and the motel key. He opened the trunk to toss my duffel bags near my feet and leered at me one more time. He got in the sedan and drove up the highway in the direction of Slade's cabin. I waited a minute or so to be certain his leaving wasn't a ploy. And with my bags in hand, I rushed into the hospital to talk to the person who freed me from serious charges.

I turned the corner of the L-shaped first floor to see Sally standing outside Major Jack's room talking with a nurse. Before I reached them, Sally covered her eyes with her left hand. The nurse reached out to give her a caring hug. I anticipated a difficult update on the major's condition.

"Sally?"

"Sir," the nurse said, "Mr. Klinkscales made it through the night okay. The doctor doesn't think he'll need surgery." She then walked back to the nurse's station.

"That's good news, right, Sal?" I approached to give her a hug, but she backed away.

"Both of you make me so mad. Just back off."

"You're right, Sal. You're right."

"Go see the major."

I dropped the duffel bags inside the major's room. I walked quietly to his bedside. In the shadows of the bathroom light, I stared at his bloated face, his protruding lips, his head and left eye wrapped in bandages, and an intravenous tube in his right hand. I reached down to squeeze his shoulder with care. Major Jack swore he would rather die than stay in a hospital for an extended period. When he awoke, he'd say he was in hell.

I leaned down to whisper, "Hey, Jack, if you can hear me, nod."

Without moving anything but his mouth, he said, "Hear you. Keep that asshole cop away from me."

"Did he harass you?"

"I . . . I pretended to be out of it."

"Listen, Jack, it's important to say this—"

"I ain't talking to anyone about anything. And I ain't going back to the VA. Let me rest."

"What's wrong with you, Zubell? Leave the man alone." Sally walked to the end of his bed. "How about being compassionate for a change."

What an untimely moment to feel the relief from prosecution billowing through me as uncontrollable as a sunrise. I grinned. I couldn't stop myself. Like it was involuntary. I had an overpowering sense of relief.

Sally noticed my facial expression. "What the hell is wrong with you? You like seeing Jack like this?"

"No, no, no. I'm just relieved—"

"I'm so happy everything has worked out for you." She gave me the middle finger. "You'd better consider the real possibility that you have lost your best friends."

"I'm—I'm—I'm not happy like that."

"Yes, you are. You'll get over us. It'll take a while, but you will."

My confusing demeanor elicited harsh criticism, which was fair.

"You're not the same person I fell in love with," she said.

Her disdain was tough to stomach. I understood why she felt that way.

"Sal, we have a lot to talk about. But first I'm gonna ask for something weird. Can you give me all the change you have?"

"Oh my God. You're kidding! You want a snack now?"

She went over to her purse for coins to toss at me. They bounced off my chest all over the tile floor. I gathered all that I saw. It must be enough to cover a long-distance call.

"I can't believe you."

It was important to deliver a personal message before the news reached the press. Closure was the reason for making the phone call now. I left the room with her saying, "Fuck you."

I walked down the hall to a pay phone in the hospital lobby. The operator came on the line to instruct me to insert coins in the slot.

When Mary Lou answered my call, I said, "Claude Sedley Senior, please."

"Mr. Sedley's office," Edna said after one ring.

"Edna, Zinny Zubell. Can I speak with him?"

At least a dozen awkward seconds passed. "Please hold."

I waited. And waited. A long-distance operator instructed me to insert more money in the slot. I deposited all the coins I had.

Finally, Edna came on the line. "Mr. Sedley is still tied up. Can I give him a number where you can be reached?"

"You told him that I was holding, right? And he shook his head, right?"

Edna was a do-the-right-thing person who was honest to a fault. Doubtful she would lie even if told to do so. Her answer: "Yes." To appease me, she said, "What's your number? I'll make sure he sees it."

"Will you give him a message?"

"Yes, I will."

"Damon Slade is dead." I hung up for maximum impact.

I turned around to find Sally right behind me. She had a disapproving frown. She backed up when I stepped toward her.

"Why did you leave such a jerk message? I'm done with you both. I'm leaving you two to clean up your own mess."

"You hungry?" I asked. "Let's get some food while Jack's resting."

"I'm in no mood for that."

"Please, Sal. It's important to tell you what's happened. Drive me to a restaurant I know. Please, Sal. Please. It's important. Then drop me off for my truck, and we'll return to see how the major is doing."

She was reluctant, shaking her head without speaking. I put my hand on the small of her back to nudge her gently to the hospital door. She pushed my hand away. She headed toward the major's room, but surprisingly stopped without any coaxing, then turned around to walk out of the hospital to her car. I followed her. After she unlocked the driver-side door, I assumed she would unlock the passenger's door. But she backed out of the parking space and drove away. To the highway and out of sight. A huge relief and a devastating loss, only minutes apart.

Bridle Path was too small for a taxi or bus service. Hitchhiking was my only option to return to the Green Mountain Inn.

Walking again. When I reached the hospital entrance, Sal pulled up. "Your explanation better be fucking awesome."

She drove us to the Mountain Morning Café. No conversation on the drive. I repeatedly glanced at her. I read her mood—angry, distraught, with every intention of slapping me at any moment. I decided to wait until we were in a public setting to talk any further.

We took a seat in a booth near the kitchen away from the other diners. I ordered the breakfast special. She ordered coffee. I waited for her to say something.

"You need a lawyer," she said.

"Not anymore."

"Oh, really? The detective said you had something to do with that guy's death."

"C'mon, Sal. I've seen too much and done too much to do something stupid like that. Believe that, if nothing else."

"So why was the detective saying that?"

"Circumstances. I didn't touch the guy."

"You denied being there? You lied to the police?"

"I never said I wasn't there. And never said I was there."

"Oh, you're clever."

"I'm covering for all of us. I had no idea Slade was dead when I got there."

"Who killed him? Jack?"

"No. He bled out from a gunshot wound."

"Then why is the detective accusing you of causing his death?"

"Cutter jumped to conclusions, which I understood. But it's simply not true. You know me better than that."

"Apparently, I don't."

"Look, Sal. The detective told me outside, just now, that he was closing the investigation on us. No charges."

"The detective came to Jack's room asking about my relationship with you. He told me that you arranged a military helo to look for the major. How did he know that? Did you tell him?"

"Of course not. The local cops saw the helo, and the doc at the hospital reported he thought Jack was beaten."

"That's why the detective started yelling at me to admit you were at that guy's cabin."

"That son of a bitch."

"He upset me so much I almost started crying. But I didn't want to give him the pleasure of seeing me like a girlie girl. That's when I lied to him. I lied, Zin. To the police!" Her tone was angry, but her voice low.

"I never wanted your footprint on this."

"Well, it is. All over it. I lied to the police and the army."

"The army? You did a legit op order."

"I shut down his questioning when I showed him the op order with Sergeant Major Zinny Zubell and Major Jack Klinkscales' names on it. That's right. I covered your asses. But that wasn't the order I filed. The official order had only Bike's name. I showed the detective a falsified op order."

I never imagined she would even consider risking a falsified order.

General Haywood wouldn't have her back for political reasons and his advancement, even though his subordinate issued the op order. Sal understood how the army bureaucracy worked and what she could get away with, especially when the flight involved a safety clearance for a major civilian contractor.

"Sal, it's gonna be okay."

"Don't you dare say that. I didn't trust your idea would work. And it didn't. You think the investigation is over? You're wrong."

"Why, Sal? The detective told me just that. It's over."

"He took the op order with him. He took it. That's when he stopped asking me questions. The detective seemed pleased with the order. He's onto something. I know it. Jack played possum the whole time. I'm really scared now. He's got what he needed. So you go ahead and believe we're out of the woods. I'm not."

She started biting her fingernails. With tears in her eyes, a worrisome frown formed on her face. Cutter taking the order bothered her. And I understood her anger over the jeopardy she believed she was facing. I disagreed. I had to convince her otherwise.

"Bike will cover us. And the army won't question anything that has to do with a legit sale to a civilian contractor."

"A falsified order is a court-martial offense. And lying to the police! Are you gonna do my time behind bars?"

Sal left the restaurant. I dropped five dollars on the table and followed her, worried she might leave me behind.

She drove me back to the Green Mountain Inn, skidding tires on the mountain "S" curves. Her eyes were red, teary. She mumbled angry words. I had a thousand words in my head to say, but they seemed frozen together. Any statement I made would be the worst thing I could say. Our fractured relationship was beyond repair.

Turning into a parking space near my truck, she slammed on the brakes.

I got out and walked around to her car door. She kept the car running and rolled down the window. "You did what you thought was best for the major. Now I gotta get in front of this."

"You mean tell the general? Don't do that. He'll say don't drag me into your fuck-up."

Sally nodded in agreement. "He'd say that."

"I can't repay what you've done."

"I always knew I could be manipulated by guys I cared about. It's like you guys can turn me over anytime you want. I don't say no."

"I'm sorry. I don't know what to say—"

"Do us a favor. Don't call me or Bike or the general. It only gets worse if the army finds out you're involved. I mean it, Zin. Stay away. Take care of Jack."

"Sal—" My plea banged against her car bumper as she backed out of the parking lot.

Her words hurt more than if she slapped me. That pain goes away. The end of a treasured friendship wouldn't.

This day was a collision of unexpected relief and heartbreaking despair. I needed time to think over what to do next. A shower and a nap might clear my head. In my peripheral vision I noticed a college-aged female walking slowly out of the motel office in my direction. She halted about ten feet away, then backed up before speaking. "Sir? Sir? Is that your truck? And you're in room one forty-six, right?"

"Yes."

"I'm sorry, sir, but the manager, he asked me to tell you that your room isn't available."

"I paid for three days."

"Sir, this isn't my doing. He made me come out here. Don't get mad, please." She backed up. "Go to the office. Ask for your money back. I don't know what else to say."

"The room is available, but not to me."

"Please, sir, I don't know what's going on."

"Miss, I'm not interested in trouble." I dropped the room key to the pavement. She was relieved.

I was in no mood to confront the inn manager. My sleeping arrangement tonight would be a hard chair in Major Jack's hospital room.

CHAPTER 23

I dozed off for about an hour in the most uncomfortable hardback chair imaginable. I stood up often to stretch my back, then shuffled back and forth in the room to ease the cramps. Despite obsessing over my aching back, I worried about Sally revealing our ruse to General Haywood. I couldn't shut off the anxiety of Sally's honest-to-a-fault approach to easing her conscience.

Sally read more into Cutter's decision to keep the bogus op order than I did. To her, he was digging to make a case. But he was done with all of us and kept the op order as evidence of his decision to close the inquiry. *What would he do if the coroner confirmed it was the major's blood in Slade's cabin? Would he reopen the investigation?* I still thought no. But Sally's disclosure to the general about the falsified op order could open an army inquiry. The moving parts of that what-if consumed me.

Sally and I approached issues thinking through the worst possible outcome. I would delve into a satisfactory scenario out of the dilemma, while Sally would hang on to the worst possible outcome a while longer.

Around 0600 the major moaned loud enough to wake me from a short nap. He turned toward me as if each inch were excruciating. I rose to be close. "It's Zin. It's gonna be all right. Remember: When asked, you fell.

Ya hear me?"

The major spoke in raspy voice. "Huh?"

"All you have to say to anyone who asks is, 'I fell.'"

"What? I didn't—"

"Because Slade's dead."

"Dead? You killed him?"

"No. You don't know he's dead."

"Oh, okay, I suppose."

The major turned his head away and closed his eyes. I waited for thirty minutes to answer any question he might have. He didn't wake up. I left for breakfast when the nurse came in to check his vitals.

The Mountain Morning Café was feeding me one more time. I needed coffee to stay awake. Returning to the major's room an hour later, the doctor who treated him and a nurse stood by his bed. They turned around when I entered. Major Jack shook his head. Painstakingly slow.

The doctor said, "Give us a few minutes."

I walked down the hospital hall with stressful thoughts about the conversation going on in the major's room. The doctor had treated enough patients to recognize the different ways someone was injured. I had no way of knowing how long or if the major would hold up during questioning about his injuries. The more I worried, the faster I paced around the hospital floor, enough so that another nurse asked if I was all right. I reassured her that I was worried about my friend's recovery.

The doctor and the nurse left his room, chatting about something I couldn't make out. The doctor had a concerned frown when he glanced up as we passed each other. Neither of them me asked any questions.

The major's eyes were open and staring at the ceiling when I went to his bedside. He spoke up before I said anything. "I fell, right?"

"You told 'em that. Good. Did the doc believe you?"

"Who cares."

"How do I look?"

"Like shit."

"Slade hit me till the bottle broke. I don't remember how many times."

"Did you stomp on his wound?"

He wet his lips. "No. Didn't get the chance. Funny, isn't it? I kinda liked the guy in a sick kinda way. Get outta here. You aren't doing either of us any good."

———

I couldn't bear another night in that chair. I returned to Charlotte for a sound night's sleep. The next morning I drove from Charlotte to the Bridle Path Hospital, passing the time with worrisome thoughts about a behind-the-scenes army investigation. Nothing acidified the gut more than the dread of "not knowing" when the "not knowing" would end. And the miles reinforced the slow burn I had for the major's stupidity for leaving with Slade.

I sat in his room most of the morning for the next two days. He said little. Only spoke of his pain and nothing else. I hardly said anything. The doc who treated him had nothing to say to me either. On the third day, I was anxious to approach the topic I had sidestepped the past two days. As usual, I allowed my anger to build up until I couldn't avoid the subject any longer. But this time Major Jack started the conversation.

"How'd you find me, Zin?"

"You ready to discuss this?"

"Go for it."

"Sal got a decommissioned helo for Bike and me to search for you. I rode along under false pretenses."

"Smart."

"Yeah, but costly."

"I bet."

"Cops thought I had something to do with Slade's death. But Sal planted a bogus op order in her files to cover our asses."

"Wow. That's pretty devious for you guys. Sounds like something I'd do."

"Well, don't think the cops are interested in us for Slade's death."

"What about the other charges against us?"

"Don't know. And I'm not asking."

"Maybe we're okay."

"I don't know. What were you thinking going off with Slade?"

"Silver's a cutie."

"You never considered the fuckin' consequences?"

"Rarely do."

I reacted to his glib comment. "You trying to get yourself killed? Is that the endgame?"

"I'm sick of everything, Zin. Yeah. Beyond that, I have no idea what I'm doing."

"I just don't know how to help you anymore."

"Me neither."

"Jack, your 'don't give a shit' attitude is driving me crazy. You're the smartest dumb-shit I ever knew."

"Roger that."

"But the worst part of your dumb-shit move is Sal may have to face an army investigation."

"For what it's worth, I got no excuse."

"And she's gonna face it by herself. We can't be involved. Only makes things worse for her. So why, Jack? I gotta know why."

"Because I do give a shit. And I don't know how to fuckin' accept myself like this." He waited a long ten count to corral his emotions. "But maybe it's time to accept me as I am."

His honesty won me over. I'd never walk away, if that were ever a consideration. Forgiving him was in play. Forgiving myself would take a while longer, accepting much of the blame for my persistent pursuit of Slade. The healing had to begin today.

"You wanna be rid of me?" he said.

"No. Not saying that. I'm here."

———

On the afternoon of the fourth day, Major Jack was feisty with the nurse on duty, who enjoyed his sense of humor. She said he recovered faster than the staff thought and was due to be released today. His VA medical cards made the checkout quick.

The major's mood on our drive back to Charlotte was like his attitude when leaving the VA—thrilled to be out of the concrete walls and a wheelchair. We didn't talk much on the trip back to Charlotte. When we reached the city limits, he asked about the prescribed meds. "We'll get them."

I walked him to his bedroom, where he slept nonstop for the next two days, waking up only to pee and eat a light meal.

———

I could feel the major's effort the days following his release to be a different person. He took his meds, used his crutches, stopped drinking beer. A few times he struggled with angry outbursts, which was understandable and an acceptable response for anyone determined to change their behavior. Sitting around with him day after day, he was less downbeat and craved sunlight. It was different enjoying the days of doing nothing with him accepting his limitations. Our history of getting on each other's nerves was a memory not to be revisited.

He brought up his disability on a beautiful fall afternoon under the sprawling magnolia tree in the front yard.

"I might just walk like this the rest of my life."

"Maybe. Never know."

"I know. It's okay. What's up with you and Sal?"

"Sal said don't call. She doesn't want anything to do with me."

"Why should that stop you from calling her?"

"Not yet."

I didn't have the acceptable words in mind to plea for forgiveness. I would rather face a squad of fierce insurgents than a woman wronged.

———

Several days later, I got antsy when I heard a siren in our neighborhood. I had no reason to expect an ongoing police investigation—no police visits or telephone inquiries about Slade's death. It was still in my head that an investigation could be in the offing. That was my punishment.

I got unexpected nerves when the phone rang. Sirens and phone calls unearthed more dread.

"Zinny, how are you?" It was Ableman.

Hearing his voice raised my anxiety. "Good. Hope there's no problem, sir."

"Well, no. I waited to call until I heard from the DA. Cecil Horry accepted a plea of life without parole for killing Edward Kelter. And with Damon Slade dead and Cecil Horry in prison, the DA agreed to drop the charges against you and Jack. No reason to continue pursuing them. That's good news."

"That's great news, sir. Thank you."

"Yes, but you know, I passed the bar to advise people about legal matters. Is there anything I should know about? I was surprised to hear about the circumstances involving you and Jack concerning Damon Slade's death."

"Sir, I would have called if the circumstances were such that I needed your counsel."

"Okay, but you shoulda called."

I tensed up. "Why do you think I need legal advice?"

"Claude asked me to get involved."

"But I never spoke with him."

"He asked me to go to bat for you. I called the police detective on your case. What's his name?"

"Cutter."

"Yes, Cutter. He confirmed he's not filing charges at this time. Of course, he trotted out his folksy 'aw shucks' manner to ask if you were willing to come forward and cooperate. I didn't fall for that ploy. Cooperate about what, Zinny?"

"What I tell you is privileged, right?"

"That's what I learned in law school."

"Well, the short story is, I carried Jack to the hospital after he was beaten badly by Slade. Police found Slade dead later and tried to pin his death on me."

"And you didn't think that was important enough to call?"

"You're right. But—"

"No buts. That doesn't work, Zinny. Cutter told me the lab reports on Slade were conclusive. He bled to death. And he isn't looking into the other blood in the cabin. Figures it belongs to Slade as well."

"I never touched Slade, sir. There's no way Jack was involved either."

An uncomfortable silence heightened my anxiety.

"I didn't agree to you coming forward unless Cutter had a warrant."

"You think he'll get one?"

"Doubt it. But we'll see. If they come to your house, call me."

"Of course. Send me your bill."

"Good afternoon, Zinny."

CHAPTER 24

I honored Sally's request to avoid any contact with her, Bike, or General Haywood. It was hard not taking responsibility for bullying my friends into highly questionable actions. But I accepted Sally's assessment of the problem I could cause raising my hand in an admission of culpability.

———

The major and I watched insipid television programs and went on short walks. We went to the movie theater to see *The Godfather: Part II*. Each day was like a lazy weekend. A quiet life with enough money to avoid working.

I never spoke of my edgy gut. Another week passed with no word from Ableman or the police or Sally. No communication was deafening—a disturbance that was the loudest when I lay in bed. My sighs grew louder and more often. The major was aware of my far-off stares and asked, "What's wrong, Zin?"

"Ignore me."

He trumpeted the elephant in the room. "You worried about what's going on with Sally, right?"

"I don't think it's over."

"Yeah, okay, then find out. Call her. Or would you rather not know what you don't know?"

"I called her apartment the past two days and let the phone ring for a while. She never picked up."

"Then you wanna agree there's no investigation, right?"

After a few seconds of doubt, I said, "I'll call her office."

I dialed Sally's direct line at the Pentagon. Any hesitation would lead to a longer delay.

A male master sergeant I didn't recognize answered. I froze. Instead of asking for Sally, I said, "Is General Haywood available?"

"No, sir, he's not. Who's calling?"

I didn't leave my name, then hung up. Maybe Sally was on vacation. Leaving my name to a staff member who might know me could draw me into an ongoing investigation and unwelcomed consequences for my friends. The thought of a criminal returning to the scene of the crime worked up a knot in my stomach.

"I don't think it's over. I feel it in my gut," I said.

The major took the high road. "Another sergeant covering for Sal is no big deal. Let's agree it's over."

———

The next morning I wanted answers, so I called Sally's desk at 0800. She was punctual, dependable. But the same sergeant answered.

"Sergeant Aberdeen, please, sir."

"She's not available."

I paused, waiting for him to ask me to leave her a message. He didn't. His tone was unhelpful.

"When do you expect her back?"

"Who's calling?"

"A retired command sergeant major." Let him figure out who was calling. "I'm not at liberty to say. Good morning."

I hung up after hearing the dial tone. I recounted the sergeant's responses to Major Jack. He again rationalized the sergeant's vague answers had plausible explanations. I disagreed. "Not enough time has passed to think it's over."

"Then get that lawyer to rep you again."

"No."

"You're gonna sit around here babysitting me and worrying?"

"Likely."

"You're gonna stop doing that—sooner rather than later," the major said.

The following afternoon I was curious about someone honking outside our home. I walked to the window to see a yellow cab in our driveway. I never called a cab. He must be at the wrong house. I headed for the front door to redirect the cabbie as Major Jack entered the living room on crutches and in his dress army uniform.

"Is that a cab? It's for me, Zin."

"When did you call a cab?"

"When you were in the shower."

"Why'd you call a cab? I can drive you wherever you wanna go."

"I know, Zin. But it's time."

"What're you talking about? What's going on, Jack? Why the uniform? I thought you said you'd never wear it again."

"I said that. I was lying to you and myself. I've been putting off something too long, Zin."

"Where're you going that you have to wear your uniform?"

"Remember when I told you about the guy who came to the VA to preach bullshit about helping wounded vets?"

I nodded like I remembered.

"Well, for some reason, I kept his card. And I called him. I'll have to admit he made sense. So the short explanation is I'm leaving to get his help."

"When did you contact him?"

"A week ago. When you went grocery shopping."

"And you're just now telling me?"

"I don't like long goodbyes. I didn't tell you, because . . . oh, I don't know why I didn't tell you. I just didn't."

"You always said no to help. Been so stubborn about it."

"I've had it, Zin. Tired of acting like I'm no good for anything. It's for the best."

"Where's this guy?"

"A lotta klicks away. California."

"I guess you haven't thought about what's next?"

"I don't know. One step, then another, and so on."

The cabbie honked again. The major went to the front door to wave at the man. He turned around and dropped his head to avoid an emotional moment. I hadn't seen him in his dress uniform in years. He was impressive—could've been a model on an army recruitment poster. He pointed at his two duffel bags beside the sofa. I went to pick them up, but he waved me off. He used his crutches to walk to the sofa, then balanced himself to reach down and swing both duffels up to his right shoulder. "I gotta get used to doing this for myself."

We stared at each other, as emotional as two old soldiers could be.

"I can't ever repay you for what you've done. Won't say goodbye. It's never goodbye for us."

"Leave me your contact info."

"Be in touch, Sergeant Major."

He stood at attention and saluted. The right words weren't available when given no time to say goodbye to your best friend. I returned the salute. I watched him walk to the cab and leave without turning back for a goodbye wave.

I should have said, "Good luck." Words were hollow.

The incident at Slade's cabin was profound for us both. His pain was taking a back seat to his decision-making. He was on a better path. Glad for that. And sad at the same time.

Major Jack was gone. My sense was he would find his footing and cut ties with the past. He never was sentimental. I considered the possibility it might be a long time before he contacted me. That thought grabbed me. It wouldn't leave.

There was no way to prepare for being alone. It was a steep climb. My eyes were a bit teary. And it wasn't allergies.

I sat on my sofa watching TV. It was difficult coming to terms with life as a still pond. The blues and loneliness, twins for a miserable attitude, ate away my energy. I initiated nothing to get me out of the house. And I wasn't in the right mindset to look for work. I was becoming sloppy, sentimental. When frustration built up too much, bedroom doors were an easy victim.

Beer was my friend, my calming influence. It never disappointed.

———

Before dinner that same day, I decided to go for a walk. Heading down the street, I saw a red Corvette parked a half block from my house. Walking slowly by the car, I saw a redhead sitting in the driver's seat—a familiar face.

"Silver, what're you doing here?"

"Hi, Zinny."

"Really surprised to see you. What's up?"

"Just driving by."

"Looks like you're parked."

"What's going on, Zinny?"

"What do you mean what's going on?"

"Nothing. Good to see ya. How're you? How's Jack?"

"He recovered. It took a while."

"He's okay, right?"

"Yeah. He's good enough to be in California right now."

"Really? Wish I were there."

No way this was a chance meeting.

"I never got a chance to say thanks, Silver."

She smiled with a hint of an uneasy acceptance.

"Slade's dead, ya know," I said.

She avoided my bait with a look-away. I caught a brief glimpse of her disturbed frown. She was noticeably edgy when I brought up Slade.

"He should've never hit Jack. He never shoulda done a lot of stuff, ya know?"

"I expected you to be there. The police asked me a lot of questions."

"Why?"

"Because they found him dead. They thought I had something to do with it."

She started to respond but stopped herself. She adjusted her position in the car seat, blocking me from viewing her face with the back of her red hair, then reached for her purse in the passenger's seat.

"It woulda gone a lot easier if you'd hung around to tell them I wasn't involved. Oh well, it's over now."

"Zinny, I had to go. You don't understand. I just couldn't take it anymore." Whispering, she said, "You okay?"

I stepped over to the driver's window as she squirmed in her seat. I leaned down. Her blouse was unbuttoned to her navel, no bra on, exposing most of her breasts. Her miniskirt above the edge of her red panties. I stared at the enticing tease.

"Lucky me finding you here when I came out for a walk, huh?"

"Not so much luck, Zinny. The truth is, I've come by a lot more than I should."

"Why didn't you knock on my door?"

"Maybe I should have."

"I'd enjoy the company."

"Really?" she said softly.

There was an awkward silence. She was tempting me to invite her inside or teasing me before she refused my advances.

"Are you in any trouble, Silver?"

"No. Why?"

"The red hair."

"I like red hair."

"Me too."

She hesitated to say something for an uncomfortable moment. "Do you want me to come inside?"

Her eyes never wanted me like that before. I stared back to be certain I was reading her right. There was a longing that many men would be excited about—the possibility of a "yes" response to an advance. It would be easy to accept her come-on, make a move without considering whether the decision was right or wrong. I had a few confusing thoughts about how much pleasure, or anxiety, Silver would bring me, but the opportunity outweighed any drawbacks. "Sure."

"Really? Ya sure, Zinny?"

"Yes, but don't be surprised if I bring up Slade again."

"Don't go there."

"Okay. But you know me. Always probing."

"Now I'm not in the mood. You just blew it. Goodbye, Zinny."

Silver was involved with Slade's death. What she knew about the last hours of Slade's life would haunt her. She drove off, squealing her tires as a signal for how upset she was.

I blew it. I baited her about future questions concerning what had happened to Slade instead of enjoying the moment of being with a beautiful woman.

Upon further thought, it was best not to be involved with her. If the police had renewed interest in Slade's death, and I was involved with Silver, they might have ample suspicion to spotlight the circumstances of his death. But that reasoning didn't hinder my sexual fantasies. The warm urges of a middle-aged, below-average-looking joe led to prolonged daydreaming about sex with a pretty young woman named Silver. That unsatisfied feeling rained all over my regret.

I went to the A&P for beer, frozen pizza, and the afternoon *Charlotte News*. The local section had a story about Claude Sedley announcing his candidacy for the Senate. My mind scrambled with memories of our troubled dealings. He buried the damaging skeletons that might waylay his achieving his political aspirations. Fairness never comes in play when the rich and powerful go after what they want.

CHAPTER 25

I waited until I could force a smile to call Sally at her apartment. After a few rings, I got a recorded message: "The number you have dialed has been disconnected." That wasn't the response I wanted. I had another round of what-happened thoughts. I then called the last number I had for Bike. His phone was disconnected.

Let the problems come to me. No. That was no longer my plan. I made up my mind to find Sally Aberdeen, no matter how long it took and where she was. Starting point was a road trip to DC.

After I loaded two duffel bags in my truck, I heard my phone ring. I had no interest in talking to anyone trying to offer me something I wouldn't buy. But I picked up the phone in hopes the voice on the other end was Major Jack.

"Is this Zinny Zubell?"

"Yes, it is."

"My name is Carl Johnson. I'm the senior partner at Johnson, Wilson, and Carter. I'm good friends with Claude Sedley. He spoke very highly of you and gave me your contact information. Do you have a few minutes to talk?"

Under different circumstances, my pulse would jump with a call from

a prospective employer. But not today. I felt like saying, "Not interested."
But I didn't.

"What can I do for you, sir?"

"We're expanding our practice and found we have a need for an in-house
investigator. Someone we can trust with sensitive matters for our clients.
Claude Sedley recommended we talk to you. Are you currently working
for a law firm?"

"No, sir."

"Would you be interested in coming to our office for an interview? I'll be
up front: Claude Sedley's recommendation carries a lot of weight with us."

"I'm planning on going out of town for a few days. Can I set up a time
to meet when I return?" *I'm stalling. Maybe I'll call. Maybe I won't.*

"Certainly. Look forward to talking with you when you return."

Mr. Johnson left his private telephone number. Mr. Sedley's payback
for abetting his cover-up was a job opportunity with another law firm. I
struggled to recall if I visited that law firm during my rounds looking for
work. A full-time investigator job was tempting, but the uncertainty was
still too strong.

I closed up my house. I backed out of my driveway, drove a half a block,
then stopped. A familiar car was parked down the street with a Virginia
license plate. Sally was in the driver's seat. I motioned her to follow me
back to my house. She parked behind me.

"Hi, Zin. Surprised?"

Stunned was more accurate. "Yes, ma'am."

"Hope it's a good surprise."

"Yeah, it is. Funny, I was on my way to see you in DC."

"Really? Why?"

"You wanna come inside?"

"I didn't come all this way to turn around and leave. Dumb question,
Zin."

She looked rested, happy, wearing makeup and a light blue floral dress and heels. We sat down on the sofa. She tucked her right leg under her left leg, getting comfortable.

"Why were you coming to DC?"

"To find you. Your phone is disconnected. And you haven't been in your office."

"Well, it's good to know you tried to contact me. But I gotta know about the dead man in the cabin."

"Coroner reported he bled to death. We're cleared."

"It didn't look good for either of you."

"You saved us. And I'm forever grateful."

"How're you, Zinny?"

"Fine. How long you been waiting out there?"

"An hour or so."

I said what was on my mind. "You look better than ever."

She frowned as if my attempt at a compliment was sophomoric at best. "Well, thank you, I guess. You really don't know much about women, do you?"

I was usually wrong regarding the nuances of a relationship due to my failures with the opposite sex. I was never good with words when uncomfortable around a woman with whom I had an issue.

"I'm really sorry I got you involved in my situation with the major. It eats me up."

"Okay. That's in the past. I didn't come all this way to hear you tell me that. Where's Jack?"

I filled her in on Major Jack's plan. She looked like she knew all about it. "He really did it, huh? He called me weeks ago to tell me that he was thinking about leaving for help. I encouraged him to do it. He said he was serious. And he told me that you would be sad."

"Yeah, well, I miss him. The crazy conversations. The shit we gave each other." I had to change the subject. "Yeah, well, is everything okay with you? I was really concerned when you weren't in your office for days, and your phone was disconnected."

"I didn't wanna tell you this on the phone." She paused, her voice cracking. "The general's promotion to NATO came through. He said it would be best for him and his wife to stay together and leave for Europe. 'Politics,' he said. Just politics and putting up a good front. But he didn't stop there. He said continuing to see me would be professional suicide because peers asked about our relationship. Of course, he denied it. He wasn't about to make the mistake of taking me to Brussels. He said he won't risk it regardless of how much he enjoyed me. That was that. He RIF'd me. Got rid of a big mistake." Tears welled in her eyes as she turned away.

"At least he's a consistent asshole."

"I didn't take your advice, Zin. I told the general about Bike taking the helo out for a test flight. Showed him the flight order. But not the one with your name on it. He was good. He really likes the contractor who bought it. He told me in confidence he may work for the company after he retires. The contractor got his helo, and that was that."

"Downsizing after 'Nam. Got a lotta good soldiers gone."

"Oh, by the way, General Haywood gave me a message for you . . .'"

Just mentioning his name raised my anxiety level. His opinion of me still mattered, so much so that I walled up for his criticism.

"He told me it was an honor to serve with you. He figured we'd be talking."

I took a moment to take in the unexpected compliment. Sally knew how I felt about the general. He should've told me that in person.

"He meant it, Zinny. Bike called to tell me that he turned in his retirement papers. Did you know that?"

"No."

"He said he landed a lucrative flying job in Costa Rica."

"Good for him."

She took a moment to gaze around my living room. She shook her head from side to side, finding nothing colorful or matching in any semblance to stylish furniture. I could read her displeasure.

"I do think about you a lot." My hackneyed line was as effective as a bent fork.

Sally took her time answering me. "I felt used and ashamed sneaking around to be with him. He promised me that he would divorce his wife. It was stupid to believe him. He treated me like he's always doing me a huge favor. No romance ever. It's like he tripped over me and couldn't get on his feet."

"Well, he—"

"Don't say it. I don't wanna hear it."

I was about to say something stupid. Instead, I gazed at her with the most attentive look I could muster.

"Very good, Zin. You're learning. Now to why I'm here. I've been thinking a lot about you too. And what I did to help the major."

"No way to thank you enough—"

"Zin, we won't talk about it again."

"Okay."

"I've made a lot of assumptions, Zin. Unsure about them, to be honest. I packed up enough clothes and things for a while. Is it too much to let me stay here to see how it goes? Do you want that? You don't have to say yes."

Without hesitation, I said, "Yes, I'd like that."

"This isn't an invite to warm up your moves. Understood?"

I couldn't hold back my excitement. "Yes, yes, okay. I won't assume anything. Just slow and friendly. See how it goes."

"Don't say yes just because it sounds right. It's been a while since you've had a woman around. Just give us time. And I'm not asking for a free ride. I'll pay my way. But please, please, don't start telling me what I should be doing with my life, okay?"

"You can have Jack's bedroom. I'll respect your privacy."

"Okay. If it makes sense and things work out, and I mean really works out, we can take your truck and a U-Haul for my stuff. I'm not wild about using rented boys' things."

"Sure. Whatever you want."

"Let's see how it goes first. How about a hug?"

We sat there, her head resting under my chin, my arms around her waist, her body snuggled against me. It was hard holding back my hands. I had to be careful not to do or say anything to upset her at this unexpected turn of events. I wanted the relationship to take an unforced course.

"You sure you're okay with me being here?"

"I'd sleep outside if it makes you feel more comfortable."

"Typical stupid statement, Zin. But I appreciate the thought. You know, the more I look around here, the more I realize your furniture really stinks. You need to spend some money."

"I agree. Time to start living like I belong someplace."

"That's the best thing you could say right now. And really, Zin, don't ruin us by jumping at everything I bring up. Just show me that you care."

"I'll try not being too stupid." *That will be hard.* "You know, Sal, I'm surprised you knew my address."

"I have my ways, Zin."

We sat together to share stories we had told each other many times, laughing at the good times, reminiscing about the struggles of dealing with lives lost. We drank beer, ate pizza well past midnight. It had taken a while, but I got it now. Give Sally the room to be herself. Together, work through everything to move on with our lives.

The next day we went shopping for a dark suit, white shirt, and red tie. I had an interview coming up. Being with Sally made me feel grounded. I was on my way to loving the right woman.

ABOUT THE AUTHOR

Steve Shockley's interest in creative writing began at the Citadel under the guidance of a dedicated mentor, Professor John Doyle, along with his college friend Pat Conroy. After graduating with honors and commissioned in the Army's Adjutant Generals Corps, he attended law school at the University of North Carolina at Chapel Hill.

Steve is a broadcasting executive, has an extensive marketing background in national sports publications, and has written and produced industrial films and television commercials. He wrote a two-act play, *Hole in the Flow*, produced by the NC Playwrights Forum with a regional theater company and staged at a local college. He wrote a sales manual, *A Business Scout's Notebook*, based on years of selling ideas and closing accounts.

Duty Strong is Steve's first novel. He lives in Charlotte, North Carolina.